time between us

time
between
us

TAMARA IRELAND STONE

Hyperion Books
New York

Corduroy written by Eddie Vedder, Dave Abbruzzese, Jeff Ament, Stone Gossard and Mike McCready copyright © 1994 by Innocent Bystander, Pickled Fish Music, Scribing C-Ment Songs, Write Treatage Music and Jumpin' Cat Music

If I Could words and music by Trey Anastasio copyright © by Who Is She? Music, Inc. (BMI)

First Edition
1 3 5 7 9 10 8 6 4 2
G475-5664-5-12243
Printed in the United States of America

Interior design by Abby Kuperstock

Library of Congress Cataloging-in-Publication Data
Stone, Tamara Ireland.
    Time between us/Tamara Ireland Stone.—1st ed.
      p. cm.
    Summary: In 1995 Evanston, Illinois, sixteen-year-old Anna's perfectly normal life is turned upside-down when she meets Bennett, whose ability to travel through space and time creates complications for them both.
    ISBN 978-1-4231-5956-8 (hardback)
    [1. Space and time—Fiction. 2. Love—Fiction. 3. High schools—Fiction. 4. Schools—Fiction. 5. Family life—Illinois—Fiction. 6. Illinois—Fiction.]
I. Title.
    PZ7.S8814Tim   2012
    [Fic]—dc23   2011053368

Reinforced binding

Visit www.un-requiredreading.com

SUSTAINABLE FORESTRY INITIATIVE Certified Sourcing
www.sfiprogram.org
SFI-00993

THIS LABEL APPLIES TO TEXT STOCK

For Michael, my daring adventure

Time is the longest distance between two places.

TENNESSEE WILLIAMS

time between us

october 2011

san francisco, california

Even from this distance I can see how young he looks. Younger than the first time I saw him.

He and his friends have been skating around Lafayette Park for the last couple of hours, and now they're sprawled across the grass, downing Gatorades and passing around a bag of Doritos.

"Excuse me."

Eight sixteen-year-old heads spin in my direction, looking confused, then curious.

"Are you Bennett?" I ask and wait for him to nod, even though I'm sure it's him. I'd know him anywhere. "Can I speak with you for a moment? In private?"

He knits his eyebrows together, but then he stands up and flips his skateboard over to keep it from rolling down the hill. I catch him looking back at his friends and shrugging as he follows me to the closest bench. He sits at the opposite end, as far away from me as possible.

Everything about him is so similar, so familiar, that I almost scoot over to close the distance, like I would have done so naturally when I was younger. But sixteen years have come between us, and that's enough to keep me on my side of the bench.

"Hi." My voice shakes, and I twist a curly strand of hair around my finger before catching myself and returning my hand to my sides, pressing both palms into the wooden slats.

"Ummm . . . Hi?" he says. He studies me through the uncomfortable silence. "I'm sorry, am I supposed to know you or something?"

My instinct is to say yes, but I stop myself, press my lips together, and shake my head instead. He doesn't know me. Not yet. "I'm Anna. Here." I reach into my bag, pull out the sealed white envelope, and smile as I hold it out to him.

He takes the letter and turns it over a few times.

"I thought it would be safer to explain in writing." My next words are the most important. After all my practice, I should have this part perfected, but I think through each word in my head again, just to be sure. "It's too easy for me to say the wrong thing today, and if I do, we may never meet at all."

His head springs up, and he stares at me, wide-eyed. No one's ever said anything like that to him before, and with that one statement, he knows that I'm in on his secret.

"I'd better go." I stand up. "Read that when you're alone, okay?" I leave him on the bench and walk back down the hill.

I keep my eyes glued to a single sailboat skimming across the San Francisco Bay so I won't turn around. After years of agonizing over this moment, I expect to feel relieved, but I don't—I just miss him all over again.

What I just did could change everything, or it could change nothing. But I have to try. I've got nothing to lose. If my plan doesn't work, my life will remain the same: Safe. Comfortable. Perfectly average.

But that wasn't the life I originally chose.

march 1995

1

evanston, illinois

I shake out my arms to get the blood flowing, rock my head back and forth until I hear a little pop, and take a deep breath of early morning air that's so cold it stings on the way down. Still, I muster a silent thanks for the fact that it's warmer than last week. I tighten the neoprene belt that holds my Discman around my waist and turn up the music so Green Day is loud in my ears. And I'm off.

I take the usual series of turns through my neighborhood until I reach the running path that hugs the glassy expanse of Lake Michigan. I twist around the last bend, giving myself a clear view of the route all the way to the Northwestern University track, and I spot the man in the green vest. As we run toward each other, our ponytails—his gray, mine unruly—swing back and forth, and we raise our hands and give each other a little wave. "'Morning," I say as we pass.

The sun is slowly rising over the lake as I turn toward the soccer field, and when my feet connect with the spongy surface of the track, I feel a new burst of energy that makes me pick up the pace. I'm halfway around the loop when the CD shuffles again and the new song transports me back to the coffeehouse the night before. The band was amazing, and when they played those first few notes the whole place exploded, everyone bouncing and head-bobbing in unison as the line that separated us local high schoolers from the transitory college students disappeared completely. I take a quick look around to be sure I'm alone. All I can see is empty row after row of metal bleachers, heavy with a winter's worth of snow that no one's bothered to dust off, so I belt out the chorus.

I'm racing around the curves, legs throbbing, heart pounding, arms pumping. Inhaling arctic air. Exhaling steam. Enjoying my thirty minutes of solitude, when it's just me and my run and my music and my thoughts. When I'm completely alone.

And then I realize I'm not. I see someone in the bleachers, hip-deep in the icy fluff of the third row and impossible to miss. He's just sitting there with his chin resting on his hands, wearing a black parka and a small smile, watching me.

I steal glances at him but continue to run, pretending not to care about his presence in my sanctuary. He looks like a Northwestern student, maybe a freshman, with dark shaggy hair and soft features. He doesn't look threatening, and even if he is, I can outrun him.

But what if I can't?

My mind jumps to the self-defense courses Dad made me take when I started running in the near dark. Knee to the groin. Palm thrust to the nose. But first, you should try to avoid confrontation by simply acknowledging the attacker's presence. Which sounds much easier.

As I come around the bend, I give him a slight nod and a glare that probably conveys a weird mix of fear and tenacity— like I'm daring him to make a move but terrified that he just might. And as I run by, staring him down, I watch his face change. His smile disappears, and now he looks sad and dejected, like I just used those self-defense skills to punch him in the gut.

But as I follow the curve of the track and start heading toward him again, I look up, right in his direction. He gives me a more hesitant smile, but it's warm, like he knows me. Genuine, like he might just be someone worth knowing. And I can't help it. I smile back.

I'm still grinning as I turn the next bend, and without even thinking about it, I flip around midstride to look at him again.

He's gone.

I spin in place while my eyes search the track for him, and then I sprint to the bleachers. At the bottom of the steps, I hesitate for a second, wondering if he was ever there at all, but I gather my courage and trudge up.

He's not there, but he had been. He left proof: the snow

is packed down where he sat, and on the bench below, two depressions show where his feet rested.

And that's when I notice something else.

My own footprints are clearly visible in the powder around me, but where his should have been—leading to and from the bench—I see nothing but a thick layer of untouched snow.

2

I race into the house and take the stairs two at a time. I turn on the shower, peel off my sweat-drenched clothes, and stand naked while I down a glass of water and let the steam fill the bathroom. My reflection in the medicine cabinet mirror fades away behind the thick fog, and when my image becomes completely obscured, I run my palm across the glass, clearing a wet, dotted path in the condensation. I consider my face again. I don't look crazy.

I spend my entire shower wondering if he was real, whom I can tell, and how I might possibly come out of that conversation sounding sane. As I get dressed for school, his face is still creeping into my thoughts, but I do my best to push the whole thing out of my mind and try to convince myself I imagined it. Still, I vow to avoid the track for the rest of the week. I know what I saw.

I shake it off as I zip into my boots and give myself one last check in the full-length mirror. I run my fingers through my curls, scrunch them up in my hands, and shake my head again. Useless.

Throwing my backpack over my shoulder, I force myself to move on to my morning ritual. I stand before the map that decorates the largest wall in my room; I close my eyes, touch it, and open them again. Callao, Peru. Good. I was hoping for someplace warm.

With my travel dreams on his mind, one day last summer Dad spent a secret hour in the garage adhering this giant paper map of the world to a foam-core board. "You can mark all the places you go," he said as he handed me a small box of red pins. I stood there and stared at it—this colorful expanse of paper, with its topographic mountain ranges and changeable shades of blue to depict the various depths of the ocean—and saw a map of the world, but knew it wasn't mine. My world was much, much smaller.

After Dad left the room, I stuck the little red pins into the paper, one by one. My class had visited the state capital last year, so I put a pin in Springfield. We once took a family camping trip to Boundary Waters, so I put one in northeastern Minnesota. We spent a Fourth of July in Grand Rapids, Michigan. My aunt lives in northern Indiana, and we go twice a year. That was it. Four pins.

At first, all I could see was that pathetic little cluster of red near the state of Illinois, but now I view the map the way

Dad intended. Like it's asking me to see every square inch of it with my own eyes, challenging me to make my little world larger and larger, pin by pin.

I give the map one last look and head down the stairs toward the glorious scent coming from the kitchen. I don't even need to hit the landing to know that Dad's standing at the coffeepot pouring out two mugs—one black, for him; one with milk, for me. I grab my cup from his outstretched hand. "Good morning. Mom already gone?"

"She left before you did. Early shift." He watches me take a sip, and then he steals a peek out the kitchen window. "Where did you run today? It's still pretty dark out there." He sounds worried.

"Campus. The usual." There's no way I'm telling him about the guy at the track. "It's freezing, too. That was a tough first mile." I pour myself a bowl of raisin bran and plop down on the stool at the counter. "You're welcome to join me, you know," I say with a grin. I know what's coming next.

He looks at me, eyebrows raised. "Wake me up some morning in June and I'll run with you. Until then, you aren't getting me out of my warm bed for that kind of torture."

"Wuss."

"Yes." He nods and raises his coffee mug in a mock toast. "Yes, I am. Unlike my Annie." He shakes his head. "I created a monster."

Dad turned me into a runner. He had been an Illinois Cross-Country State Finalist in high school. With his glory days behind him, now he's the crazy guy in a professorial sport coat standing at the end of the course, clapping wildly and cheering me on in a booming voice that threatens to take down the forest's most sturdy oaks. It's gotten worse now that the cross-country season has ended and I'm running track, where he's never out of sight and there are no trees to muffle him. Even though he's beyond embarrassing, he's devoted. In return, he's the only one I still allow to call me Annie.

Dad goes back to his paper while I down my coffee and finish my cereal in comfortable quiet. Unlike Mom, who seems compelled to fill silence, Dad lets it stick around like a member of the family. But then the low horn of Emma's car breaks the calm.

Dad drops one side of the newspaper. "There's your Brit."

I give him a peck on the cheek and head outside.

The car is humming in the driveway, and I walk toward it as quickly as I can without banana-peeling on the ice-covered concrete. I let out a little breath of relief when I swing open the door of Emma's shiny new Saab and fall into warm leather.

"'Morning, love," Emma Atkins chirps in her British accent. She throws the gearshift into reverse and flies out of the driveway. "Did you hear?" she blurts out, like the words have been locked up in there for hours and she's finally setting them free.

"Of course not." I look at her and roll my eyes. "Why would I hear anything before you do?"

"New kid starting today. He just moved here from *California*. That could be good, right?" While Emma's seen the world, she hasn't seen much of the States beyond the Midwest. California seems like a fantastic American oddity to her, like frozen custard or a hot dog dipped in cornmeal and impaled on a stick.

"Anything new is good," I say, and when I turn to look at her, I see that she's wearing more than the usual amount of eye shadow, extra accessories, and the uniform miniskirt she had hemmed to make it "mini-er." Clearly the new guy's been heavy on her mind since she woke up this morning. When we stop at the light, I watch her stretch her neck to look into the rearview mirror and blot her lipstick with her fingertip. Not that she needs any extra help. She's English, but she looks more like a Brazilian supermodel with her high, defined cheekbones and dark, sultry eyes. Today I didn't even bother to put on lip gloss, and when we walk into school together, whether Emma's all dolled up for the new guy or not, I know which one of us turns heads.

Even more extraordinary than the extra effort she's taken with her appearance is the fact that she hasn't bothered to put on music. I reach into the glove compartment and start sifting through the pile of CDs, loose and scratching up against each other, until my fingertips feel suede. I unearth the hot pink case I bought Emma for her birthday last year, and start slipping the disks into the little plastic sleeves.

"Hey, why aren't you more excited? This is big news, Anna.

We haven't had a new student since . . ." She trails off as she thumps her fingers on the steering wheel, like she does when she's deep in thought.

I don't even look up from my project as I finish her sentence. "Me."

"Really?"

I shrug and nod. "Yeah. Eighth grade. Zits and braces. Frizzy hair. That horrible plaid Westlake jumper." I wince at the thought of that last one. "New kid. Me."

"Really . . ." She stares out the window and thinks about it, like there's a chance I'm wrong. Then she says, "Huh. I guess so." She reaches over and pinches my cheek. "And see what a good day that turned out to be! Without you, I'd be singing all by myself. Speaking of which, we're going to be at school before you choose one. Here." Emma reaches over and grabs the disk on top. "*Vitalogy*. Perfect."

We've been playing the new Pearl Jam CD practically non-stop for the last three months. She slips it into the stereo and turns up the volume as high as she can without distorting the bass. She looks at me and smiles, moving to the beat as the opening guitar notes of "Corduroy" start out quietly, then build, escalating at a steady rhythm until the car is filled with sound. I lean back into my seat as the drums join in, softly at first, then louder. We hear the last five notes of the intro and that's our cue—we look at each other and sing.

The waiting drove me mad. . . .
You're finally here and I'm a mess. . . .

We sing every word, loud and off-key, but the final minute of the song is instrumental, so that's where we really let go. I air-guitar and bob my head while Emma drums on the steering wheel, her hands flying around and slapping the leather, but as close to "ten and two" as I've ever seen them. As if she were capable of choreographing our arrival, she pulls into her usual parking space just as the last guitar notes fade to black and twists the key in the ignition. "Pearl Jam's coming back to Soldier Field this summer, you know? You should get Freckles to get us tickets."

"Stop calling him that." I stifle a laugh. "His name is Justin. And yeah, he can probably get us tickets. . . ."

She looks at me sideways, eyebrows raised. "*Probably?* Come on, he'll do anything you ask. That boy has it *bad* for you."

"No, he doesn't. I've known him since I was five. We're just friends."

"And is *he* aware of this?"

"Of course he is." My parents and Justin's have all known one another for years, and for most of them, he and I were inseparable. But things have changed. Justin Reilly used to feel like a comfortable pair of sweats, but now he's more like a prom dress. Lovely but itchy.

"Fine, then would you kindly ask your *friend* if he can score us Pearl Jam tickets?" She's just about to get out of the car, but she stops, seeming to have had a new thought. "Wait, what if he can't get them? Then what?"

I stare at her. "Do you want to see Pearl Jam this summer, Em?"

She nods. "Of course."

"And when was the last time you didn't get what you wanted?"

I wait while she thinks about it. Then she shrugs and smiles. "Am I that spoiled?"

"No," I lie. Emma gives me her puppy dog look, and I say, "Sometimes, but I love ya anyway," and that gets a smile.

Emma and I walk from the student lot to the side entrance. Inside, we stamp our feet on the doormat, watching as the heater above us melts the snow on our boots and makes it drip, and for the first time all morning, I have an opening. If I'm going to tell anyone what happened at the track, Emma is the one, and now is the time, but I don't know where to start. How am I supposed to tell my best friend that a guy appeared out of thin air, smiled at me, and disappeared before my eyes, leaving me with nothing more than an impression of his butt and a nagging mystery to solve?

"Em?"

"Yeah?"

"Can I tell you something . . . weird?" I look around to be sure no one can overhear me, because it's one thing to tell your best friend that you may be losing your mind and another thing entirely for the news to catch fire and start making the loop.

"Of course."

We walk toward our lockers and stop, but just as I open my mouth to tell her, Alex Camarian comes around the corner, wearing his basketball jacket and a huge grin, and throws his arm over Emma's shoulder.

He sticks his face between the two of us, and I hear him murmur into her ear, "Good morning, gorgeous."

"Ugh, Alex," Emma says, giving him a small push but still egging him on with a half smile. "Can't you see we're having a conversation? What do you want?"

Before he can answer her question, the first bell rings. "I'll tell you what I want . . ." he says, pulling her to his chest, ". . . if you walk The Donut with me."

Emma looks at me. Then at Alex. Then down the circular hallway dubbed The Donut.

She gives me another glance, this time asking silent permission, and I give her what I think is an encouraging smile as Alex offers her his arm. "May I?" His pseudo-sexy voice is matched by an earnest expression that makes him look like he's trying out for the lead role in a cheesy soap opera, and I watch as she lets him thread his arm through hers and lead her away. She looks back at me with a shrug and a grimace, like she has no choice but to go with him, and mouths the words *Later, okay?*

Maybe Alex's intervention is a sign: if I am seeing disappearing guys, that information may best be kept to myself. I reach into my locker, grab books for my next three classes and a piece of gum for the road, and stand up.

And that's when I spot him. I freeze, staring at him like the apparition he must be. Dean Parker's arm is draped over his shoulders in a fatherly way as he guides him through the hall, past the throng of students, pointing into doorways and calling his attention to the signs on the walls. Directing him to his first class on his first day at his new school.

The new student. The one from California. A guy with dark shaggy hair—and there's no question in my mind, the same guy I saw at the track.

They pass right by me, neither one giving me so much as a glance. I stand there, slack-jawed and pale, as the two of them round the corner out of sight.

3

I'm usually the first one through the door, but today I make it to Spanish just as the fourth-period bell rings. Señor Argotta watches me with this surprised look on his face, like I'm the last person he expects to be late for his class. He waves the bright yellow tardy slip back and forth in front of me as I walk by. *"Hola*, Señorita Greene." He tries to look stern, but he can't hold the expression for more than a second before his face relaxes back into a grin.

"Hola, señor." I race past him with my head bowed at first, but then I turn around and give him an apologetic smile as I collapse in my chair. I remove my spiral notebook from my backpack and dig around for a mint while I contemplate the mystery this day has become.

He's real. And he's *here*.

I can't stanch the flow of questions racing through my head. First: Where has he been all morning? I've walked

The Donut between every class so far and he's nowhere to be found. Second: Why would a high school kid who's new in town be hanging out at a university track at 6:45 a.m. on a Monday? Third: Why did he look at me like he knew me, but pass right by me two hours later like I was a total stranger? Unless . . . maybe he just didn't see me. If I could just find him, I'd know.

Where is he?

Alex flops into the seat next to me, and Argotta picks up the pad of tardy slips and waves it at him with a scolding voice and matching expression. "You're late, Señor Camarian," he says in his thick accent. But within seconds he returns the pad to his desk, and Alex gets the same understanding smile Argotta gave me.

"Sorry, señor," Alex says toward the front of the room, and then he leans across the aisle, well into my space. "*Hola,* Anna." I blink from the glare of his teeth, blinding under the harsh fluorescent lights.

"Hey, Alex."

He opens his mouth to say something else, but before he can verbalize the thought, Argotta clears his throat at the front of the room and begins speaking.

"Attention, please! Today we are welcoming a brand-new student." I look up and my breath catches. "This is Bennett Cooper." Argotta pauses dramatically while the new guy shifts his weight from one leg to the other and adjusts his backpack over his shoulder. "Everyone, please welcome our new amigo and make him feel at home here." Argotta points at a seat behind me and one row over, and the new guy starts walking toward it. "Now, essays, please, everyone."

Twenty sets of curious eyes follow him, settle on him for a moment, and turn their attention to their respective bags to unearth stapled essays on Spain's admission to the European Union. My eyes are among those that look at him, but are also the only pair that can't seem to look away.

Bennett. His name is Bennett.

He's looking down at his desk and playing with the pages of his textbook like he's embarrassed by all the attention, but after a few moments, he slowly raises his head. I watch his gaze land on the door at the far end of the room, move clockwise around the perimeter of the classroom, and come to a sudden stop when he sees me. Because I'm still staring at him.

I don't know how long my face has been frozen like this, but as soon as I realize that he's caught me, the flush creeps up my neck and into my cheeks, and I feel myself do the only thing I can do at this point: I smile. And I wait for it to be returned, with not just any smile, but *that* smile. The one from the track. The one filled with warmth and recognition and . . . interest. But his expression contains none of the above. Instead he shoots me a small, almost shy smile. The kind of smile one might give a total stranger.

I can't possibly look that different in my uniform than I did in running clothes. *Why is he pretending he doesn't recognize me?* I realize I'm still staring at him, and now the tips of my ears are burning and my face has fully ignited. I flip around in my chair and reach down into my backpack, searching for a distraction. My hair starts to tickle my nose, so when I sit back up, I grab a handful of curls, twist it around my finger, and stick my pencil through the middle to hold it in place.

Twenty minutes later, Argotta snaps my attention back to the room when he holds his arms out wide and exclaims, "Let's do four practice groups today, okay?"

I look down at my notebook and discover that its pages are covered with words and phrases and conjugations, which is surprising, because I don't think I've heard a word Argotta's said. He points to Courtney Breslin in the front row and says, "Count us off, señorita! *Por favor.*"

"*Uno.*" And the count-off continues, snaking its way around the room until it comes to me.

"*Cuatro,*" I say, and then I listen. And work hard not to move my head at all. A few minutes later, I hear what I've been waiting for. The voice over my shoulder says, "*Uno.*"

At the end of the count-off, Argotta yells, "Bring your stuff," and we begin moving around the room to our newly assigned sections. I'm in Group Four and Bennett is in Group One— clear across the room—and this is where we will stay for the remainder of the class. As quickly as he appeared behind me, he is now as far away from me as possible; but at least I can study him better from this angle.

His uniform is the same as the rest of the guys': Black pants and a white oxford shirt under a black V-neck sweater. I think he's wearing Doc Martens, but it's hard to tell from here. It's easy to see what's different: his hair. Most guys wear theirs in some conservative, neatly parted style. Others sport ultrashort Caesars or leave it a little long on top but shaved on the sides. But their hair is never *this* long. Bennett's is unkempt, hangs just a little over his eyebrows, and looks like it hasn't seen a brush in days. I can't remember what he was wearing at the track, but the hair . . . That's definitely the same. The hair I remember.

When the bell rings thirty minutes later, everyone stands up and moves for the door, blocking my view. I rise and reach for my backpack, quickly deciding to talk to him on his way to lunch, but all I catch is the blur of his head as he vanishes through the doorway.

When I go through the double doors to the dining hall, I spot him right away. He's sitting alone at a table in the corner, with his back to the floor-to-ceiling windows. I make my way through the salad bar, grab a banana, and fill a large cup with Coke, all while stealing glances in his direction. As it turns out, I'm in no danger of being caught. In the five minutes it takes me to get my food, he doesn't look up once. He just sits in his chair, holding a paperback in one hand while he picks at his food with the other.

Danielle is already planted at our usual table, and as I set my tray down, I steal another quick look in Bennett's direction. He spoons out bites of red Jell-O without looking away from his book.

"Scoping out the new guy already?" Danielle asks.

I look at her with surprise, then panic. "No." I sit down and reach for my drink. "Why?"

"Oh, come on! I've been watching you. I've never seen anyone work a salad bar with her eyes glued on someone twenty feet away. It's impressive. Quite a skill."

The tips of my ears begin to burn. Again.

She laughs and takes a sip of her Coke. "You're talented, Anna, but you're hardly subtle." She moves close and gives my arm a reassuring pat. "Don't worry. He didn't notice. I don't think he's looked away from that book once."

Emma arrives breathless, plops her tray down on the table, and takes her seat. "So . . . what do we think?" She draws out the last word in a higher inflection.

Danielle shrugs and tilts her chair back, balancing on the two back legs and not even attempting restraint as she stares at him across the room. "He looks . . . oblivious. Do you think he knows there are other people in the room?"

"He looks older, or something," Emma chimes in.

I pretend to look around the room before letting my eyes settle on him again. It's not that he looks older—he's actually got a bit of a baby face. Danielle was closer. He looks indifferent, like he doesn't seem to care that he's here—or care that we're all staring, wondering *why* he's here—and that alone makes him even more interesting. At least to me.

"Hmmm . . . I think I'm disappointed." Emma stares straight at him, taking stock of every detail. She turns back to look at us, eyes wide, nose crinkled. "He's definitely not what I was hoping for. He looks like every other guy in this cold, dreary town. No tan. No hot blond surfer hair." She takes a bite of a bread stick. "I shouldn't have gotten my hopes up."

"Maybe that is surfer hair," suggests Danielle. "How do you know what surfer hair looks like?"

"You know, it's long." Emma wiggles her fingers next to her head. "It looks cool. Not like"—she directs her thumb toward Bennett's table—"that mop top of his."

"Come on, you guys. Give him a break." They both turn to me, their professionally shaped brows raised in matching expressions, and stare. "What?" I shrug and take a deep pull on my straw, letting the cold liquid slide down my throat and cool my face.

Emma finally picks up a forkful of salad and directs it toward her mouth, and for a split second, I think I'm off the hook. But then she stops. "Okay, I'll ask." The lettuce and tomatoes hover in front of her. "Why do you care what we think?"

"I don't. It's just . . . You're just being mean."

"We're not being mean!" Emma looks at Danielle. "Are we being mean?"

Danielle shakes her head no. "I didn't think we were being mean."

"We're just observing. Like . . . scientists." She shoots me a smart-ass grin and pops the fork into her mouth.

I let out a sigh and pick at my sandwich. She's right. Why *do* I care what they think? It's not like I know him. And since

I don't seem to be at all familiar to him, I'm starting to wonder if the thing at the track this morning even happened.

Emma and Danielle are watching me intently and exchanging meaningful glances as they eat. Then Emma shoots Danielle her "don't worry, I've got this one" look, turns to me with those soft eyes, and begins to do what she does best: make people tell her things they don't want to tell her. It's like a superpower or something. "Anna?" she sings. "What's going on?"

I look at her like I know this trick, like I'm not about to give in to it, but then I fold. I bury my face in my hands. "It's nothing. It's just weird." I try to say it under my breath, but it comes out loud enough for them to hear. Emma gently pulls my hands away from my face and makes me look at her.

"What's weird?" Then she remembers this morning, and things click. "Wait, like the weird thing you were going to tell me before class?"

I look around the room, checking for anyone else within earshot, and when I turn back again, I find Emma and Danielle leaning in so close to me their cheeks are nearly touching.

I look around the room again before moving in toward them. "Fine." I let out a sigh. "So . . . I was on my run at the Northwestern track this morning. I ran around a couple of times, and all of sudden, I looked up in the bleachers and saw this guy sitting there, watching me. I ignored him at first—I just kept running and he just kept staring at me—but when I came around the bend . . ." I stop and scan the room one more time. "He was gone. And I mean, *gone* gone. He just . . . disappeared." I leave out the part about how he smiled at me.

"Okay, that's definitely weird," Emma says and looks at me wide-eyed. She must see something in my expression that tells her there's more. "And?"

I gesture with my chin toward Bennett's table. "And that's *him.*" Out loud, it sounds even weirder than it did in my head.

Emma and Danielle spin in their chairs and take him in again. "Are you sure?" Emma asks without taking her eyes off Bennett.

I look past them, directly at his table. "He looks like the same person. Same build. Definitely the same hair. The weirdest thing was that at the track, he looked at me like he . . . knew me or something. But he doesn't even seem to recognize me now." They're still staring. "Please stop looking at him."

"He's not that bad, I guess," says Danielle.

"Yeah, if you look past the hair he's sorta cute," Emma agrees. But when she turns around again her expression is stern, maternal. "But you know, the track thing is sorta creepy."

I look past them, watching him. If he's noticed the three of us talking about him, sizing him up, he never lets on.

"I know!" Danielle says, and I peek up at her with optimistic eyes. "Go up and ask him."

I roll my eyes at her encouraging smile, but before I can even reply, I hear Emma say, "Good idea." She slaps her palms on the table and pushes herself to standing, with an emphatic "Let's just go get this sorted."

"What? No!" I shove my hair behind my ears. "Please don't. I swear if you go over there, I am not speaking to you."

She stops and turns on her heel. "I'm helping."

I grit my teeth and stare her down. "Emma. Atkins. Seriously; please don't."

Emma walks back to our table. "Look, he was watching you and he creeped you out and now he's acting like it never even happened. I want to know why." She turns and starts back toward him, and before I have time to consider bolting from the room, she reaches his table. Danielle and I watch, frozen and lame, as Emma invades his space with a little wave. They shake hands and exchange a few words before she points back in our direction.

He dog-ears his page and stuffs the book into his backpack, then grabs his tray and follows a beaming Emma to our table. I'd probably get more than detention if I reached out and strangled her upon arrival, but that doesn't stop me from considering it.

"Ladies"—Emma extends her arms toward our guest—"this is Bennett Cooper."

He smiles at the two of us and then looks expectantly back at Emma.

"Take a seat here." She pulls an empty chair out from the table and returns to her own. "So, Bennett, this is Danielle. And this"—she pauses in a pathetic attempt at dramatic effect—"is our track star." She gestures toward me, and Bennett's eyes follow until they rest on mine.

"Cross-country," I correct her.

"Whatever." Emma shrugs at me and turns her attention back to Bennett. "She's a runner." She twists in her chair to face him straight on. "But you already knew that, right?" Her accusatory glare is fierce and unrelenting.

Oh. Dear. God.

He looks at her, then back at me, then back at her. "I'm not sure what you mean."

"Didn't you two see each other at the Northwestern track this morning, Bennett?" she asks, sharp and critical, like a lawyer cross-examining her witness. Emma rests her hand on my shoulder. "She runs there at the crack of dawn. She saw you there. You were watching her."

Yes. Emma is going to die.

"Northwestern?" He furrows his brow and stares at us. Like he's never heard of the university that dominates this town. "I'm sorry, but that's impossible. I just moved here over the weekend. I've barely seen *this* campus, let alone the university." He looks straight at me and smiles—kind and sincere, like he's telling the truth—and even though it's not the same smile, it's much closer to the one he shot me at the track. Close enough to make me all the more certain I've got the right guy. "You must have me confused with someone else."

I don't. I stare at him with nervous anticipation, waiting for him to tell me he's just kidding and reach across the table to give me a friendly punch in the arm. But he just sits there.

Looking at me like this is the first time he's ever seen me. And like maybe I'm nuts. "Are you sure? You were wearing a parka," I finally say.

There it is again. His smile is still tinged with confusion, still lacking any sort of recognition, but it's warm. Sweet. The *same*. "I'm sorry, I don't own a parka," he says. "It wasn't me." I want to believe him, but I can't, and when I look over at Emma, she's still wearing a questioning expression that makes me think she doesn't either.

Still, I decide to let him off the hook, and I try to match the warmth in his eyes. "You just look . . . exactly like him. I guess I was mistaken." I hope my expression is masking my lie. And my embarrassment. I reach across the table. "I'm Anna."

He was already reaching his hand forward to meet mine, but it stops midway. "Anna?" He stares at me in disbelief. "Your name is Anna?"

"Ummm, yes. . . . Should it be something else?" I say, surprised to hear a flirtatious inflection creeping into my voice.

"So now her *name* rings a bell!" Emma says to Danielle, far too loudly.

He's still staring at me, and for just a split second, I see a trace of recognition in his expression that reminds me of the look he gave me at the track this morning. But then he snaps out of it and reaches for my hand again.

"Nice to meet you, Anna." Now his voice sounds forced, his handshake is stiff, and anything that looked like recognition has been replaced by a certain stoniness. He lets my hand go and turns to Emma and Danielle, giving each of them a formal nod. "Nice to meet you, too." He stands and carries his tray to the garbage bin in the middle of the room, and I see him shake his head as he walks out through the double doors and disappears into The Donut.

"Okay, *that* was weird." Emma sighs. "But at least it's done." She brushes her hands together as if she'd just completed a nasty chore.

I know she only wanted to protect me, but that doesn't make me feel any better about looking like an idiot. Words like *beyond awkward* and *mortifying* and *why?* pop into my brain, and I want to turn them into cohesive sentences and spit them out; but I can't think straight. Besides, Emma knows that I'm nothing if not true to my word: I'm no longer speaking to her.

⁓

The little bundle of bells that has been hanging on the bookstore door as long as I can remember makes its jingle, and Dad looks up from behind the counter. I lug my backpack over to him and let it land with a thunk.

"What happened to you?" His voice is full of concern.

I left without saying good-bye to Emma and walked two miles through the frozen tundra. My teeth are still chattering, my face is red and chapped from the wind, and there's not a pencil on earth large enough to wrangle my curls into place at this point. "Nothing." I smooth out my hair and distract him with a question. "Has it been slow all day?"

He glances around the empty bookstore my grandfather bought when he retired from teaching at Northwestern fifteen years ago. "Typical March. It'll pick up after finals."

Dad watches as I remove a T-shirt from my bag to change into, then extract textbook after textbook and pile them on the desk. "Good God, how many books can you fit in there? That backpack's like a clown car." He laughs, but I know he's genuinely perplexed by how different my high school experience at Westlake Academy seems from the one he had at Evanston Township.

"You're the one who wanted me to go to that fancy school," I remind him as I wave one of my heftier books in the air.

He grabs it, grimaces like it's far too heavy for him to lift, and lets it crash onto the desk. "You're a rock star." He kisses me on the forehead and heads for the door. "It's supposed to start snowing soon," he says, zipping his parka and wrapping his scarf around his neck. "Give me a call if you want a ride home, okay?"

"It's only three blocks, Dad."

"And I know you're fearless and indestructible, but call me if you change your mind, okay?"

I roll my eyes. "Dad. Three blocks."

He's just about to push the glass door open when I realize that tomorrow morning's walk will be much longer. And colder.

"Hey, Dad." He turns around, one hand resting on the metal bar of the glass door. "I'll take a ride to school in the morning . . . if that's okay?"

"Oh. Does Emma have a doctor's appointment or something?"

"No."

He looks like he's about to ask me what's going on, but he must decide against it, because he just shrugs and says, "Sure," and the little bells jingle behind him.

4

"What am I doing?" I ask out loud as I add a second layer of lip gloss. Staring into the girls' bathroom mirror, I apply a coat of mascara, then roll my eyes at my reflection.

So he's cute. That hardly makes him worth the considerable effort it took me to decide on lip gloss this morning. I'm not a makeup-in-the-bathroom kind of girl, and I feel like I've lost it completely. Yesterday, I thought I was crazy because I was seeing things. I think I prefer that crazy over this one.

As I leave the bathroom and head to fourth period, I start to feel it—the adrenaline rush that I usually associate with the last half mile of a race. I stop outside the classroom for a moment to catch my breath and remind myself to enter the way I planned—looking cool and disinterested. I shake out my arms, rock my head back and forth, and take one last breath before I walk through the door.

I spot Bennett right away. He's reclining in his chair, twisting his pencil back and forth between his fingers. I expect him to look away when we make eye contact, but he doesn't. In fact, his face seems to brighten, like he's happy to see me or something. Then he looks down, still smiling to himself, and starts doodling. He doesn't look up again.

I take my seat and let out the breath I didn't realize I was holding. For something to do, I start extracting my homework from my backpack while everyone else ambles in.

When the bells rings, Argotta throws his arms high in the air and shouts, "Pop quiz!" Thankfully, the chorus of collective groans and the noise of paper being ripped from notebooks drowns out the sound of my heart pounding against my rib cage.

My palms are sweating, and I'm pretty sure the heat from my body alone is about to make my curls frizz up. Without thinking, I sweep my hair back, gather it into a ponytail, twist it around my finger, and hold it in place at the top of my head with one hand while I search through my backpack for a clip. I feel books, a collection of gum wrappers, a roll of Certs, a jewel case, but no clip, no hair band. I look over at the pencil on my desk, which always works in a bind, but I have only one and I need it for the test. My elevated arm is falling asleep and I'm just about to give up when I hear a noise behind me.

"*Pssst.*"

I whirl around, still holding a handful of hair.

Maybe it's because he's leaning so far forward he's practically lying on top of his desk, but he seems so much closer to me right now than he did yesterday. Or perhaps it's not only his physical proximity; it's also the combination of the distance and the expression on his face. His eyes aren't vacant like they were when I stared him down in class yesterday, or confused like they were when my best friend accused him of being a creepy stalker. Today his eyes are soft, like they're smiling completely on their own, and I notice that they're an interesting shade of smoky blue, dotted with little gold flecks that catch and reflect the light. When I finally realize what I am doing—staring into his eyes like a complete moron—I lower my gaze to his mouth to find that it's not only his eyes that are smiling. His mouth is too. Like he's amused. Like he's laughing at me. And that's when I realize I'm missing something.

He points with his chin, attempting to direct my attention away from his face and toward the hand he's been extending in my direction this entire time. The one holding a pencil.

I look at it, and then back at his eyes, puzzled. Then understanding takes over, and I reach forward and take it from him.

Thanks, I mouth.

I turn toward the front of the room, stick the pencil through my hair, and get self-conscious when I realize that in the process I'm revealing the flush creeping up the back of my neck. I take a deep breath and force myself to pay attention to the quiz, which has already begun, but I can't stop the smile creeping onto my face.

He *was* paying attention to me yesterday. He noticed me put my hair up.

It's probably just a plain yellow Dixon Ticonderoga

number two pencil—exactly the same as the one I'm using to complete this ridiculous quiz—but perched in my hair, holding the strands in place, it feels a lot like what we had at the track yesterday: a connection.

Somehow I've managed to go all day without running into Emma. Until now.

I just finished track practice and I'm walking out of the locker room, heading for the student lot and chatting with a few of my teammates, when I see her. She's striding toward her car with her field hockey stick swinging by her side as she moves, and even though I assume she broke into a sweat at some point you'd never know now. Her makeup looks perfect, and her knit cap and gloves match the piping on her warm-up suit. I look down at my sweats. I came straight out of the shower, towel-dried my hair, and piled it under a baseball cap to keep it from freezing on my walk home.

"I'll get the heat going!" she yells when she sees me. After she opens the door and starts the engine, she gets out of the car and relaxes against the hood, waiting for me.

I take a quick look up at the sky and see a mass of dark clouds moving into formation, preparing to send down fury in the form of hard snow. I look down again and see Emma, smiling and beckoning. For just a split second, my resolve melts a little and I picture myself collapsing into the heated seat. I really don't want to walk home. But there is no way, *no way*, I'm letting her off that easy.

I keep walking with the group, straight past her car.

"Anna!" I can hear the shock and hurt in her voice. "Wait." The sound of her tennis shoes padding cautiously behind me closes in and I pick up my pace a little. "Seriously, can't you just stop and talk to me? I'm trying to apologize." My teammates look at me and then at one another. I wave them on and slow down so Emma can catch up.

She grabs me by the shoulder. "I really am sorry." Her remorse looks genuine and her British accent makes her sound so sincere that I'm tempted to throw my arms around her and forgive her without another word. But I haven't forgotten how mortified I felt yesterday, how she made a fool of me. And so instead, I just stare at her.

"I'm sorry," she repeats, and hugs me. I want to hug her back but instead stand rigid.

Her grip loosens, and when she steps back from me I can see how hurt she looks. But then her expression softens and she reaches forward, takes my face in her hands, and squeezes my cheeks in a soft-mittened vise grip. "I was an ass. Please don't be mad at me anymore. I simply can't take it."

I let out a sigh. "That was really uncool." My voice comes out garbled since she's now squeezing so hard my lips are pursed in a fish face.

"I know. But you love me anyway, right?" She wiggles my cheeks. "Right? Just a little?" And that's all it takes. Because I do. When I try not to laugh, my lips must look even funnier, because Emma lets out a snort, and that makes us both crack up.

She finally stops squeezing, but keeps holding my face. "I really am sorry. I just got carried away. I wasn't trying to embarrass you."

I bite my lip. "You did."

"I know."

"Please don't do it again."

"I won't," she says with a smile and a hard shake of her head. She grips my shoulders and air-kisses each of my cheeks. They still feel red from all the squeezing. "Can we get in the car now?" She clenches her jaw and shivers.

When I nod, she leads me to the Saab. She even opens my door and ushers me in before going around to her side and taking her place behind the wheel.

"Where to?" she asks. "Want to grab a coffee?"

"I can't. It's Tuesday."

"Right, family dinner night." She backs out into the nearly empty parking lot. We're silent for a few seconds, and I think she's going to reach over and crank the stereo like she always does, but instead she turns to me. "So, do you still think the new guy was the one watching you at the track?"

I shrug. "I don't know." I start to tell Emma about the pencil, but I stop myself. To someone who already considers him creepy, it might sound weird rather than charming. Come to think of it, perhaps *I* should have found it weird rather than charming. I reach up and touch the top of my head, having forgotten that I'm now wearing a baseball cap and the pencil is tucked safely in my backpack.

"Do you want my opinion?" Emma asks.

"Do I have a choice?"

"No. Stay away from him. I don't know what it is, but there's something . . . off about him."

"Oh, come on. That's just because of the track thing. He made it clear he'd never been to Northwestern. I must have been wrong." I'm not sure why I'm defending him, and I'm still sure I am *not* wrong, but I think I sound pretty convincing.

"What about how he reacted to your name?"

Yeah. That was weird. I shrug.

"Look at you. You think he's cute." She draws out the words as her accent intensifies.

"I don't even know him."

"You don't have to know him to think he's cute."

"Sure I do." I glare at her. "I'm just . . . curious about him, that's all." But if I'm being completely honest, Emma may be right. I exchanged a few meaningless glances and a pencil with him, and that somehow gave him the right to creep into my head and settle there.

The car skids to a stop in front of the house, leaving a two-foot space between my door and the snow-covered sidewalk. Emma turns to face me. "I missed you this morning, by the way."

"Me too." I finally reach over and hug her. I get out of the car and shut the door behind me, and she peels away, kicking up a flurry of dirty snow.

"Grab a knife!" Mom's singsong holler carries from the kitchen into the hallway, over Pavarotti's booming tenor. I follow the tantalizing smell of roasting peppers and onions and see Mom hard at work in the kitchen.

"Hi, honey!" Mom looks up with a smile and returns to her sauce. She's wearing a black apron over her scrubs, and her dark curls—the ones she passed down to me—are piled into a clip on top of her head, though a few loose ringlets have escaped to frame her face. She hums along with the Italian music as she draws a blade through ripe tomatoes. "Can you start slicing the mozzarella?" She uses her knife to point at the ball of slimy white cheese on the counter. "How was school?"

I twist around to watch Mom slide the last of the tomatoes into the stockpot, give them a little stir, and take a seat on one of the bar stools facing me. She rests her elbows on the counter, and I stop cutting to glance up at her. She's waiting for me to tell her everything, because it's Tuesday—the day we cook and I tell her who's dating whom, who's fighting with whom, and who's not quite cutting it on the track. Then I ask her what's going on at the hospital, and even though I imagine it's all fairly mundane, and often a sad place to spend a day, she makes it sound like she works on the set of *ER*, crafting dramatic stories about people who have pulled through even when there seemed to be no hope, and doctors who flirt with nurses, and patients who flirt with doctors. I'm glad she enjoys her job, especially since I know the only reason she went back to work was to help cover my Westlake tuition. It was my parents' idea to send me there, but it takes two salaries to pay for it. Tuesday-night dinner is pretty much all they ask for in return.

"Well?" Her eyes are wide, and she looks like she's about ready to burst. "Go ahead. Tell me about your week so far. Anything juicy?"

I hear myself say, "It's been fine," and I cast my eyes down at my cutting board, run the knife through the mozzarella, and watch it cluster onto the wood. "How about you? How was your day?" I ask in a voice that sounds far too high-pitched, and fake.

I don't look directly at her, but in the periphery I can see her squirm in her seat, like she doesn't know what to do with herself, and the seconds drag on until she speaks again.

"Oh, come on!" she finally says. "It can't be my turn yet." She gets up to check the sauce, hums along with the music again while she gives it a stir, and returns to her spot at the counter. "Come on," she repeats, beaming and practically begging. "There must have been *something* interesting."

I want so much to tell her the truth. Yesterday, someone disappeared right before my eyes. I almost got a tardy slip for the first time in my life. I walked home from school, because, until thirty minutes ago, my best friend and I weren't speaking. And there's a pencil sitting in my backpack that shouldn't feel quite so important. I want to tell her that, so far, nothing about this week has been normal, and that alone is interesting.

Mostly, I want to tell her that there's a guy at the center of all of the excitement, so she can ask me if he's cute and I can blush and nod. Instead, I keep my eyes on the cutting board and say, "I got an A on that anatomy paper you helped me with last week."

She gives me a small, forced smile. "Oh. Well . . . that's good." I can still feel her watching me slice and hoping I'll say more, and I move slowly, waiting for the right amount of time to pass so I can turn the subject back to her. After a few minutes, I hear her start drumming her fingertips on the counter. Finally, when she can no longer stand the silence, she sits up, her back straight. "Okay, I'll go," she says, and she launches into a long story about one of the nurses who got caught kissing an EMT out by the ambulance bay.

Fifteen minutes later, I hear the front door open and close. "I'm home!" Dad yells from the foyer. When he arrives in the kitchen, Mom and I are standing side by side at the counter, layering noodles, sauce, and cheese in a deep casserole dish.

"Hi, Annie." He leans down and kisses the crown of my head.

"Hey, Dad." I lift my cheesy, tomatoey fingers out of the lasagna and give him a little wave.

But before he can take another step, Mom turns around and grabs his face in her sauce-covered hands. "Hi, honey."

Dad takes two steps back, bright red handprints on both cheeks, and we both watch him, eyes wide as we wait to see how he'll react. He just stands there, stunned. Then he shakes his head and gives Mom a peck on her nose. "I'll just go wash up," he says.

"You do that," Mom says with a laugh, and the two of us crack up while we top off our creation with handfuls of shredded cheese. Then the dish goes into the oven, Mom heads for the shower, and I trudge up to my room to start on my homework.

I plop down on my shag rug and open my backpack. In the small zippered compartment in the front, I spot the pencil, right where I left it, now blanketed in gum wrappers. I take it out and run it back and forth between my fingers, just like Bennett was doing this morning as I walked through the door. I close my eyes, picturing the way he smiled as he held it out to me. And I start concocting a plan to return it.

5

Stalling.

There are more details behind my brilliant scheme to return Bennett's pencil, but that's basically what it comes down to— stalling. I intend to dawdle on my way to Spanish so I won't have time to return it before class. Then, when the lunch bell rings, I'll stand up, turn around to block Bennett's path, and give it back to him. If everything goes according to plan, I'll be able to keep him talking all the way to the dining hall.

My heart is racing as I arrive at the door. The bell rings, right on cue, but as I walk into the classroom and pass Señor Argotta, he claps and announces, "Conversation practice! Time to move, everybody!" He bursts out with it like he's declaring a celebration.

No. Not conversation practice. This is the worst of Argotta's clever little group exercises. I've timed my arrival perfectly, but it won't matter if Bennett ends up on the other side of the room again.

Argotta's walking through the rows of desks, breaking us up into pairs, and passing out laminated cards that depict a situation no one would ever find themselves in on a trip to Spain—or anywhere else in the world, for that matter. He gives me my card, and I shut my lids tight, fearing the worst. I open one eye and read: *Partner number one, you are interviewing for a job as a waiter/waitress at one of Madrid's finest restaurants. Partner number two, you are the restaurant owner.* I look over at Alex, my usual partner, and he winks.

Señor Argotta stops and turns back. "Señorita Greene, partner with Señor Cooper, *por favor.*"

What? No. I'm sorry, señor. I cannot partner with Bennett Cooper. All night I've pictured how I'm going to return his pencil. How I'm going to ask him again—when he's not under Emma's and Danielle's scrutiny—if he was at the track on Monday. I'm going to ask him why he seemed to know me then, but now he doesn't. I've pictured the whole discussion, right down to the last detail; but I've never pictured talking with him in *Spanish.*

I consider running for the door. Faking a seizure. I could move across the room and take the open seat across from Señor *Kestler,* as if I've misunderstood Argotta's accent. But it's too late. Bennett has heard the instructions just as plainly as I have, and now he's eyeing me with this "don't worry, I won't bite" look. He lifts his chin like he's commanding me to stand up, and when I do, he turns my desk around to face his.

"Hi," I say when we're both settled again.

"Hi. Anna, right?" Bennett looks completely relaxed, and the act of verbalizing my name doesn't seem to cause the odd reaction it did in the dining hall two days ago.

"Yeah." I look down at the table, trying not to look at his eyes for fear of getting trapped in there again. "Bennett, right?"

He nods.

"Do you ever go by 'Ben'?" Where did *that* come from? Oh, God.

He grins. "No. Just . . . Bennett."

And here comes the flush. I wonder if he is as curious to know what I look like without a red face as I am to see him with a haircut. "Thanks for the loan." As I pass him the pencil, I can feel all my questions just sitting there, waiting for me to launch them one by one, but I can't seem to find my voice now that he's sitting here across from me.

"Any time," he says as he sets it in the long groove at the top of the wooden desk. The pencil must have magnetic properties, because it seems to be pulling both of us into it. "So, what's our assignment today?" he asks as he leans forward, and I swallow the questions down.

"I'm afraid it's a tough one." I reach over, bridging the gap between our two desks, and set the card down with the words facing him.

He picks it up, and a grin gradually spreads over his face. "Oh, this should be easy." He leans forward, like he has a secret. "I've interviewed for several waiter jobs in Madrid before."

"Really?"

"No." He smiles. "I'm kidding."

I laugh too loud. "Well, good." I take a deep breath to steady my nerves and press my palms flat on the desk to keep my hands from shaking. I move in toward him and say, "I have no idea how to hire someone in this country or any other one." I take the card from his desk and lean back, trying to look comfortable. "So," I begin in my most practiced Spanish diction, "tell me about your experience as a waiter, Señor Cooper."

Bennett launches into a lengthy description of his work at various fictitious restaurants throughout Spain. In perfectly crafted sentences, he describes his expertise with a crumb scraper. He explains how he can talk any customer into getting the special of the day instead of the dish they really wanted. He can handle ten tables at once, including large parties, and he always overtips the bussers. He says it all with a straight face and the smallest trace of a glint in his eye.

I understand his Spanish, but I have to work to hear the words he says. He speaks beautifully. His voice is steady and strong, the cadence is balanced, and I'm completely transfixed, pulled into the richness of his voice. He tells about another fictitious job in a restaurant in Seville called *El Mesero Mejor.* The Best Waiter.

By the end he has me smiling. Laughing. And more than a little bit in awe. He concludes in his perfectly confident Spanish: "So you see, I am a perfect waiter for your restaurant." I'm not sure how much time passes between the completion of this sentence and his next word: "Well?" He raises his eyebrows and waits for my reply.

When I realize he's caught me staring again, I bite my lip and wait for the flush to spread over my face, but this time, nothing happens. I go with it. "You're hired," I say with a shrug.

"Wow? Just like that?" he says in English. "You're an easy manager."

I try to think of a clever response, but my mind is blank. "Your Spanish is really good," I say instead.

"I did a study abroad program in Barcelona last summer."

I smile when I think about living in Barcelona with a local family. "I'd love to do that. It must have been fun to *live* there. To really get into another culture."

"It was pretty incredible." He rests his forearms on the desk. "How about you? Have you been to Spain?"

"No," I say under my breath. "I haven't been . . . anywhere. I work at my family's bookstore, and I spend a lot of time in the travel section. That's about as close to the rest of the world as I get."

"I'm surprised to hear that." He leans in even closer, like he's got a secret to divulge. "This is only my third day here, but it seems like a fairly well-traveled bunch."

"It is." I shrug again. "I'm just not . . . part of that particular bunch."

"So, you work in a bookstore." It's a statement, not a question. "And read travel books."

I look at him and try to think how to respond. I'm long past the point of being embarrassed by the fact that I'm the poorest kid in this incredibly wealthy high school, but he doesn't need to rub it in. "Something like that. I take it you travel a lot."

"Me?" He looks down at the table. "Yeah. You could definitely say that. . . ." He trails off and seems to be suppressing a smile. "I love traveling." My expression must show my confusion, because his face gets serious as he clarifies. "Yes. I travel a lot. . . . As much as I can."

"Lucky you." The words sound bitter as they leave my mouth, and I immediately wish I could pull them back.

"I'm sorry. Was that rude? I didn't mean it to be."

"No." It's not his fault I've barely left the state. "You weren't rude."

"Look, anyone who wants to travel can find a way to do it. You just have to get creative."

Señor Argotta suddenly turns the corner, coming within earshot, and Bennett switches back to Spanish. He looks me right in the eye. "You know what they say, *La vida es una aventura atrevida o no es nada.*" He looks out of the corner of his eye, thinking. "I can't remember who said that."

I laugh under my breath.

"What?" Bennett's smiling along with me, even though he has no idea why I'm so amused.

"Helen Keller," I whisper, picturing the poster that hung on the wall in Miss Waters's English class back in seventh grade, its white sailboat fighting against the current in the foreground and the quote *Life is either a daring adventure or nothing* in block letters below.

"She probably didn't say it in Spanish, then."

I try to stifle my laugh but it's hopeless. "No, probably not." We're both still smiling and watching each other, but I break the connection when I look up to be sure Argotta can't hear us speaking English. He's clear across the room, kneeling down next to another team and helping them through a translation. When I look back at Bennett, I discover that his eyes haven't left me.

"Well, whatever language it's in," I say, "I have to agree with her. I, for one, am ready for a *lot* more adventure and a lot less nothing."

His smile fades, and he looks at me with a serious expression. I think he's about to say something significant, but he presses his lips together. I watch him, waiting him out, until it's clear that he's planning to stay silent.

"Were you going to say something?" I finally ask.

He gives me a little grin. "Yeah . . . actually . . ." But then the bell rings. "Never mind," he says rising and heading for the door. "I'll see you later, okay?"

I watch him walk across the room and out into the hallway. When I look down at the desk I see the pencil, still sitting in the groove, right where he put it. I twist my hair and hold it against the back of my head with one hand while I stick the pencil in place with the other.

<hr />

See you later. That's what he said three days ago—*See you later.* But I didn't see him later at all. He wasn't in the dining

hall, I didn't run into him in The Donut, and he wasn't in the student lot.

He was in Spanish on Thursday and Friday—and I'm certain he was watching the door for me both days, because the minute I walked in he looked down at his desk. But there was no satisfied grin when he saw me, no smile on his face as he doodled—and he didn't look up again before I took my seat. Each day, I'd tried to return the pencil, but he bolted for the door in perfect synchronization with the bell. And it was as if our conversation had never even happened.

6

The storm that starts on Saturday morning rains out my track meet, keeps me awake all night, and doesn't let up until afternoon. I walk to the bookstore in a daze, and when I manage to make it to the corner without breaking anything, I decide to reward myself with a latte. Even with the stop, I have fifteen minutes to kill before my shift, so I head into the record store.

"Anna!" Justin yells over the loud, steady backbeat of music coming from the ceiling, godlike and omnipresent. He walks out from behind the counter and pulls me in for a hug. "I was hoping you'd come by this weekend."

"Hey, buddy," I say, and silently scold myself for calling him that. It's probably worse than calling him Freckles, but words like *buddy* or *pal* or some other brotherly sounding term seem to pop out of my mouth whenever I see him. He pulls back and looks at me, and even though it's only for a brief flash, it's there. A twinge, like I just insulted him.

"What's this?" I ask, pointing up at the music.

He leans in close to me. "I scored." He looks around the store to be sure no one's listening—and no one is, since we're the only ones here. "The drummer from Nirvana just cut a demo, and Elliot let me borrow it." I don't know who Elliot is, but I imagine he's someone important at Northwestern's student-run radio station, where Justin has been interning for the last three months. While I dream of visiting far-off places, he dreams of moving into a high-rise dorm just down the street so he can major in broadcasting and spend his college years as a DJ for the station's legendary *The Rock Show*.

"Do you want to borrow it?" he asks as he steps even closer to me.

"No, really, that's—" I'm shaking my head, but it doesn't matter. He's already walking away, and when he ducks down behind the counter, the music stops. He comes back carrying the CD. "Here, take it. Tell me what you think."

"Really?"

"Absolutely. Just bring it back sometime next week."

"Thank you. That is so cool of you," I say as I press it to my chest.

"I think you'll like it."

"I'm sure I will. You know I trust you completely." I look up and find him watching me, and that's when I feel it. Him wanting to kiss me.

"Any other new stuff?" I try to turn his attention toward the rest of the new releases on the wire rack.

"Not there." He shoots me a smile and gestures for me to follow him to his usual spot behind the counter. Then he disappears and pops up again, placing a jewel case on the counter between us. The paper cover is painted in watercolors: blues and reds and greens, all swirling in interesting patterns and fading off at the sides. Like any watercolor, it's unique. One of a kind. Still, it matches all the others on my shelf in my bedroom.

"A new running mix!" I pick it up, flip it over, and read the track names. "You have no idea. I'm so tired of skipping through tracks on my CDs. I always run best to yours."

"I have to say, I outdid myself this time." He smiles and blushes, and I watch how the hue makes his freckles disappear. He's kind like no other guy I know, and I wish for a moment that I could think of him as more than a friend.

"I'm sure you did." And there it is again. In his mind, this is the moment in the movie where I leap over the counter and rip the buttons off his shirt. Instead, I look at my watch. Three fifty-nine. "Shoot." I gesture across the street toward the bookstore. "I've got to run and release my dad from duty. Do you need any books?" I hold up my new CDs. "You know the deal—one for one."

He nods. "Actually, I wanted to ask you some—" Justin trails off and we both turn our attention to the front door, watching as a girl in sorority letters walks in, comes straight to the counter, and stands next to me, waiting. Justin shoots me an annoyed look. "Never mind. I'll just try to come by the bookstore later."

Once my back is turned, I let out a sigh of relief and silently thank the Tri-Delt for buying me a bit more time.

⌒

Time seems to have slowed to a crawl. Northwestern students come in and look around, then leave. Mothers come in with their toddlers in tow, browsing the Book Club Recommendations table while their kids destroy the picture-book section. I scan credit cards, adjust books into place until all the bindings are even and the newer books are displayed with prominence, and read the Michelin guide to the Côte d'Azur. At 8:50, I total the day's sales, zip the cash into the green vinyl envelope, and lock it in the safe in the back room. I flip the sign on the front door to CLOSED and click the dead bolt in place.

The coffeehouse is already packed. Finals week at Northwestern has just ended, and no one's studying tonight. In fact, most look haggard and worn, like they've been celebrating since Friday afternoon.

As I walk by, I casually look in the window to see if I can spot Justin with his radio-station friends. He seemed so eager to talk to me earlier, but he never came by the bookstore tonight.

I keep walking, and round the corner to my dark and quiet block. I see a sudden movement in the park across the street and I slow my pace, squinting into the darkness. It's hard to see any details, but there's definitely someone there, and I narrow my eyes again until I make out the shape of a person, doubled over on the park bench, rocking back and forth. I step onto the grass to get a closer look. I gasp, because even from this distance, I'm pretty sure I know who it is.

My feet seem to move toward him on their own, and when I'm within earshot, I whisper, "Bennett? Is that you?" There's no response, but now I'm close enough to make out the sound of groaning, low and weak. "Bennett?" I take small steps, moving in a little closer. "Are you okay?"

"Go away," he grunts. He tries to raise his head, but it drops farther into his lap, and he rubs his temples, making that guttural sound again. I realize he's saying something, so I bend in closer. "I can't leave," he's whimpering. "I've got to find her." He's rocking and moaning and repeating the words, and I'm watching and shaking and starting to freak out.

Suddenly, he stops moving and his eyes find me. He seems surprised to see me standing next to him. "Anna?"

"Yeah, it's me. I'm going to go get you some help. Stay here, I'll be right back."

"No!" He says the single word with force, but it's tinged with agony, and I know there's no way that I can handle this alone.

"Bennett, you need help." I pivot on my heel to leave.

"No." He reaches out and grabs my wrist. "Please. Don't. Go." I stop cold and whirl around. It looks like it's taking all his strength for him to lift his head. "It's . . ." He takes another deep breath. "It's easing up now." But I don't believe him. In spite of the temperature and the frozen bench he's planted on, sweat is beading up on his forehead and running down his cheeks. He looks like me after a sprint, concentrating on each inhale and exhale. "Please. Just. Sit."

I look around the pitch-black park, drop my backpack on the ground by his feet, and kneel down beside it. I can't bring myself to sit on that cold bench.

"I'll be okay." He rubs his temples again and slowly raises his head. His voice sounds a little stronger now. "It's a migraine," he says between breaths. "I get them when . . ." His voice trails off. "Just sit with me, Anna? Please?" I look back toward the coffeehouse.

I start to lean forward to rub his back like my mom would, like a friend who knows him much better than I do might, but I catch my hands and force them to my sides. For the next five minutes, the only sound between us is his labored breath.

"Keep breathing." It's the only thing I can think to say, even though I realize it's not helpful.

Finally, he sits up a little straighter. "Do me a favor?" He hasn't even told me what it is and I'm already nodding. "Don't tell anyone about this."

"I won't." I shake my head and watch the sweat still dripping down his cheeks. "But can I please go get you some water? I'll be fast."

He doesn't say yes, but at least this time he doesn't argue. Before he changes his mind and stops me, I stand up, leaving my backpack at his feet, and sprint back to the coffeehouse. The girl behind the counter gives me a cup of ice water, and I run back to the bench.

"Here you—" I start to say, but my words hang in the air. My backpack is still on the frozen ground, but Bennett is gone.

7

Bennett's not in Spanish on Monday. Or on Tuesday. I'm starting to lose my mind with worry, but Ms. Dawson in Administration is less concerned.

"Can I just get his phone number?" I beg. "I just want to be sure he's okay." I use my most responsible voice, but it doesn't have the desired effect.

True to my word to Bennett, I've omitted large sections of the story I told her—like the park, the sweat beading up on his face, and the fact that he was moaning about needing to find someone. I'm not sure which part of "Don't tell anyone about this" Bennett wanted me to keep under wraps, but I hope it didn't include the migraine, because I can't think of any reason to be asking about his personal information without disclosing that part.

"I know you just want to help, Miss Greene, but you know I can't release another student's confidential information. I'm sorry." Her tone is patronizing and not at all apologetic. "I'm sure he'll be here tomorrow."

How the hell do you know? I want to say, but instead I mumble, "Thanks," and shuffle out the door. I never should have left him there. All he wanted me to do was sit with him, and instead I left him alone on a bench in a dark deserted park, sweating and panting.

I head into the locker room and change, but as I listen to the team chatter, I start to dread the idea of running in a circle on an overcrowded track. I duck out before anyone notices and make my way to the abandoned and frozen cross-country course instead. And as I run, I try to listen to the sounds of the wind and the woods, the rhythm of my feet sloshing through the mucky trail, but all I hear is his voice in my head: *Just sit with me, Anna? Please?* I feel horrible.

As it turns out, Ms. Dawson was wrong. Bennett isn't at school on Wednesday. Or on Thursday. By Friday afternoon, as I'm walking The Donut between fifth and sixth—and freaking out about facing the entire weekend without knowing what's happened to him—the solution hits me out of nowhere. It's my only option.

I rush to Emma's locker and wait, but she doesn't show. When the bell rings, I pull out my spiral notebook and scribble, *I need to talk to you.* Folding the paper into a small square, I feed it through one of the vents and sprint to class.

After the bell rings again, I race back to Emma's locker

and find her there, reading my note. "I need your help, Em," I blurt out. "Do you think you can get something from the office for me?"

"Probably."

"I need Bennett Cooper's phone number. I asked Dawson and she wouldn't give it to me. But she likes when you come into the office and talk about your auction-party planning, so maybe she'll tell you." She starts to say something, but I stop her. "Please don't ask why I need it."

Emma presses her lips together and raises her eyebrows. She stares at me and does that *tell-me-everything* superpower thing.

"Look. I ran into him last Sunday night, and he was . . . sick. Now he hasn't been here all week. I just want to be sure he's okay." I'm standing there, bracing myself against her locker and preparing for the inquisition, when she breaks into a huge grin.

"You wanna shag Shaggy!" She laughs as I look around wildly to see if anyone's heard her. "Come on, just say it. You like this guy, don't you?" We stare at each other. I don't reply. She repeats herself. "Don't you?"

I let out the breath that's been constricting my chest. "I'm just worried about him."

She stares at me with big eyes.

"Okay, maybe."

She grins. "See. You did it. The first step is admitting you're powerless," she says, bastardizing the first of AA's Twelve Steps. "Let me see what I can do. I'll meet you at the car after school."

"How are you going to get it?"

"I don't know yet. I'll think of something."

An hour later, in the warmth of the Saab, Emma is euphoric, boasting about her skills in crafty manipulation.

"I really can't take any credit for the first thing that happened. That was absolute luck," she says as she whips the car out of the parking space. "Get this. I walked in and Dawson's on the phone—with Argotta, I assume—saying she needs this week's Spanish work so she can take it to Bennett Cooper's house tonight." Butterflies come to life in my stomach at the sound of his name. Someone, please shoot me. "So I offered to take his homework to him."

"She gave you his homework?"

"No. She said she couldn't do that—it wasn't allowed. *Not even for you, Miss Atkins.*" She mimics Dawson's voice to a tee.

"So you didn't get it?"

"Of course I got it."

"Great. Where is it?"

"I'm getting to that part." She turns in to the street and the driver she cuts off lays on the horn. "So I start asking her questions about the auction—so she thinks that's why I came in, right?—and Dawson starts telling me about this great cabin in Wisconsin that the Allens own. . . ."

"Oh, please. You're killing me. Get to the point."

"Okay, okay. So we're talking about the auction, and Señor Argotta comes in and drops a stack of papers on the counter. She thanks him, he leaves, she goes to the monitor—now she's telling me about some antique photos someone else is donating to auction off—grabs a Post-it, writes down the address, and sticks it on the pile."

"And?"

She pauses for dramatic effect. "Two-eight-two Greenwood."

"What about the phone number?"

She flips around to face me. "Are you kidding? No *Thanks, Emma*? No *You're amazing, Emma*?" She brings her attention back to the road, shaking her head.

"I just wanted to call—"

"Well, she didn't write down his phone number, and I couldn't see the screen. But don't you see? I got the better of the two!"

"But now I have to go there!" I wince at the thought.

She shoots me that satisfied smile she wears when she gets her way. "Exactly."

~

I can't believe I'm doing this.

I peek out from behind the tall hedge again and stare at the house. Impressive. Two, maybe even three, stories. Tudor style. A carriage house out back, if I'm assessing accurately from this distance and the three times I've walked past the house, chickened out, and hidden behind shrubbery.

Why am I doing this?

I let out a heavy sigh as I move from behind the bushes, walk toward the house again—this time with a determined stride—and turn onto the recently shoveled walkway. It's only 5:30, but it's almost completely dark, and I'm shaking as

I climb the steps. When I reach the top, I pick up the lion's-head door knocker and take a deep breath before I bring it down.

I wait.

There's no answer.

I knock again, tightening my coat against the wind, and glad I've traded my tights and skirt for jeans.

Just as I turn to leave, I hear footsteps. "Who's there?" asks an elderly-sounding woman from the other side of the door.

"I'm sorry. Never mind." I back away and head for the steps. "I think I have the wrong house."

The dead bolt makes a heavy *thunk* and the door opens slowly. She's older but not elderly, and striking, with long gray hair and smoky blue eyes. She's wearing a red silk scarf over her dark, loose-hanging clothes, and smiling at me with a curious expression.

"Hi." She opens the door, wide and welcoming.

"Hi. I'm looking for someone named Bennett, but I'm so sorry. I think I have the wrong address." I start to turn away again.

"No, you don't; Bennett's here. Come on in and warm up." She moves back to make room for me in the entryway.

"I'm Maggie." She holds out her hand.

"Anna." I shake it, still wondering who she is.

"You must be a friend from school."

"Yes." I'm not sure I qualify as a friend, but it's the simplest answer. "I'm sorry to impose, ma'am." Yes. I'm an idiot for coming here. And I'm just now realizing this.

"No imposition, dear." She gestures toward the room on the other side of a wide arch. "Have a seat, and I'll go up and get him."

I peek inside as she turns and starts up the staircase. The living room, with its massive windows, is beautiful, tastefully decorated with dark antique furniture that makes it even more welcoming than I expected it would be. The fire is warm and creates a soft glow.

Instead of sitting on the couch, I walk around, taking a closer look at the room. The wall surrounding the fireplace is lined from top to bottom with dark-stained bookcases filled with a collection of classics that puts the bookstore's section to shame. With the exception of a large black-and-white portrait of Maggie and her husband on their wedding day, framed photos of a little girl—dark hair, bangs cut straight across her forehead—take up every available surface. Some include her mother. A few feature both parents. It's hard to miss the framed snapshot in the center of the mantel: the same little girl, sitting in a chair and smiling up at the camera, clutching a tiny baby with a tuft of dark hair.

"Those are my grandchildren," says a quiet voice behind me, and I jump. I hadn't heard her return. "That's Brooke. She's two. And that's my new grandson." She runs her finger across the glass.

"They're really cute," I say.

She returns the photo to its shelf and picks up another one. "This is my daughter." She points to a photo of a woman with the same little girl on her lap.

"Do they live here in Illinois?"

"No. San Francisco." She lets out a sad sigh. "I keep trying to get them to move back home, but her husband's job keeps them in California. I haven't even met the new baby yet."

Suddenly, I have the strange sensation that we're no longer alone. I glance over my shoulder and find Bennett standing in the archway, watching us. His hair is stringy, his skin is masked by patchy stubble, and the heavy circles under his bloodshot eyes make him look as if he hasn't slept in days. The vacant expression on his face ups the severity.

"What are you doing here?" His voice is tight, and he blinks involuntarily, like his eyes are adjusting to what little light there is in the room.

Maggie jumps in before I can find my voice. "I was just showing your friend photos of my new grandson, Bennett." She turns back to me. "Can you believe that ? I've never met anyone with the first name Bennett, and now I know two of them!" She shakes her head at the impossibility.

I look back and forth between them, confused. Bennett winces.

"Do you two want some tea?" Maggie says, seemingly unaware of the tension that's hanging around us. "I was just about to make some."

"No," Bennett answers before I can, shifting his weight back and forth.

Maggie ignores him and looks at me, her eyes still innocent and questioning. "Anna?"

"No, thank you, Mrs.—"

She rests her hand on my shoulder. "Call me Maggie, dear. Maggie's just fine."

I return her smile. "Thank you, Maggie."

Bennett gestures for me to follow him, and we leave Maggie alone to make her tea. We climb the staircase in silence and continue down a dark hallway. Like the living room, its walls are lined with photos, but these are more dated.

His bedroom is nearly dark, insufficiently lit by a small lamp that barely brightens the wooden desk. Coffee cups and empty plastic water bottles are scattered everywhere. Books and papers are strewn all over the floor and across the surface of his twin bed. The antique furniture is beautiful, but hardly reflects the tastes of a high school boy. He looks out of place in the sea of mahogany.

He reaches over my shoulder to shut the bedroom door, and the proximity makes my heart race. Until I realize that he smells like sweat and dirty socks. My face must show something that looks like disgust, because he drops his gaze and takes a step backward. "I wasn't expecting company."

"It's okay . . . I'll just . . . I'm sorry. I'm interrupting you, aren't I?" He doesn't give any hint that he's accepting my apology. He also doesn't clear space for me to sit down on any available surface, so I stand, awkward and nervous, leaning against the doorframe.

"I'm sorry about my grandmother," he says, so quietly I have to strain to hear him.

I'm confused. "Your grandmother? Maggie is your grandmother?"

"She has Alzheimer's." He looks past my eyes and studies the door as if considering his next words. "In her mind, I'm— I'm like an infant."

"Really?" I play back the conversation in the living room. "But . . . the pictures stop seventeen years ago. . . ."

He nods. There's a long, uncomfortable pause, and I feel bad for bringing the pictures up. "They just upset her. We had to take them away."

"So, who does she think *you* are?"

"After my grandfather died, money was tight and she was lonely, so she started to rent this room out to Northwestern students." He makes a dismissive gesture and stares down at the floor. "I guess she thinks . . ." He trails off, and the room goes silent.

He looks horrible. His skin is sallow, and his red eyes are half closed. "Are you okay? You look tired."

He stares at me, and when he finally talks, he doesn't answer my question. Instead, he draws his eyebrows together as he asks one of his own. "What are you doing here?"

The way he asks the question makes me even more nervous. "I haven't seen you since last Sunday night in the park. When you were . . . you know . . ." I wait a moment for a response, and when none comes, I blurt out the rest. "You didn't show up at school this week, and I got worried, I guess, and I . . . I just wanted to make sure you were okay." I reach behind me for the doorknob. "And now I know you're alive. Which is . . . you know . . . really great. So I'll just go now." It hits me like a shot that a phone call would have been much more appropriate, and I want to kill Emma. What was I thinking, showing up at this guy's house like I *know* him?

"Sunday." He squints past me. "That's right. I forgot about that."

I let go of the knob and stare at him. Forgot? How could he have forgotten?

"Are you sure you're okay, Bennett?"

"Yes. I'm fine. I just . . ." He looks worried. No. Panicked. "How did you find me, anyway?"

I feel my hands start to shake. "I got your address from the office." It's true. There's no sense in bringing Emma into this if I don't need to.

"Someone in the office just *gave* you my address?"

"No. It was on a Post-it." Also true.

He looks at me, confused, and he opens his mouth to speak. But suddenly, all the color leaves his face. He wobbles a bit, feeling for the wall as he steadies himself.

I reach forward and grab his arm. "Are you okay?"

He tries to talk, but nothing comes out. He draws in a few labored breaths.

"I'll go get your grandmother." I start to release his arm, but he reaches out and grabs me by the wrist, just like he did in the park.

"No! Don't!" It sounds like he's trying to shout but he can only manage a whisper. He lets my arm go and starts steadily exhaling. "I mean . . . that's okay." He takes a slow, deep breath. "I just need to lie down."

"Are you sure?"

He opens the door. "You need to go." He takes a deep breath. "Now."

"But, I can—"

"No. Now. Please."

I fold my arms across my chest. "You can't make me leave you like this—not again."

His eyes are cold and frightening as they bore into mine. "This is my house. And I'm telling you to leave. Right now."

As soon as I'm in the hallway, the door slams shut behind me, so hard I can't help wondering if he has just collapsed against it. I take a few steps back and stand there watching it and wondering what to do. I step forward again with my arm raised, prepared to knock. But I stop myself. I back away again. And I turn and walk slowly through the hall and back down the staircase.

I stop at the foyer to pull my coat off the hook. As I fasten the buttons, I run through what I'm going to say to his grandmother. *I think he's sick again* or *I think you should check on him.* But I think of his firm *no* and the *don't,* and against my better judgment, I decide I need to hold on a little tighter to his secret this time. So I peek into the kitchen, tell Maggie it was a pleasure to meet her, and assure her that she doesn't need to get up—I can let myself out.

8

"Oh, good, you're here." Like the bells that have just announced my arrival, Dad is way too chipper for me in my current state of mind. "Do you mind if I take off?"

Mind? God, no. Please go so I can pace through the empty bookstore and wonder if I've just left Bennett dying alone in his messy antique bedroom. "That's why I'm here," I say, trying to make my voice as light as his.

"Thanks. Your mom has already called twice, wondering when I'll be home. She might be a little too excited about this party."

He looks handsome. I reach up and adjust his tie.

"We'll be at the Chicago History Museum. We should be home by midnight, but don't wait up. You know how your mother and her friends can talk."

"Go. Have fun." I grab his shoulders and pivot him toward the front door.

He takes a few steps forward, then stops and turns back. "Thanks again for working on a Friday night. We didn't interrupt your social life, did we?"

"Sadly, no."

As soon as Dad's gone, I walk around the store, straightening books and thinking about the look on Bennett's face. When I walk past the front door, I pause, tempted to turn the BACK IN TEN MINUTES sign around and sprint to his house. When I pass the back room, I have the urge to go to the phone and call Emma so I can tell her everything that just happened. When I pass the window and see the police car parked down the street in front of the coffeehouse, I want to run down there and send them over to 282 Greenwood. But I don't do any of these things. Instead I march over to the children's area and grab the denim beanbag chair, drag it over to the travel section, and plop down with Lonely Planet's guide to Moscow.

I'm crouching down on the floor of the back room, spinning the dial on the safe, when the bells jingle. I lean on my hands and see someone in a wool cap holding a black coat standing at the front counter.

"Sorry—we're closing!" I yell. I select the last of the three numbers, pull up on the heavy steel handle, and throw the vinyl cash bag inside.

I'm looking down at my watch as I walk back toward the counter. "Sorry, we close at—"

Bennett turns around to face me, and a small smile moves slowly across his face.

I stop in my tracks. "Hi." I can't imagine I'm doing a very good job of hiding my surprise. He already looks much better than he did just three hours earlier. The dark circles are gone, and his eyes are no longer bloodshot. He looks different, relaxed, in dark brown chinos and a light blue sweater that does something sort of magical to his eyes. And I can't help noticing that he smells shower fresh. He looks better, but still tired.

"Hi, Anna."

"You're okay?" I'm so relieved that I want to run over and hug him.

"Yeah. I'm okay." He smiles. "So . . ." His eyes move around the store. "This is where you work?"

I nod.

"It's nice." He takes a few steps toward me and leans against the counter. "I'm glad you're here. I wasn't sure if you worked on Friday nights."

"I don't. My parents went to a party in the city." I don't know what to say. I walk to the counter and mirror his pose.

"Hey, I wanted to apologize. I didn't mean to be so rude earlier."

"It's okay."

"No, it's not. It was really nice of you to come over." His expression is soft, his voice kind, and any trace of annoyance is gone from his eyes.

"I should have called—or something—instead."

"No, I shouldn't have left the park that night. I didn't

remember you were there until you told me." He looks at me like he's trying to figure out what I'm thinking, gauging where to go next. "Anyway, thanks for helping me. I'm sorry I didn't say that earlier."

"You're welcome."

His eyes stay locked on mine, and he smiles even wider. "Can I make it up to you?"

"Make it up to me?"

"How about a coffee?"

"Coffee?"

"Yeah. Coffee. Unless"—his eyes circle the empty store—"you're busy."

I feel my forehead wrinkle. "Are you sure you're well enough for coffee?"

He shrugs. Nods. "Actually, it helps my migraines. Come on. It's the least I can do after kicking you out of my house."

While he stands there, waiting for my answer, I think about Emma's words in The Donut earlier today. *Just say it*, she insisted. *You like this guy, don't you?* I don't feel like I know him well enough for it to be true, but it is.

"Okay. Sure." Maybe by the time we've finished our coffee I'll know him better. Maybe I'll even have answers to all the questions he keeps adding to the pile.

I walk around the store, shutting off lights as I go, and flipping the sign from OPEN to CLOSED. As I'm locking the dead bolt, Bennett lifts my backpack off my shoulder and throws it over his own.

We walk in silence to the end of the block. I can hear the noise from the coffeehouse growing louder as we get closer, and smell the aroma as it floats up through the frozen air and disappears into the clouds above. As soon as we walk in, I notice a group just leaving, and we weave through the crowded tables and collapse on the crushed-velvet sofa in the corner.

"What can I get you?"

"A lot of explanation." I reach down to pull my wallet out of my backpack. "And a latte, please."

"I've got it." He touches my hand, and I silently chastise myself for the shiver it creates. He leaves and returns with two small, froth-filled, glass mugs, each with a chocolate-dipped biscotti balancing on the rim.

He sets them down on the table and returns to his spot on the couch. I look at him expectantly. "Big talks require biscotti," he says. Now I let him have a smile.

He picks up his mug and breaks through the froth with his Italian cookie, and after a few dunks, he pops it in his mouth and chews. When I realize I'm staring at him, I turn my attention to my own cup. The coffee is warm and soothing.

"So. Where should I start?" He dunks his cookie while he looks at me. "I guess Sunday night. The park? I have to admit, my memory's foggy in some spots, but I take it I told you about the migraines?"

I feel my face soften with concern, and I nod again.

"I honestly don't know what happened. I was walking around town, and I felt a headache coming on. Before I could even process what was happening, it just hit me—" He takes another bite and a sip before continuing, "Anyway, I'm not sure how long I sat there in that park before you found me. All I remember is trying to get home."

"I would have helped you. Why didn't you just wait for me to get back?" I look down at my mug and take another sip. When I look up again, I find him watching me.

"I left as soon as I could walk again." He pauses, searching the air for something I can't see, then looks back at my eyes. "I'm sorry. I don't remember why you left."

"I ran back to the coffeehouse to get you some water."

He nods, like it's all coming back to him. "I'm sorry, I didn't mean to take off on you. I just wasn't thinking straight." He shakes his head as if casting off the memory of that night.

I've never been that out of it, but I can see how it would be disorienting. "And you've been sick all week?"

"On and off. I planned to go to school on Thursday, but I felt another headache coming on when I woke up, and I was worried that it might happen again. It would have been embarrassing to pass out on my second week at school." I'm surprised to hear that he cares what any of us think. "And now I have a ton of homework to catch up on this weekend. A woman from the school came by with all of my assignments after you left."

"Ms. Dawson."

"That's who I thought you were. I guess that's why I was so surprised to see you."

"Surprised?" I raise an eyebrow. "Is that what you call that?"

He drapes his arm over the back of the sofa. "I'm really sorry I made you leave earlier tonight."

He's smiling and leaning, and I find myself doing the same. "That's okay."

"You just kind of . . . threw me."

"I threw you?"

He looks down, then back up again, and shoots me a bashful grin. "I looked horrible. A beautiful girl shows up at my door, and I'm in sweats, smelly, and looking like I hadn't slept in a month." His eyes never leave mine. "I shouldn't have been so rude."

"Don't worry about it." I smile.

"Thanks for not telling Maggie. I don't want her to worry."

"Sure." He's still staring at me, and with all the tension in the air, I latch on to the change of subject. "Your grandmother seems nice," I say. I watch his face light up.

"Yeah, she's great."

"So, you moved from San Francisco to live with her?"

"For now. I'm only here for a month, you know, while my parents are in Europe."

"Oh," I say. My head falls forward as my heart sinks. "I didn't know that." I guess that explains why he hasn't bothered to meet anyone.

"Yeah, well . . . I feel like I can tell you the truth. Can you keep a secret?" He waits for my nod. "It's not just that my parents are traveling."

"Oh?" I take another bite and chew. I hope he knows that means he should continue talking.

"I was supposed to go with them, but I made a mistake," he says. "I blew it pretty big. My parents understand, but let's just say Evanston is the best place for me to be right now. Taking care of Maggie is much better than spending a month with them—or in reform school." The huge grin on his face makes me think that's supposed to be a joke.

"And?" I ask.

"And what?"

"And you aren't going to tell me what you did to deserve this frozen version of hell?"

He shakes his head and gives me a dismissive little laugh. "Trust me, you don't want to know."

"Oh, come on, it can't be that bad. You didn't kill anyone." I stop in mid-dunk and look at him. "Did you?"

He swirls the coffee in his mug, looking into it for answers, as if there were tea leaves inside. "No, I didn't kill anyone. But someone . . . disappeared. And it was my fault."

I picture him on that frozen park bench, rocking back and forth and mumbling about needing to find someone. I start to tell him what I heard and to ask him what it means, but I look at his face and something tells me not to. When the silence continues, I press him for more information. "That doesn't give me much of a secret. Is that really all you're going to tell me?"

"For now." His face brightens as he asks, "So, how long have you lived in Evanston?"

I stare at him. "We're going there now?" I ask.

"We're going there now," he says.

I decide to let him off the hook for the time being but give him a look that signals that he has more explaining to do. I sigh. "All my life. Same house my dad grew up in. Same house my grandfather grew up in."

"Wow." He looks at me with what I think at first are soft, understanding eyes; then I realize what's really behind his expression: sympathy. Like I'm a hobbit who's never left the Shire.

"Yeah." I feel small. "Wow."

He leans in even closer, filling what's left of the space between us, looking like he's genuinely interested in my pathetically simple life. "Do you ever feel . . . trapped?"

I want to tell him about my map and my plans to travel the world, but as the words start to form in my head I realize they sound as pitiful as his stare. Yes, I'm trapped for now, but I won't be forever. Still, deep down, I can feel the reality I live to ignore percolating to the surface: I can dream all I want. It's more likely that I'll be here when I'm old and gray, rocking and knitting on my porch when I'm not at the bookstore I own and run with the help of my grandchildren, who think I'm a crazy old bat because I refuse to go near the Travel section. Trapped doesn't even begin to cover it.

"Every day," I say.

"I can't imagine being in one place that long." I shrink back away from him, but he props his head against his hand and fills the space I've just created. "I've traveled everywhere. I've seen more than most people get to see in a lifetime." This isn't helping. He must realize that, because he suddenly shifts gears. "But you have something I've never had." His expression softens and he looks almost sad. "Deep roots. A history of a place. You've watched the kids you knew in kindergarten grow up right before your eyes. Aside from my parents and my sister, I feel like everyone I know is somehow"—he pauses to search for the right word—"temporary."

It's my turn to look sympathetic. I've known Justin longer than I've known my other friends, but I can't imagine thinking of any of them as temporary.

"Don't tell me you're going to Northwestern." He keeps smiling, so I just keep talking, like I've been injected with truth serum.

"God, no. At least, I hope not. I'll apply, because everyone does, but it's definitely my last choice." I tell him about running and my plans for a scholarship, and he looks at me like he's hanging on every word, and I can't, for the life of me, figure out why. But his eyes are wide with interest, and this time, when I picture my map, I decide I can tell him. "There's also the other plan," I say, "the one my parents don't know about."

He smiles excitedly. "I get a secret too?"

"Yeah, except, see, I'm actually planning to tell you the whole thing," I say, and that makes him grin so wide his eyes narrow into little slits. "I'm thinking of taking a year off after graduation to travel. I know I'll go to college, but I feel like I have this one window after high school, you know, to see the world." I look down at the sofa. "But of course, my parents would never approve of this plan."

"Why can't you travel after college?"

Of course he'd have to ask. I've seen where he lives. "I'll need to go straight to work to pay off my student loans," I explain. "Even if I get a cross-country scholarship and financial aid or whatever, I won't get a full ride." His smile encourages me to continue. "I guess I'm afraid that if I don't go soon, I never will, and I just . . . need to."

He's staring at me. I can't tell what he's thinking.

"What?" I ask.

"You're interesting." His mouth curves into a half smile. *And beautiful,* I want to add. *Earlier, you said I was beautiful.* "I had a feeling you'd be interesting." He watches me, and I hope he can't tell that my stomach has started doing those damn flip-flops again.

And as I stare back at him, I realize that over the last hour I've let myself forget all the little—and big—things that have haunted me for the last two weeks. How he disappeared into thin air at the track that day and then denied it. How strangely he reacted the first time he heard my name. How I found him in the park that night. Even that bizarre trip to his grandmother's house just hours ago. I don't see what he's learning about me that's so interesting, but I know I'm a little too fascinated by everything I don't know about him. I just want to complete this puzzle, but the most important pieces keep dropping on the floor, landing upside down and just out of reach.

But the questions disappear again when he reaches forward and slowly traces the line of my jaw to my chin. I close my eyes as his thumb slides toward my mouth and brushes my lower lip, and I can feel myself moving in closer, like I'm being pulled into the gravity that surrounds him. He starts to kiss me, and I close my eyes and take a little breath as I wait for the touch of his lips.

But the kiss never comes. Instead, I feel him pause. His breath travels past my cheek, and the words *I'm sorry* fill my ear in a whisper.

"About what?" I murmur.

"This." He sighs. "I'm sorry. I can't—"

"What about daring adventures?" I hope he can hear the smile in my voice.

I feel him laugh into my neck and he sighs again. "I'm afraid I'm already on one. A different one." I pull back to see his eyes, and wonder why he looks sad. He rubs my cheek with his thumb and pulls away from me.

He looks at his watch. "I should really get back to Maggie. Can I walk you home?"

I sink back into the chair, confused. Dejected. "That's okay. It's just a few blocks."

"I'd feel terrible if something happened to you."

"If I went missing?" I ask sarcastically. "Yeah, it sounds like you have that effect on people." I'm still close enough to see how his face falls, and then hardens.

"Thanks." He scoots backward, and the part of me that's upset he didn't kiss me feels satisfied. "I'll be right back." He walks toward the bathroom, leaving me alone on the couch to berate myself.

"Bennett, I'm so sorry," I say as soon as he returns. "I was trying to be funny."

He bends forward and picks my backpack up off the floor. "It's okay. Don't worry about it." We maneuver into our bulky jackets and walk in silence past the couches and tables and out into the street. We walk side by side, but there's a visible gap between us. We hardly say a word for the next three blocks, and I can't help noticing that the Bennett I just spent the last hour talking to isn't anything like the one who's now walking me home.

"This is mine," I say when we arrive at my house. I watch as Bennett looks up at our nineteenth-century Craftsman, with its flaking yellow paint and wraparound porch that serves as its only exterior asset. The kitchen light is on, but there's no activity inside, and my parents won't be home for hours. "Do you want to—"

"No." He cuts me off, his voice sharp. He sets my backpack on the ground by my feet. "Look, you were right . . . about what you said back there." His voice is softer now, but it's almost like he's forcing it to sound that way.

"Oh, come on. I was kidding." I try to get him to lighten up, but he stuffs his hands into his pockets and refuses to look at me. I didn't think my comment was that insulting, but it was enough to send him into the bathroom as one person and emerge as a completely different one. The first one was just about to kiss me. This one can't wait to get away.

"You don't know anything about me."

I step closer and give him a flirty smile, hoping I can bring back the Bennett from the coffeehouse. "I know two of your secrets." Something about that near-kiss in the coffeehouse makes me feel brave enough to reach forward and grab on to the lapels of his wool coat. "That's got to be good for something. Isn't it?"

He moves in close to me, just like he did on the couch, but this time his face is tight and he stops far short of my lips. He reaches up and grabs hold of my wrists to remove them from his lapels, and I reflexively loosen my grip. His expression turns even colder.

I can't believe my comment has offended him so much. "What's wrong with you?"

He takes a big step backward. "Listen. This is *not* going to happen again. Do you understand, Anna? This," he says, motioning back and forth between us, "is not going to happen this time."

"I have no idea what you're talking about! What do you mean 'this time'?"

"Nothing." He crosses his arms tight across his body and stares right into my eyes. "Look. I'll be here for another two weeks, and only because I don't have a choice. Then I'll leave and you'll never see me again. So please, go back to your life." He turns on his heel and I watch him march off through the snow.

april

9

Thirty-five days. Bennett's been in town for thirty-five days, which, by my definition of a calendar month, means he should have left town four or five days ago. Yet when I walk into Spanish each day, he's still here. We've barely spoken since the night in the coffeehouse three weeks ago, and he never looks at me; if our eyes do accidentally connect, he gives me a perfunctory smile, and I avert my gaze. But everything about that night still haunts me, and I can't quite figure out how he's still managing to turn my world upside down while simultaneously allowing it to stay exactly the same.

"I have news!" Argotta sings, beaming and spreading his arms wide. He glances around the room, holding all of us hostage with his words, and we stare at him as he walks back to his desk and sits on the edge of it. "How many of you have heard about my Annual Travel Challenge?"

A few of us raise our hands. "Good," he says. "Well, this

year, even *you* will be surprised. Because this year, I have a really big, very exciting reward."

He hops down off the desk and pulls on a long tab marked MEXICO. The giant, color-coded map of the country unrolls from its home in the ceiling. "But first, let me tell you about the assignment. Each of you will be planning a fabulous two-week vacation in Mexico. You must depart from our lovely O'Hare International Airport, but you can land anywhere you like. From there, you must create an itinerary that will allow you to see as many Mexican destinations as you can in fourteen days. The person who creates the most logical, interesting, and cost-effective travel plan will win the challenge."

He walks forward to the front of the room and stops. "Sound good?" Twenty heads nod in unison. "Great. Travel plans are due next Monday—a week from today." He turns his back to the class and erases the whiteboard.

The room is silent. We look around at one another. Finally, Alex clears his throat and raises his hand.

Argotta spins around and throws his arms up in the air. "Oh, wait a minute!" He walks back and forth in front of the class, grinning. "I bet," he says slowly, drawing out each word, "you want to know what you get if you win, right?" He stands there at the front of the room nodding and smiling while we nod back at him. Alex lowers his arm.

"Of course, of course." He paces his words to build tension in the room. "I have this friend, you see, who works for one of the major airlines." I bet he's practiced this all morning in front of the bathroom mirror. "I told this very good friend about my Annual Travel Challenge, and he thought it was such a great idea he arranged for his company to donate a five-hundred-dollar travel voucher to the winner."

We all look around the room at one another. I can't help looking at Bennett and when I do, he gives me an obligatory grin and shifts his gaze to the window.

"So, what do you think?" Argotta searches the room. "Could anyone here put a five-hundred-dollar voucher to good use?"

Sure, everyone here could use it. But I'm the only one who thinks it can change my life.

~~~

I sit cross-legged on the carpet in front of the shelf marked with the word *Mexico* and scan the book spines. The store is empty and, given the storm that's been raging outside all afternoon, likely to stay that way. Which is perfect, since I have a vacation to plan.

I pull *Let's Go Mexico* from its home on the shelf, and place three more thick books on top of it.

I thumb through the pocket-size Michelin Green Guide and remove a slim book that opens into a giant road map. Pretty soon, I have a stack of guides, each valuable to the planning effort in at least one way. I pull out my spiral notebook and stare at the stack. And decide I need a latte.

I pull on my coat, hang the BACK IN TEN MINUTES sign on the door, and lock the dead bolt behind me. It's only six, but it's pitch-black outside, and if it weren't for the calendar, no one would know that there should be grass on the ground and leaves on all of these bare wooden sticks. We're two months away from summer vacation, but it's snowing hard. Again.

I buy my latte, take it back to the store, return to my spot in the travel section, and start dividing the books on the carpet into smaller stacks. I know what I want: A balanced combination of archaeological sites and beaches, where I can run on sand and swim in a real ocean. I draw a line down the center of the paper and begin my list.

The left column quickly fills with archeological sites: the Mayan ruins in Tulum, Chichén Itzá, and Uxmal. The right column, as it turns out, is more challenging. Cancún has the Great Mayan Reef, so that has to be on the list, but I'm not sure if I want to include better-known destinations like Los Cabos, Acapulco, Cozumel. They all look pretty, so I add them, along with small question marks in the margin.

The hail is pounding against the window, and one of the branches of the giant oak outside keeps scraping against the pane. I've stopped jumping every time it happens, but it's still unnerving. I try to ignore it and let Mazatlán's quaint village squares and the open-air pottery and ceramics markets of Guadalajara take me away from the snow and wind.

But when I hear the noise again, I stand up, peer around the bookcase, and creep toward the window. The storm is still whipping the tree around, but the branch that was screeching against the glass is now limp and broken, dangling silently over the sidewalk below. Then I hear a sound behind me, and I spin in place. This time it's not coming from the street at all—it's coming from the back room, and it's not the sound of the storm—it's a voice. I hold my breath and listen.

My heart's racing as I move to the phone at the counter. "Who's there?" I yell toward the back room while I pick up the receiver and dial 911 with trembling hands. I stand completely still and listen, watching the back door as I wait for someone to pick up. "Answer!" I whisper into the receiver.

Suddenly, the front door bursts open, and I whip my head around in the opposite direction as the bells jingle without their usual pleasant ring. I put the phone back on the cradle and rush toward the door. "Hi!" My voice is shaking. I rest my palm on my chest, like that will help steady the pounding, and try to act as if everything were normal. "Can I help you?"

He looks past me, searching the store, and then over his shoulder at the street. Just as I'm about to ask him if he'll help me check out the noise I heard in the back room, he pulls the door closed so hard the bells slam against the glass and rolls his hat down to cover his face. Then he locks the dead bolt.

"Cash." His voice is deep through the wool, but my attention is on the shiny metal knife he pulls from his baggy jeans. He points it straight at me. "Now."

It's hard to gesture toward the front desk when my limbs are shaking so badly. "Over there. It's not locked. Take it all." It's hard to speak, too.

Before I can move farther away, he pulls me toward him, presses the knife to my throat, and pushes me past the register. "The safe!" he yells into my ear as he tightens his grip.

"In the back—" The words come out wobbly, but I stick to the plan Dad laid out when I first started working here.

"The combination is nine–fifteen–thirty-three. We don't have an alarm. I won't call the police. Just take the cash and leave."

I calculate in my head. The register might have fifty dollars in it, if even that. The safe would have closer to a thousand.

He pulls me around to the register, opens the drawer, and releases his grip on me for just a moment while he dumps the cash into his bag. He grabs me again and pushes me to the back room, while I keep my gaze on the floor and try not to think about the cold steel of the blade on my neck or his heavy breath in my ear. "Move!"

I feel a wave of nausea pass through me.

I figure that's why I'm seeing things.

I narrow my eyes so I can focus on the movement near the bookshelves. I'm somehow certain I saw it, even though I know it's impossible. The store was empty, the door locked.

I squint over the tops of the bookshelves and see a dark patch of hair moving toward the aisle. I jerk my head up to get a better view, but stop when I feel the cold blade tight against my throat. When we reach the back room, the man removes the knife from my neck and shoves me inside, and I land hard on the floor in front of the safe.

"Open it," he orders. I spin the dial—right, left, right—and pull down on the heavy handle. The door opens wide, and he pushes me away.

That's when I see the movement again, slowly emerging from the shadows at an angle where only I can see him, and I watch, stunned, as Bennett puts his finger to his lips. There's no way the two of us could ever overpower a man with a blade and a fierce sense of desperation, but my first feeling even so is one of relief.

He moves out of my direct line of vision but I can see him from the corner of my eye, creeping with careful steps toward me. I stay silent and still.

And while the thief is distracted by the contents of the safe, three things happen, so fast and overlapping that they seem to take place simultaneously. Bennett disappears completely, and suddenly he's kneeling next to me on the floor. He grabs my hands and closes his eyes, and I must follow suit, because when I open them, the store is gone. The robber and his knife are gone. And Bennett and I are in the exact same positions—him kneeling, me sitting, still holding each other's hands—only now we're next to a tree in the park around the corner, the wind throwing snow violently around us.

10

Bennett releases my hands and holds my face instead, and I hear him say the words, but it's like he's far away, muffled. "You're okay, Anna. Breathe and don't talk. Just listen carefully and do what I say. I'll explain everything, but right now I need you to listen to me."

I nod, wide-eyed and blank.

"First, I need you to run to the coffeehouse. Order me an espresso and two big glasses of tap water without ice, and sit down and wait for me." He looks into my eyes. "You can do this, Anna. I need you. Can you trust me?"

I nod again.

"Okay, run. Don't talk to anyone, just order the coffee and water and sit down."

I turn and run to the coffeehouse.

I'm trembling so hard I can barely get the words out, but

the barista is kind and offers to carry my drinks to a table for me. I lead him to the couch by the window and collapse.

The sirens grow louder and louder until two police cars skid to a stop in front of the bookstore. I can't make out much from this angle, but I see their headlights shining on the building, and I watch the cops draw their guns and creep toward the entrance. They quickly disappear from view, and I press my forehead to the glass to try to see what's going on. I'm waiting for them to reappear when I feel a weight next to me.

Bennett falls forward, his elbows on his knees, his fingertips gripping each side of his head. He lets out a small groan between heavy, labored breaths, just like the night in the park.

Without even letting myself question it this time, I begin rubbing his back. "What can I do?"

"Water . . ."

I leave one hand on his back and give him the water glass with the other. He lifts his head and empties it in three giant gulps. "More . . ."

After the second glass, his breathing becomes more regular.

He looks up at me and smiles. "Hey, you're still here." He reaches for the shot of espresso and throws the hot liquid down his throat. I stare at him. I want to say something, but I can't, because every time I take a small breath, my own body seems to shoot it right back out. I try a deep inhalation, the kind I know will slow my heartbeat and get my limbs to stop shaking, but my lungs won't cooperate. *What the hell just happened?*

I don't realize that I'm staring at him until he wiggles his fingers in front of my face and says, "You're in shock." He holds up one of the empty glasses, waves toward the barista, and gestures toward me.

"Drink this," he says. I take the glass with both hands, since I can't trust my shaking limbs to pull off a task as complicated as lifting a cup to my lips. Bennett speaks in measured breaths. "I need you to listen to me, Anna. We have to go talk to the police in a couple of minutes—they've probably called your parents, and I'm sure they'll be looking for you." He grabs my shoulders and pivots me around to face him. "I promise, I'll tell you everything that just happened, but for now I need you to stick to a story. Can you do that?"

I finish my water and nod.

"Good. Keep the first part true: The man stormed into the store and he forced you to open the safe. But then say this: when he wasn't looking, you saw a break and you ran out the back door into the alley. I saw you there and stopped to help. We waited down the street and returned once we saw the police had arrived." He lifts my chin. "Can you do this?"

I nod again, eyes wide.

"Don't worry. I'll do the talking. Just stick to the story." I can't seem to do anything but nod.

We head toward the window to look out at the last two remaining police cars parked outside, their lights swirling. I stand in the store, mute, while Bennett explains what happened. The officer captures every detail of the break-in and my escape through the back door in his black leather–bound notebook. I listen, still nodding, but I know that Bennett's lying, because I'm well aware of what happened. I did *not* run into him in the alley. *How did he get into the store? How did we get out?*

The officer reviews his notes. "Stay here," he says. "I'll be right back."

I'm surprised to hear my own voice say, "Officer?" He stops and turns to face me. "Did you catch him?"

"Yeah. We caught him when he had some trouble with the lock on the back door. This long winter seems to be making some people pretty desperate. But don't worry, he won't be going anywhere for a while." He turns again to walk away.

"Officer?" I repeat and he turns back to me. "How did you get here in time?" Bennett puts his arm around my shoulders and gives me a light squeeze as the cop flips through some of the pages in his notebook.

"Looks like it was an anonymous tip. Someone called and reported a robbery in progress." He looks up at me with a sympathetic smile. "One of your neighbors must have seen him break in. You have a guardian angel, young lady."

Dad bursts through the door with Mom on his heels. Bennett must have stepped back from my side, because suddenly there's room for both of them to surround me, enveloping my body in two familiar sets of arms. "Anna . . ." Mom says, hysterical, stroking my hair and stopping every so often to kiss my forehead. "I'm so sorry," Dad whispers repeatedly while he rubs our backs.

We all hear the officer clear his throat, and we look up.

"Excuse me. I'm sorry to interrupt, but I need you and your daughter to come down to the station to press charges." The police station is the last place I want to be. What I want is a hot cup of coffee and an hour alone with Bennett.

I look at my dad and ask, "Can we have a minute first?" I point to Bennett. It's the first time my parents notice him standing there, but now he has their full attention.

"Hi, Mr. Greene, Mrs. Greene." He offers his hand to Dad first, then reaches toward Mom. "I'm Bennett Cooper."

"Bennett is a . . . friend. From school. He's been helping me since—" My voice trails off when I see Mom's face become contorted. But it relaxes and she smiles after I lie to her about the details, just as Bennett told me to.

"Well, thank you, Bennett." She shakes his hand and keeps her other arm around me as her eyes dart between us. "I'm not sure what you were doing walking around in a snowstorm, but I guess it was a lucky coincidence." She looks at me sideways and raises her eyebrows. I just shrug.

"Can we just have a minute?" I repeat to Dad.

"Keep it to five," Dad says, looking at his watch.

I lead Bennett to the Self-Help section and we're finally alone again, if only for a few minutes.

"So . . ." I look at him, my expression serious. "I take it this is the big secret?"

"Yeah." He laughs under his breath. "Pretty much." He reaches over and grabs both of my hands in his. His hands are warm and soft. "I have a lot to tell you."

"Good."

"Are you sure you want to hear it?"

I nod.

"Think you can angle to stay home from school tomorrow?"

I look at my watch. It's only eight thirty, but it feels closer to midnight. By the time I'm home from the police station, it may be that late. "I think my parents would be cool with that, under the circumstances."

"I'll come over at ten a.m. We'll go somewhere we can talk."

I look at him for answers I don't want to wait until tomorrow to hear.

He leans close and whispers, "Are you afraid of what I can do?"

I look around the room, toward the police and my parents, and back at Bennett. I'm not afraid, although I suspect I should be. Right now, I'm just happy to be alive. And to see that the pieces of this puzzle that Bennett has been since the day I met him are finally starting to fit together, snapping into place and forming an image I may someday comprehend. "No," I say. "Not even close."

11

My room is still dark, but I sense that it's morning. I roll over and stretch and steal a glance at the digital clock radio on my nightstand. Nine fifteen. I can't remember the last time I slept past seven, especially on a school day.

Then everything that happened last night comes rushing back, and it hits me—Bennett will be here in forty-five minutes.

I leap out of bed, pull on my sweats, and bound down the stairs. I haven't eaten anything since lunch yesterday, which explains why I'm starving. I find a note on the counter by the toaster:

> *A—*
>
> *Glad you're sleeping in. Dad's at the bookstore and I'm at work. Call if you need <u>anything</u>. We'll both be home by 5. Relax. And please, no running today.*
>
> *XO,*
>
> *Mom*

I grab a bowl from the cupboard and fill it to the top with cereal. I'm eating so fast I can't really taste anything, but the cornflakes and milk are filling the uncomfortable void in my stomach. All of a sudden, I start to feel nauseated again. I had a knife at my neck. I was in danger, and in an instant, I wasn't.

Bennett can disappear. And reappear. He can make other people disappear and reappear. He has a secret talent, I'm the only one who knows about it, and today he's going to tell me everything.

I shower and wash my hair, and as I'm drying off, I reach for the body oil that smells like vanilla and makes my skin soft. I apply a little mascara and some lip gloss, and dart to my closet to find something to wear.

When the doorbell rings, I fly down the stairs and land with a thunk in the foyer. I take a deep breath and fling the door open. "Hi." I'm beyond giddy.

"Hi." He looks confused. "God, you look . . . actually . . . excited to see me. You do remember what happened last night, don't you?"

I smile at him. "You saved my life. And today, I'm going to find out how you did it." He still looks confused. "You *are* still going to tell me how you did it, aren't you?"

He raises his eyebrows. "Do I have to tell you from the porch?"

"No. God, I'm sorry. Come in." I step back to give him room and close the door as he looks at me with a relieved smile. I hang his coat on a hook and he follows me into the kitchen. "Coffee?" I ask, but I don't wait for the answer before I begin pouring. I hand him an oversize mug with a picture of the Northwestern Arch on one side, and we sit opposite each other on the kitchen bar stools. It's silent as he sips his coffee, and I watch, perched on my seat and ready for him to disappear into thin air again at any moment. He doesn't appear to be going anywhere, but he does look a little bit terrified.

"Are you okay?" I'm holding my coffee cup, but I haven't even had a sip yet, so it can't be the caffeine that's making me twitchy, ready to burst out of my skin.

"Yeah." He shifts on the stool, plays nervously with the handle of his mug. "I'm just not sure where to start."

I give him an encouraging look. "Start from the beginning."

"You have to know you are, literally, the first person I've ever told." He stops and looks at me, like he's expecting some kind of reaction. "My parents know, my sister knows, but I never *told* them. They sort of found out by accident. But that's it—my family, and now you." I nod so he'll continue. "I honestly had no intention of telling anyone else. If last night hadn't happened—"

I get it. He barely knows me, and there are probably countless other people with whom he'd prefer to share this precious secret. But I'm not about to let him off the hook. I can't. Not now. "You can trust me. This is your secret, not mine. I won't tell anyone."

"Thanks," he mutters, and then he's quiet again. "The thing is . . . you don't know how big this is. I don't want to freak you out."

I rest my elbows on the kitchen counter and look at him. "I promise I will not freak out." He narrows his eyes, as if to say that I shouldn't be making this promise. "I will try very hard not to freak out," I revise.

He leans forward, elbows on the countertop. Those smoky blue eyes are striking, especially in contrast with his skin and that hair of his. He looks adorable like this, all nervous and jittery.

"Look, Anna. This—" he says, motioning back and forth between us like he did that night on the sidewalk, the night he almost kissed me in the coffeehouse. "This is a really bad idea."

"Probably," I agree.

He laughs and shakes his head, like he's kicking himself for giving in to me. "I'll make you a deal. When I've told you everything, you can decide what to think, and if it's all too much, I'll totally understand. I'll go back to being the transient weirdo, and you can go back to your friends and your life."

"Or?"

"Or . . . you'll think it's all very interesting. And maybe a little exciting. And somehow that will offset the fact that I'm a complete freak of nature."

"You're not a freak. And besides, I've already seen what you can do, Bennett, and it's huge. If that didn't scare me, I can't imagine what else you could do or say to change the way I feel about you." Crap. I didn't mean to say that last part. I pull back from him so I can see his expression.

He doesn't look fazed at all, though, and I think I may have even made him happy. "That's good to hear. But you only know part of it."

I let out a nervous laugh. "How much more is there?"

"More." He stares at me. Then he pushes back from the counter and stands up. He takes his mug to the coffee machine, tops it off, and drops in two ice cubes from the dispenser in the freezer door. "Where do you keep your water glasses?" He's all business, like a salesman preparing to demonstrate a miraculous new cleaning product.

"That cabinet there," I say, gesturing, "to the right of the sink."

He pulls out two matching glasses and fills them with cold tap water. He sets the glasses and the cup on the counter and comes back around to sit on the stool.

"Okay." He takes a deep breath. "I want you to sit here and watch. I'm going to go away, but I'll be back in one minute." He checks his watch. "Are you ready?"

"Yes." I nod and try not to look anxious.

He looks at me for a moment and smiles. Then he closes his eyes. And I watch him become transparent—I can see through him to the photograph of my parents and me on the wall behind his translucent frame—and he's like that for less than a second before he's gone. The stool is empty. I walk around to his side of the counter and touch the surface.

Yep. He has disappeared completely.

I feel my breathing become shallow as I wait for what seems like more than a minute, never taking my eyes off the stool, and suddenly he's back. Exactly where he had been. Opaque and solid as he is supposed to be. As if it had never happened. But it did.

He gulps down both glasses of water, then chugs the coffee.

"Do you need anything?"

He shakes his head no, looking down at the tiles.

"Where did you go?"

"My room. I counted to sixty and came back." He looks up and watches me with a tentative expression as he weighs my reaction.

"What's with the water and the coffee?" I remember the specificity of his requests last night at the coffeehouse, the water bottles and coffee mugs strewn around his room that night I visited him uninvited.

"Traveling makes me dehydrated, and caffeine helps with the migraines. I don't usually experience pain when I travel *to* a location. It's the returning that kills me."

"Like the night in the park."

"Exactly."

"Okay, so you can disappear and reappear? That's it?"

"You make me sound like a third-rate magician." He laughs. "That's not enough for you?"

"Of course," I say nervously. "I just meant—"

"I'm kidding." He gets serious again. "Actually, that's just the first thing."

"The first thing?"

"Yeah. I told you. There's more."

I look at him. "How much more?"

"Two." He shrugs. "Two more."

"Wait a minute," I say. "The fact that you can disappear is the first of *three* things?"

He nods. "I told you. I won't explain everything today, but I'll tell you . . . a lot."

"What? You don't think I can take it?" My heart starts beating fast as I question my own question. Or maybe it's just that Bennett's face is so close to mine.

"If anyone can take it, you can. But it's still a lot of information to process." He looks at me like he's waiting for me to argue with him. Which I'm considering. "Look, today I'll tell you how I got you out of the bookstore last night. And eventually I'll tell you the rest. Trust me on the baby-steps thing, okay?"

He looks determined. Like arguing with him won't pay off anyway. "Okay." I straighten up in my chair and give him my full attention. Which takes zero effort. "I'm ready. Start from the beginning."

⌒

Bennett matches my posture, sitting straight up in his chair too, like we've discovered a cure for this magnitude of nervousness. He takes a couple of deep breaths to prepare, and then he begins.

"One night, when I was ten, I was in my bed reading this book on Greek mythology—I was really into gods and myths when I was a kid—and I thought how cool it would be if I could go there. So I sat up in bed, *Star Wars* pajamas and all, and I tried to 'will' myself there. I closed my eyes and pictured ancient Greece and repeated the date over and over again. And . . . well, nothing happened. But I started thinking about the next best thing, and it got me thinking: picturing the rows and rows of mythology books at my school library. So I closed my eyes, pictured the library, and focused. And the room felt cold—a lot colder than my bedroom—and when I opened my eyes I was standing in front of a metal bookshelf. That's when I kinda freaked out. It was dark, and everyone was gone, and I took off running for these big steel doors that led outside. But I stopped. Forced myself to calm down. I closed my eyes, pictured my bedroom, and focused. When I opened them, I was back home."

He reaches for his coffee and takes a deep sip, and I just sit there hanging on every word, watching his mouth pucker against the rim of the mug and his tongue lick the residue from his lips.

He rests his coffee cup back on the counter, and I force myself to look at his eyes instead of his mouth. "Wait. You actually *went* to your school? In the middle of the night?"

He nods. "I did it a few more times again that week, staying close to home—the park, the movie theater, the grocery store. I never stayed more than a minute or so. Eventually, I started interacting with people to be sure they could see and hear me, and they could. I was *really* there."

"What about the migraines?" I ask.

"I didn't have them in the beginning—it wasn't painful at all. The big problem back then was that I had no idea how to tell my parents. I was terrified they'd take me to doctors or just straight to a mental ward."

I can't imagine keeping that kind of secret from my parents. Not at sixteen, let alone ten.

"When I was twelve, I decided to find out what happened to me when I left. I set our video camera on a tripod, pressed record, and focused my mind on a seat in the back of the theater just down the street. I sat there and timed myself with my stopwatch, waited exactly ten minutes, and returned. The video shows me sitting in my room with my eyes closed; then I disappear, and the film continues, taping an empty chair. Ten minutes later, I reappear."

He stops and looks at me, then continues. "A few weeks after that, my parents found out. My mom woke up in the middle of the night and found my bed empty. She combed the house, and when she couldn't find me, she decided to call the police. She'd already pushed nine and one when I reappeared before her eyes. Scared the crap out of her." He smiles at the memory. "I told them everything that night. Showed them the video."

He stops again. "How are you doing with this?"

"It's sinking in." At least, I think it's sinking in. I can feel my head nodding, so I must comprehend it at some level. "So, what did your parents do when they found out?"

He rolls his shoulders backward and gives his arms a little shake. "Mom freaked out. She still hasn't gotten over it. She wants me to see doctors and psychiatrists—anyone who can 'fix' me—even though I'm not allowed to tell them what's 'wrong' with me. But my dad . . . Now, Dad loves it. He thinks I could be, like, some comic-book hero or something. And he sees that I have total control over it, so he doesn't worry, but he's gotten a little pushy." He looks down at the counter. "Anyway, they see it differently, so when my parents aren't fighting with me about my 'gift,' they're fighting with each other about it."

I feel sad for him. "You saved my life last night. Tell your parents about that."

"Last night was fun." His eyes light up with excitement. "I've always worried about doing so many sequential hops, but last night I did a bunch in a row without getting the headache until the very end. I'm thinking it has something to do with the adrenaline—" He stops short. "But it was so stupid. If the migraine had hit me when I moved from the bookcase to your side, that guy could have killed you."

"But it didn't happen that way."

He closes his eyes tight, then opens them and looks at me. His voice is sincere, regretful. "I didn't think first, Anna. I just saw you in trouble and I reacted. I can't do that. I have to plan and calculate so I don't . . . screw anything up."

I just grin at him. "Well, if it's all the same to you, I'm going to be grateful anyway."

He smiles and watches me, but I'm not sure what he's looking for.

"What?" I ask.

"What would you think about taking this conversation somewhere else?"

"You want to go out in that?" I point toward the kitchen window at the snow and hail, still falling hard and adding inches to the thick blanket that buried the lawn during last night's storm. The driveway is nowhere to be seen.

"I was actually picturing someplace warmer. Someplace . . . tropical." My expression must show that I'm still confused, so he just comes right out and asks, "Do you want to try it?"

"I can go with you?" I guess I should have put the pieces together faster; even as I'm saying the words I'm aware of how dense I sound.

He nods and a huge grin spreads across his face. "If it's too soon, I totally understand."

"No, no . . . I'm just—" I stammer. "Will it hurt?"

"My sister gets stomachaches. My mom's never tried it, but my dad isn't affected in either direction. Technically, you've already been the third person to travel with me." I flash on the park last night and remember how queasy my stomach felt, but I don't want him to change his mind, so I keep it to myself. "This will be a bit of an experiment."

"I can handle that. I think." I let out a nervous laugh. "How long will we be gone? What if my dad comes home?"

Bennett explains that he plans to return us back to this exact spot, just a minute after we leave. "But while we're gone," he tells me, "time will continue as usual for everyone here. You might want to call your dad, just so he doesn't worry if he comes home before we do." I'm not sure I fully comprehend it all, but I dial the bookstore anyway and explain that I'm awake and feeling good, and Dad sounds relieved. While I talk, I watch Bennett fluttering around the kitchen, filling and refilling coffee cups and water glasses.

"Ready?" he asks after I hang up, and I smile and nod, mostly to convince myself that I am. Bennett walks over to the kitchen window where I'm standing and takes both of my hands in his. His are warm, strong, and for some inexplicable reason I feel safe, even though I'm completely terrified.

"Close your eyes," he commands, and I do, smiling in the seconds before my stomach begins to contort. My intestines feel like they're being twisted, kneaded from the inside, and while it isn't painful, it certainly isn't pleasant, either. Just as I feel the nausea, I see a bright light through my eyelids that forces me to shut them more tightly. Then I feel warmth on my face and a hot breeze that lifts my hair away from my forehead.

He squeezes my hands. "You can open your eyes. We're here."

12

We're standing exactly as we had been back in the kitchen, facing each other and holding both hands. Only, when I look down, my feet are in sand.

I squint against the sunlight and look past him at the bright blue-green water that stretches out as far I can see. The cove is small; I can look in both directions and see its entire length. Giant boulders hold back the tranquil, turquoise bay until it meets the sea, and high, jagged rocks reach for the sky, like bookends holding the white sand between them firmly in place. I turn around and look behind me to find nothing but a dense collection of trees. There is no one here. Not anywhere.

Bennett's watching me. He's still holding my hands, which is a good thing, because I'm pretty sure I've stopped breathing. "I know, it's a lame cliché. A secluded beach on a deserted island—" He stops short and looks at me. "Anna? Are you okay?"

I can't take my eyes off the view. This can't be real. "Where are we?" I must drop his hands, because now I'm walking away from him, like I'm being pulled by force toward the water.

His voice follows me. "It's one of my favorite places in the world . . . Ko Tao. It's a tiny island in Thailand. You can only get here by boat, and there's no pier. You actually have to wade through—"

"No way." I stop and turn around to look at him. "We're in Thailand? Right now . . . we're in Thailand?"

"Welcome to Thailand." He smiles and spreads his arms wide.

"I'm in Thailand." Repetition may help it sink in. My feet move toward the water, expansive and sparkling before me. It's like a mirage in a cartoon that looks refreshing and beautiful until one of the characters leans forward in disbelief, and the moment their fingertip touches the water it's enveloped in sand and disappears from sight. I'm so prepared for that same phenomenon that I'm surprised when I kneel down, touch my fingertip to the water, and feel the wetness of the ocean.

I can feel him watching me as I look around, spinning slowly in place, taking in every square inch of this island. Every palm tree. Every boulder. Every wave. Every shell. I can feel the expression on my face. My eyes are wide and my mouth is open and my forehead's all scrunched up, and I think I must look ridiculous, until I look over at Bennett. He's got a smile on his face, this look of wonder, like he's the one who's awestruck. I close my eyes and inhale . . . everything.

"You okay?"

I nod.

"Good. Come on." Bennett takes my hand and we walk along the shore. The water runs over our feet and washes back out again, and we squish through the sand until we pass the giant boulders. Bennett leads me up a slope to a secluded patch of sand that's warm and dry, and I take my sweater off so there's nothing between my skin and the hot sand but my T-shirt. I lie back and melt.

"This is much better than my kitchen," I say to the sky, and then I look over at him.

He's stretched out in the sand, propped up on his elbow and watching me with a satisfied grin, and I roll onto my side and mirror his pose. We each have one hand occupied, holding up our heads, but neither one of us seem to know what to do with the other one. I don't know if it's the physical warmth of the sand or how good he looks in his thin T-shirt and jeans, but all I want to do is reach over and rest my free hand on the small bit of skin peeking out between the two. I picture him pulling me into a kiss and rolling around in the sand like we've just been dropped into a photo shoot for some cheesy designer cologne. But then I remember the night he walked me home after coffee and I summoned up the nerve to grab the lapels of his coat, only to find myself standing alone and rejected in the snow. I can't bring myself to touch him, so I bring my fingertip to the sand and start making little circles there instead. "So . . ." I say, "Thailand."

He shoots me a confident smile.

I watch him for a moment, wondering why he was so worried about bringing me here. Who wouldn't want to have a small part in something so impossible? So magical? "I don't get it. What's not to like?"

When he smiles at me I can tell I've just passed whatever test I'm supposed to pass to get to the next level, like he's got a mental list with an empty box next to the words *teleported to deserted island / didn't freak out.* Check.

But I know he still has more to tell me. Two more things, in fact. I should probably just sit here in the sand and enjoy the view, but I can't. I need answers.

"How did you know I needed help last night?"

"I didn't. I came by to get a book on Mexico. For Argotta's travel assignment."

I'm confused about a lot of things that happened last night, but I'm certain I was alone when the thug with the knife came in. "No way. You weren't in the store."

He reaches forward and my heart starts racing with the idea of him touching me, but instead he grabs a fistful of sand and lets it fall through his fingers. "Are you sure you want to hear this part?"

I stare at him, and finally I nod.

"The robbery didn't happen exactly the way you remember it." When all the sand has fallen from his grasp, he brushes his palm against his jeans and looks at me to gauge my reaction.

I just raise my eyebrows and wait.

"I came into the bookstore. You and I talked about Mexico. Then the guy burst through the door."

"No way. I remember that. I was definitely alone—"

He cuts me off. "Let me explain. The way you remember it, you *were* alone. But that's not the way it was the first time."

"The *first* time?"

"The first time I was in the bookstore. We were talking about our travel plans. When the door blew open, you got up off the floor to help the man you thought was a customer, and he grabbed you. But he didn't see me. I had time to disappear."

I flash on the trick Bennett just showed me—God, how long ago was that? Fifteen minutes or so?—where he was sitting on my bar stool one second, vanishing into thin air the next, and reappearing right where he left a minute later. Even if he disappeared last night, that doesn't explain how I went from having a knife to my throat to standing underneath an elm tree during a blizzard.

"I disappeared from the bookstore, went back five minutes earlier, reappeared in the back room, and called nine-one-one from your phone."

The voice. The sound from the back of the store. "I heard you. . . ." The details are coming back in bits and pieces, but they still don't make any sense. What does he mean by *the first time*? "Wait a minute. Did you just say you went back? Five minutes earlier?"

He nods. "Yeah. I went back."

"In *time*?"

He tilts his head up and smiles shyly. "I . . . do that too."

"You went *back* in time. And *changed* what happened?"

He's wearing a sheepish grin, like he's sorry, but he just can't help it. "It's, like, a do-over."

"So, why didn't you just tell me someone was about to rob the store? Or, like, lock the dead bolt before he came in?" I don't mean to sound ungrateful, but I can't help thinking it would have been nice not to have a knife to my neck in the first place.

"I don't do that," he says. "I don't *stop* events from happening, but I'll change smaller things, little details that might affect the outcome. If I'd stopped the robbery entirely—and I've never done anything like that, so I'm not even sure I could have—something even more horrible could have happened. That guy might have robbed someone else at knifepoint but not gotten caught. He might have seen you walking home a couple of hours later and . . ." His voice trails off and he's silent for a moment. "Anyway, I just make it a rule not to change the big stuff."

"So you couldn't *stop* the robbery. But you could go back five minutes *earlier*?"

He nods. "Technically, I shouldn't have even done that, but yeah."

"And call nine-one-one from the phone in the back room."

He nods again.

"Why didn't the police come?"

"They did, just not fast enough. After I called, I snuck out and hid behind a bookcase. By the time he got you back to the safe, I decided I couldn't wait for the cops anymore. I had to get you out of there on my own. Just in case."

Suddenly everything hits me: Bennett doesn't just disappear and reappear in different places, he can travel backward through *time*? I want to appear brave, unflappable, and worthy of hearing the next thing, but I can't quite wrap my head around it all.

"I take it this is the second thing?"

He nods. "Part of it."

"*Part* of it?" My eyes widen. I lie back in the sand and stare up at the sky.

"You okay?" he asks. I feel my head make a little divot in the sand when I nod. But he's right—this is a lot to process. I throw my arm over my eyes to block out the sun, and we just lie there in silence for a few minutes. One arm is over my eyes, and the other is resting in the sand between us. Suddenly I feel the tickle of warm granules slipping across the surface of my arm and slowly piling into my open palm, and I look up to find Bennett leaning over me, watching the sand trickle from his hand into mine. "See," he says with a grin, "I told you I could freak you out."

"I'm not freaked out."

"Yeah," he says with a nervous laugh, "you are *definitely* freaked out."

I prop myself up on my elbows, ruining his little sandpile, and look at him. Then I look around at this beautiful setting—palm trees and white sand and turquoise water— this postcard he's just magically inserted the two of us into, and I start to understand how implausible the whole thing really is. It should have taken at least two planes, a boat, and more than thirty hours to get here from Chicago. I should be many time zones away, and it should be dark. I should be complaining about the windchill factor, not enjoying this warm little breeze on my skin. Above all, I should be in AP World History. I look back at Bennett and give him a sincere smile. "Thank you for bringing me here."

He looks relieved. "You're welcome."

"What you can do is . . ." Every word that comes to mind sounds inadequate, but I finally settle on *amazing*.

"Thanks." I haven't heard the rest of the second thing, but I can tell I'm baby-stepping my way toward it.

"Look, I know I can't give you all the answers you want, but at least for today, I can give you that daring adventure." He stands up and brushes the sand off his jeans, then holds his hand out to me.

"You know, I've never been in an ocean before." I try to make my voice light and flirty, like this isn't weird at all.

"I know. You told me last night. You were trying to figure out which beaches to add to your travel plan so you could do your morning run on the sand and swim in the ocean."

Okay, that's weird. "And I assume you had a suggestion."

"La Paz," he says matter-of-factly. Yes, this *is* weird. And I'm not crazy about the fact that we've had a conversation I can't remember. But I don't have time to be irritated, because he wraps his arms across his chest, grabs the bottom of his T-shirt, and lifts it over his head. His arms are more muscular than I'd pictured them and his chest is perfect and I think my jaw just dropped.

He reaches his leg forward and, with his big toe, draws a line in the sand in front of us.

"It's not La Paz, but there's sand and water." He beams and leans forward in a racing stance. "Take your mark, Greene."

I'm not sure if he expects me to strip down to my bra and underwear, but the thought alone brings heat to my face that has nothing to do with the temperature here. I look down at my bare feet, my jeans. I wonder how transparent my gray T-shirt will become. But when I look out to the water and squeeze the sand between my toes, I decide I don't care. Laughing, I lean into my lunge.

"Get set." He turns to me with a sly smile. "Go!" he yells, and we bolt forward, running as fast as we can until the sand turns darker and colder and wetter and eventually the waves carry us away from the warm beach.

I swim out into the current. I dive under. I feel the waves lap against my body as I push myself against them. When I look to my side, I find Bennett there, his arms cutting through the water as he starts to dive again, and I follow him under, letting the water burn my eyes. Letting the taste of salt fill my mouth. Enjoying every minute of every stinging sensation. And wanting it never to end.

Four hours later, we return home to find that one minute has passed. Steam rises from the coffee mugs. The water is still ice cold. And I'm about to throw up.

"You don't look so good." Bennett leads me to the living

room couch and instructs me to lie down. A voice that sounds far away says, "I'll get you some crackers," and in the distance I hear cabinets creaking open and shut. He comes back carrying a giant box of saltines.

He sits on the edge of the sofa, rubbing his temples, and looks down at me. "Interesting." He's watching me with a fascinated stare, like I'm a glob of unidentifiable goo in a petri dish. "It hits me in the head, and you and Brooke in the stomach."

I see a white cracker coming toward me but I can't even take it, and I cover my mouth and close my eyes to keep the room from spinning. *Please, God,* I beg in my head. *Please don't let me throw up in front of him. Please. Just this one thing.* And I'm not sure if it's time passing or the work of a higher power, but after a few horrible minutes the feeling washes away and I can open my eyes again. He's still here. Still looking guilty and still holding that little cracker. This time I take it, nibble on the corner, and then try a larger bite.

"I'm so sorry," he says, but I stare at him, confused, and even though my mouth is full I try to talk. "What did you say?" he asks. He looks so worried.

I swallow hard. "Worth it." I give him a weak smile and grab another cracker. I eat a few more and sit up when he offers me a glass of water and orders me to take small sips. The room comes into clearer focus.

I run my fingernail up my pant leg and bring it back to examine the caked, wet sand. We're home, back in the cold snow, and I'm wet and covered with sand from a Thai island. "No way." My energy is starting to return. I laugh, shaking my head in disbelief. "This is so cool." I look over at Bennett and find that his pants look the same.

I stand up, feeling just a little bit closer to normal again, and he follows me up the stairs to my parents' room. I dig out an old pair of sweats and a T-shirt from my dad's dresser, pass him the folded pile, and show him where the bathroom is.

When I'm alone in my room, I peel my clothes away from my skin. I take off my shirt and shake out my hair, watching in awe as sand flies though the air and sprinkles itself across my bedspread, and I can't help giggling. I pull on a pair of tight-fitting black sweats and a sweatshirt from some 10K race I ran last year, and go back to sit on the bed. I run my palm across the granules and think about Ko Tao. About the heat of the sun and the salt of the ocean, and suddenly I'm so grateful for every last speck of sand—on my bed, on my carpet, in my hair, glued to my clothes—because they're the only tangible things I have to remember this day by.

"Where should I put these?" Bennett's voice shocks me back to reality, and I turn around to find him standing in my doorway, looking adorable in Dad's Chicago Marathon sweatshirt.

I gather my sandy clothes up from the floor and meet him at the doorway. "I'll take them," I say, as I add his pile to mine.

He gently grabs my arm as I walk past him. "Hey . . . you okay? You looked sad for a minute there."

"No, not at all." I laugh it off. "I was just wishing I had a souvenir, like a postcard or something. It was silly. I'll be right back." I float down the stairway, my feet barely touching the wood.

I've left Evanston.

I've left the *country.*

I put the pile of sandy clothes on top of the dryer and walk into the kitchen to grab a plastic bag.

And Bennett's in my bedroom.

I return to the laundry room, looking up the staircase as I pass.

Bennett just closed his eyes, held my hands, and took me to Thailand.

I scrape our clothing, collecting as much sand as I can inside the little bag, and zip it shut.

And now we're back. And he's in my *bedroom?*

I throw the clothes into the washing machine and stand there holding the bag of sand, listening to the water fill the drum, and thinking back to last night. I remember the expression on Bennett's face as we stood in the bookstore's Self-Help section, his voice quivering as he asked me the question. *Are you afraid of what I can do?* I wasn't then. Am I now?

I'm not afraid of the fact that he can disappear and reappear. I'm not even afraid of the fact that he can travel back in time. I'm not afraid of what he can do. I *love* what he can do. But there's more I don't know, and the moment I have the thought I feel a knot form deep in my stomach. I *am* afraid—I'm afraid of whatever's next. Whatever it is that might make me question whether or not I want to know him, even after we have spent the afternoon swimming in a sea so salty we were literally buoyant. Whatever it is, it can't be bad enough to make me not want this daring adventure. And I picture him, alone in my bedroom, and suddenly I can't wait to see him again. With the bag of sand tightly in my grasp, I run up the steps, taking them two at a time.

13

Bennett is standing in front of the wall of built-in shelving, examining my trophies and racing numbers. "Wow. How many races have you been in?"

"Eighty-seven." I cross the room and drop the bagful of sand on my nightstand. It makes a little sound as it hits the surface and I'm happy for this confirmation that it's real.

Bennett walks around the room, analyzing each trophy and photo. "This is incredible. You're really good."

"You sound surprised."

"No." He looks me in the eye and I feel my breath catch in my throat. "I'm impressed. Not surprised."

He turns his attention from the trophies to what's in between them: my CDs. He paces past the shelves, running his finger along the plastic spines of the jewel cases until he finds one, pulls it out, examines the cover, and then returns it to its alphabetized home. I lean back against my desk and watch him check out Blink-182, *Cheshire Cat*. Bush, *Sixteen Stone*. The Smashing Pumpkins, *Siamese Dream*.

"This is quite a collection."

It probably looks like I've spent all my bookstore earnings on CDs. "My dad and the owner of the record store across the street are good friends. We swap books for music. It's pretty much for my benefit."

He removes a few more cases and pauses, letting his fingertip rest on one of the mixes. "What are these?" He removes one of the twenty or so cases painted in Justin's trademark watercolor swirls.

"Running mixes. My friend, Justin, makes them for me. His dad owns the record store."

He nods and turns away again before I can see the look on his face. While he continues examining my music collection, I press play and then shuffle on the stereo, and the lyrics to "Walk on the Ocean" start up immediately.

We spotted the ocean
At the head of the trail

"Hey, I've seen these guys," he says without looking away from the bookshelves. "At a little club in Santa Barbara. They were pretty good."

"You've seen them live?" I heard him the first time, but I have to say something, because my chest feels heavy as I stand here, picturing secluded Ko Tao, and listening to the song tell a story about traveling to a faraway ocean, stepping on stones, and coming home without any pictures to prove it.

"It's sort of a hobby."

"Who else have you seen?"

He shrugs and gestures toward the shelves. "Just about everyone here." As if the exotic world destinations weren't enough.

"Really?" My eyes wander to the bulletin board above my desk, where my lonely Pearl Jam stub is pinned, and I sigh. Even the things I'd treasured a couple of days ago look pathetic and trivial when I see them through his eyes.

He follows my eyes to the desk, then walks over and examines the stub. "No way."

"What?"

He shakes his head hard, like he's trying to dismiss a thought he doesn't want to have. "Nothing. I've got this giant bowl of ticket stubs—" He holds his arms out wide to demonstrate the size of the bowl and confirm my assumption. He probably can't believe I've only been to one concert.

And that's when he spots the map. Now I really feel insignificant.

He walks over to get a closer look, and stands there, arms crossed, serious, examining it like it's a piece in an art gallery. I cover my eyes in embarrassment and force myself to go and stand by his side.

"My dad made it for me. It's supposed to mark all my travels." I flash back to the night we sat in the coffeehouse when I told him about my plans to see the world someday, and I steal a sideways glance at his face. I wonder what he's thinking. No,

I *know* what he's thinking. Like the lone ticket stub, the four little pins on my map must make a pretty sad statement, especially to someone who has never known limits. "As you can see, I'm off to a fine start."

But he just looks at the map and says, "It's fantastic." After a long pause, he steps backward so he can take it all in. "See, now, I've never been to any of these places." I laugh. "I'm serious," he adds. Right. Like he wasn't making fun of me.

I hold my palms flat like a balancing scale and lift them up and down like I'm weighing the destinations. "Let's see. It's a Tuesday. Should I go canoeing on Boundary Waters or rafting on the Amazon? The Amazon or *Boundary Waters?*" I stress the last destination like it's the more interesting and exotic of the two. "It's okay, Bennett. You don't have to pretend to think it's 'fantastic.'" I look past him instead of into his eyes. "To tell you the truth, the map used to make me a little sad. I guess sometimes it still does."

He steps in to close the distance that separates us, and I think I stop breathing when I feel the warmth of his skin next to mine. The oversize sweatshirt doesn't show off his body the way his T-shirt did, but that doesn't keep me from picturing the strong shoulders underneath, the way his arms cut through the water, and the way he pulled his body out of the surf. "Why does it make you sad?"

As I look at him, my chest is tight with the feeling of holding back what I really want to say. "Four pins," I finally squeak, as I shoot him a fake smile and try not to look like I care quite so much. We stare at each other but say nothing.

Then Bennett reaches past me into the clear plastic container of pins and takes one by the sharp silver point. He holds it up. The tiny round red tip looks enormous in the small space between us.

"Five," he says, extending his hand.

I reach out to take the pin from his fingers and stare at it, pressing my lips together so I won't cry. "I don't even know where it is," I finally say with an embarrassed laugh.

"Right there." His voice is kind, not at all condescending, as he points to an unmarked speck in the Gulf of Thailand.

I consider the dot on the map, not much larger than the tip of the pin itself, and wonder how something so tiny could mark the most extraordinary four hours of my life. Then I look at Bennett, dressed in my dad's sweats, his shaggy hair still peppered with sand. His expression is sweet and soft and, if it's possible, even more grateful than mine. He gave me this gift today, but I can't help feeling like I gave him one too.

I consider the pin once again and step forward to meet the map. I'm still fighting back happy, overwhelmed tears as I reach out, hands shaking, and press it firmly into the tiny island of Ko Tao.

⁓

I make grilled-cheese sandwiches and we sit on the couch, eating and trying to think of something to say. He's not starting in on the rest of his secrets, and we're way beyond small talk, so I turn on the TV and flip channels just for something to do, but there isn't much to watch at two thirty on a weekday.

Not that Bennett seems to care; he finds the commercials far more amusing than the actual shows, but refuses to tell me why. More important, he doesn't seem at all concerned that our day's running out, and he still hasn't told me everything. I still don't even know the rest of the *second* thing.

I lift the remote with a dramatic gesture, stare at him, and click the power off. The room goes silent, and he turns to me. "I'm ready for the rest of the second thing."

"Haven't you had enough for one day?"

I shake my head.

"Okay." He sits back against the cushions again and twists to face me. He props his arm up on the back of the couch, and for a moment, it's as if we're back in the coffeehouse, telling each other our secrets. He gives me a little grin, and the small, insignificant gesture makes me want to lean over and kiss him to get it over with. But I'm afraid if I do, I'll never hear the rest.

He takes a deep breath. "I can go anywhere in the world, but *when* I travel is . . . restricted. I can go into other *times*, but only within certain dates." He stares at me like he's waiting for me to react, and when I don't, he opens his mouth to continue.

"Wait." I hold my finger up in front of me and listen.

"What?" he asks.

I hear a car door slam. Mom or Dad would have come in through the garage, so it can only be one person. "Emma," I say in a panic. I'm not ready for Bennett to leave, but I'm also not prepared to explain why he is sitting in my living room.

"Don't worry. I'll go." He grabs my hand and gives it a little shake. "I'll see you tomorrow," he says. I watch as his hand, still holding mine, becomes transparent. Then it's gone with the rest of him. I wonder if I'll ever get used to this.

She knocks hard on the front door and then rings the doorbell for good measure.

"Coming!" I yell as I slide the two plates and their leftover grilled-cheese passengers under the couch and inspect the room for other signs that I haven't spent the day alone. When I open the door, Emma practically falls through it. "Oh, my God!" she yells as she drops her backpack on the floor and wraps her arms around me. "I heard what happened last night! Are you okay?"

Last night? The robbery? Was that *last* night?

"I'm fine," I hear myself say over the deafening thump of my own heartbeat.

"I've been trying to get here since I heard, but Dawson caught me trying to leave campus, and I couldn't escape after that!" Her voice is high-pitched and dramatic. "I've been so worried. Are you seriously okay? Do you want to talk about it?" She plops down in the exact spot Bennett was just sitting in.

"Not really," I huff. But I can tell from Emma's eager eyes that the protective side of her needs to know I'm okay and the gossipy side can't help wanting to hear every detail. Since I can't tell her that I spent the day on a Thai beach and I'm not sure I'm ready to tell her about Bennett, I figure I might as well give her what she wants. "It all happened so fast."

14

"No." I use the firmest voice I can muster this early in the morning. "You're not serious?"

"Afraid I can't keep up?" Dad's dressed in his winter gear, stretching into an almost comical runner's lunge against the refrigerator, like I imagine he did in the olden days.

"No." I cover my eyes. "Listen, I'll stick to the streets. I'll stay off campus. *Seriously*," I beg, pointing toward the kitchen window, "I don't need a babysitter. The sun will be up in a few minutes. I'll be fine." The last word comes out in a whine, and I feel like the ten-year-old he seems to think I've reverted into. This overprotective parent thing had better pass quickly.

"Ignore me." He takes a long drink of water from his sport bottle and lunges to the side. "You don't have to talk to me or even look at me, but I'll be right behind you, kiddo." Evidently there's no convincing a father of his daughter's safety when she's just been robbed at knifepoint.

"No, it's okay. We'll run together." I set my Discman on the hallway table, already mourning its absence. I need my music to help get my head straight before I see Bennett at school.

Dad follows me out the door and we run side by side toward the lake. In unison, we wave to the man in the green vest with the gray ponytail. We run around the track four times, through campus and past the clock tower as it chimes seven. I race him the last half mile to our lawn, which turns out to be a mistake, because now he can't catch his breath.

"Are you sure you're okay?" I keep asking.

He's red and blotchy, but he nods and forces a smile anyway. "Just. Fine," he pants. "Why. Do you. Ask?"

"You overdid it." I scold him—just like I know Mom will when he can't move tomorrow. I stretch into a lunge next to him. "What, are you going to drive me to school now, too?"

"Nope. I trust Emma with that duty."

"Clearly you've never seen her drive." I finish my stretch, shake out my legs, and run toward the steps.

"Hey, Annie," Dad calls, and I stop and turn around. I rest my hands on my hips while he tries to keep from having a heart attack.

"Invite Bennett over to dinner. Your mother and I want to meet him. Properly."

I glare down at him from the porch. "Dad. We're not even *close* to that." The mere fact that he'd ask is mortifying.

He gives me his best stern-parent voice. "Okay, but if this is serious, we want to meet him."

⁓

"'Morning, love." Emma chirps out her usual greeting and pinches my cheek. "My brave little friend." I don't feel brave. I feel nervous about seeing Bennett. I feel guilty about not telling Emma about him yesterday. I feel tired, because I have barely slept.

She slams the gearshift into reverse and backs out of the driveway. Dad's standing at the kitchen window, staring out at us with a look of mild panic on his face, and I give him a little shrug as we tear away from the house.

"Em," I begin, "If I tell you something, do you promise not to get mad?"

She shoots me an irritated look. "Now, see—I don't understand why people ask that question. How can I promise I won't get mad if I don't know what you're going to tell me?" The look on her face makes me think this might fall into her Stupid Americans category. "Just spill it."

I spit the words out quickly, before I can change my mind. "I didn't tell you the whole story yesterday, about the robbery." I take her back through the high points, but I don't tell her the whole truth. How can I? Even if I hadn't promised Bennett I'd keep his secret, she'd never believe me. Instead, I include the story Bennett crafted for me, including the part where I take off out the back door and run into him. Then I tell her he skipped school yesterday to spend it with me.

"What?!" She swerves dramatically, nearly hitting a parked car. "Crap! Okay, I'm good. I'm good." She looks at me again. "You spent the *day* together."

I smile, picturing the look on Bennett's face when he drew the line in the sand with his toe and challenged me to race him into the ocean. In my head, I watch the slow-motion video of his body floating on the turquoise water and his arms cutting through white-tipped waves.

Yes, we spent the day together.

And I can't tell my best friend about the best parts.

"He was worried about me." The words come out as squeaks, but Emma doesn't seem to notice.

"Now that I think about it, I didn't see him in English Lit—"

The little movie in my head comes to a halt.

"Great. I didn't think about that. Everyone in Spanish knows we were both absent yesterday." I wonder if Courtney has already started speculating aloud.

"Oh, don't you go trying to change the subject. Go back to telling me all about how you two *made out* in your empty house all day." She raises an eyebrow and turns her attention back to the road, waiting me out as only Emma can.

"Hardly. He didn't even kiss me." I can hear the disappointment in my own voice. "We talked. We listened to CDs. We ate lunch. He—" I almost say the word *disappeared*, but I catch myself. "He took off just before you got there."

"And why didn't you tell me any of this yesterday?"

"My dad came home."

She grimaces and rolls her eyes. Here it comes. "Oh, of course. Say, do you have a phone? I do. I have a phone. It's great for telling your best friend the biggest news of your life when you can't do it in person." I don't even have time to squeeze out an apology.

We pull up to a red light and she turns to face me. "What are you doing, Anna?" She sounds like my mom when I'm not washing the dishes the right way, or stuffing way too many clothes in the dryer. "Didn't he tell you that he's, you know, *leaving*?" She stresses the last word like it alone is enough to make me know better.

"Yeah." I can't say anything else. I don't need her to tell me that I'm crazy for walking into this thing with Bennett, whatever it is.

"And it's worth the inevitable heartbreak?" she asks. "For a brief fling you know is going to end?"

Not a brief fling. A daring adventure.

"Yeah, Em. To me it is."

She bites her lower lip hard. "This isn't going to end well."

I study the all-weather floor mats. She's right, and I know it. But the truth is, I couldn't stop now, even if I wanted to. I've spent the whole night thinking about how it will end, but right now, there's only one thing I want to think about: there will be a middle.

"I like him, okay? There. I said it. I really like him." I look right into her eyes. "I know it's probably a mistake, but please, just . . . let me enjoy this?"

We stare at each other.

"Green light." I gesture with my thumb toward the windshield.

She keeps staring at me. She doesn't press on the accelerator, but she nods, and I know that means she'll be on her best behavior. At least for today. When the driver behind us lays on the horn, Emma finally pulls into the intersection. We're silent for the next two blocks, but I know what she's thinking.

"So, while we're coming clean and all, there's something I wanted to tell you yesterday, too." Okay, maybe I don't know what she was thinking. I stare at her and wait for her to continue. "Your friend from the record store, Justin, sort of asked me out."

"Justin? *My* Justin?" As soon as the possessive leaves my mouth, I wish I could pull it back in. Bennett's little do-over trick would come in handy in moments like these, when my foot is stuck firmly in my mouth and all I want to do is go back in time for *one* minute so I can say the right thing instead. "I'm sorry, I just meant—" I don't even know what I meant. "It's just . . . I'm usually with you when he's around, and I've never picked up on . . ." I really should just shut up now, before I say what I'm thinking: *But I always thought he liked me?*

"Well, not always. You know, I stop in the record store sometimes after I drop you off at work." No. I didn't know that. "A few weeks ago, we started talking about music. He knows a lot about music." Yes. This I do know. I've known Justin since I was five. "And then he asked me out for coffee, and we went out to dinner the night before last."

"You went out to dinner?" I ask. "You and Justin had coffee and then went out to *dinner*? Why didn't you tell me any of this, like—I don't know—last week? Yesterday?" But I feel a little guilty when I remember that I never told her about the night I hung out in the coffeehouse with Bennett. It was just too weird, especially when nothing ever came of it.

She gives me an apologetic look and a guilty shrug. "He said he tried to talk to you about me once, when he was first thinking about asking me out, but . . ." Emma trails off, and I flash back to that day in the record store last month. He'd wanted to ask me about something, and I'd avoided him because I'd thought he was trying to ask me out. Now I feel like an idiot on two fronts: first, because I read him wrong, and second, because he and my best friend have been talking about me, bonding over my lameness. "I know he's your friend," Emma continues. "And you know, I always thought he liked you, but—" She likes Justin? Emma and Justin? It doesn't even sound right. "Anyway. I really didn't think anything would ever come of it. I mean, I thought he was nice, but I didn't think we'd hit it off or anything."

"But you did."

"Yeah, I guess we did."

And now it's quiet. I can't remember a time when Emma's car was this silent for this long. A few blocks later, she finally talks again. "We're going to spend the day in the city together on Saturday." She keeps her eyes on the road and tries to play it cool, but she breaks into a huge grin.

"That's great, Em."

"You sure?" She turns to me. "You *are* okay with all of this, right? I mean, especially now."

It's weird, but yeah, I'm okay with it. I have no right not be. "Of course I am," I say, but I feel a little pang of sadness, too because it's Justin. It's Emma. And Justin. *My* friends. Before I can stop myself, I wonder how this will change my friendship with them, if they'll wind up liking each other more than they like me, and which one I'll have to stop talking to if this whole thing doesn't work out. And most selfishly, if Justin will still make me running mixes.

Emma lets out a dramatic sigh. "Good. As long as you're cool with it." She brightens again as she changes the subject back to me. "So—you and Bennett," she begins with a little teasing tone in her voice. "What happens at school today?"

I let a nervous laugh escape. "I have absolutely no idea."

She turns in to the student lot and makes a beeline for her usual spot. "Well, you're about to find out," she sings, and I follow her gaze to find Bennett, standing there on the lawn, waiting for me. I feel sick.

"Oh. My. God." Emma snorts as she throws the gearshift into park. "What did you *do* to that boy? Just look at him." Bennett has gotten a haircut. It's still a bit long for my taste, but he looks crisp and clean in his uniform and nothing short of gorgeous—although after yesterday, it's hard not to picture him in his thin T-shirt and those jeans that rested so perfectly on his hips. And that's when I remember that his clothes are still in my dryer, and I panic for a moment until I realize it's not laundry day. "He's adorable!" Emma gives him a flirty little wave and I slap her hand down.

"Oh, please; you're just saying that to be nice." I'm grateful for the change of heart, even though I know it's fake.

Emma turns and looks at me. "I don't say anything just to be nice, love. Even to you."

"Fine. Then please continue to act like a loyal friend and don't embarrass me." I'm still struggling with the butterflies in my stomach and the latch on the door when Emma gets out of the car and pokes her head back in to say, "Ahhh, it's going to be a *good* day."

She slams the door behind her and struts up the small incline toward Bennett, abandoning all concern about my future heartbreak. "Well, hello!" I hear her say as I scramble to join them before Emma has the chance to talk too much.

"I know!" I can hear her say in a voice as exaggerated as her smile. "I don't think we've talked since your first day here, have we?"

When I reach the two of them, Bennett turns his attention to me. God, he looks cute. "Hey," he says. His smile is so warm I think the snow has just started to melt around his feet.

"Hi."

"So, Bennett, I noticed you weren't in Lit yesterday," Emma says, and he takes his eyes away from mine to look back at her. "Were you sick?" She stares him down, and I shoot her a warning glare.

"No. I spent the day with Anna," he replies, and then he looks straight at me again. We used to be strangers because he insisted on it. Today, we're standing here like friends because he decided he could trust me with a secret so large, so implausible, I wouldn't have believed it if I hadn't seen it with my own eyes.

"Oh. Well." She looks at him, then at me, and then back at him. She reaches up and musses his hair. "Don't cut too much more, or I'll need to find you a new nickname, Shaggy. See you at lunch, Anna." She starts to walk away but pivots on her heel and turns back to us. "Speaking of lunch, will you be joining us today?"

"Yes," he says, still looking at me, and I grin.

"Shaggy?" he asks when Emma's out of earshot. "Is that the best she can do?"

I roll my eyes and look up at the top of Bennett's head and smile. "When did you manage to cut your hair, anyway?"

He shrugs.

I look around to be sure no one's listening. "You traveled?" I ask.

He moves even closer to me and whispers in my ear, "No. I went to Supercuts."

I crack up.

People keep staring at us—walking by, watching us, whispering to each other.

Bennett says, "I just wanted to be sure you're okay. You know, after . . ."

"Anna!" Three of my cross-country teammates burst in on us, cut Bennett off without even looking at him, and start talking over each other. "Oh, my God! I heard about the robbery!

Are you okay?" They all have the same look of concern on their faces.

The robbery. That's why everyone's staring. Of course, a fellow student's being held at knifepoint would make the Westlake grapevine.

"Yeah, thanks, guys. I'm fine."

They all express their relief and we chat for a few more seconds before they each give me a quick hug and rush off. Bennett and I watch as one of them skids on the ice and nearly plows into the rosebushes.

"Anyway, I just wanted to be sure you were okay . . . with everything."

"Yeah." I smile. "I'm okay. But I still want to hear the rest." I wait for him to say something but he doesn't.

"You will."

"We should probably get to class," I say, at the exact same time he says, "I have something for you."

"You do?"

He reaches into his backpack, pulls out a piece of paper, and gives it to me. I let out a gasp when I realize what it is. What he did to get it. I look down at the postcard from Ko Tao and smile at the photo. "You went back? For this?"

He shrugs and gives me a sheepish grin. "You needed a souvenir." The bell rings in the distance, making us both officially tardy. "I'd better get to class. I'll see you at lunch." He turns to walk away, but I call out, "Bennett." He turns around to face me again.

"Yeah?"

"I still have your clothes." That doesn't come out the way I planned, and I quickly look around to be sure no one has overheard me.

His mouth turns up into a satisfied grin. "Good. I guess I'll have to come by and get them."

⌒

Argotta asks me to stay after class, and I reluctantly send Bennett off to the dining hall alone. Argotta asks if I'm okay and goes over some things from yesterday's class, and five minutes later, I walk into the dining hall to find Bennett planted at our usual table with Emma and Danielle. He looks like he's holding his own.

"You're just in time," Emma says as I set my tray on the table. "Bennett was just telling us all about himself." She turns to me and says, "He's not really into sports, you know?" She shrugs and takes a bite of her sandwich.

"Well, like I said, skateboarding *is* actually a sport," Bennett says.

"Oh, I guess it could be. But it's really more of a mode of transportation, isn't it? I meant, you know, school sports. Football. Basketball. Baseball. Lacrosse. Hockey. Those types of sports."

"Team sports."

"Well, no, you could swim, I suppose. Or play tennis. Those are sports too."

"Or, you could skate," he says calmly. I can see the wheels in Emma's head turning as she attempts to land on the perfect retort. She glances at me sideways, and I give her a warning look, reminding her with my eyes of the promises she made me this morning: To be nice. To not embarrass me.

"Sure. You could skateboard, I guess." Emma looks back at me for confirmation that she has said the right thing, and I give her a grateful smile. And silently will her to stop talking. She looks back at Bennett. "So, what other hobbies do you have?"

So now it's a hobby. I just look at him, the boy who doesn't need a sport or a hobby, because what he can do counts for more than either one in my book. Bennett looks ready to jump back into the skateboarding-as-a-sport debate, so I answer for him.

"He travels," I say, and all three of them look at me. "He's been everywhere. Haven't you?"

They turn their attention back to Bennett, and he shrugs like it's no big deal. I sit back and listen as the three of them spend the rest of lunch talking in animated tones about the places they've seen. I've been on this side of the conversation before, but this time, I don't feel left out. Instead, I'm completely captivated, mentally taking notes, and wondering which of these beautiful-sounding destinations Bennett might take me to next.

15

Emma pulls up in front of the bookstore to drop me off, and before she even has the car in park, her head whips around in the direction of the record store across the street.

Okay, this is already a little weird.

"Are you going over there?" I ask as I open my door and step out onto the curb. I lean back in to hear her answer.

"No, not today. Today he should wonder if I'm going to pop in, and then, you know, miss me a little bit when I don't."

I roll my eyes. I don't think that's Justin's style, but then I realize, since I completely missed his attraction to my best friend, maybe I don't know much about Justin's style after all. "Okay, Em. See you in the morning."

"Bye, love," she says, and I watch her drive off.

The bells on the bookstore door give their standard jingle, but an unexpected chill goes through me when I hear them today. I usually associate them with happy memories, like coming in on a Saturday morning to help my grandfather stock the shelves, or the first time Dad gave me my own set of keys and let me lock up for the night. I've spent the last two days being grateful that the intruder was caught before he could take any of our money, but until now, it hadn't occurred to me that he robbed me of my bells.

"Hey, Annie." Dad's at the counter, punching numbers into the calculator, and making a small stack of the day's receipts.

I plant a kiss on his cheek. "Hi, Dad." He pecks my cheek in return and goes back to the accounting. Neither of us acknowledges that the store is different today, but I know we both feel it.

"I'm going to run to the bank and make the deposit," he says without looking at me. "From now on, I don't want you to do the night drop. I'll take care of it." I liked making the night drop. I watch as Dad collects all the receipts and staples them together, and stuffs the cash from the register into the zippered pouch. "I made arrangements to have an alarm system installed this weekend. It sounds pretty fancy. It even has a remote control, so you can just press a button from anywhere in the store and it will call the police immediately."

I look at him sideways. "Which is great, as long as you're carrying the remote."

"Well, yeah, I suppose." He laughs. "That's a little intense, isn't it?"

"No, not at all. We can get matching leather belts, with little holsters." I reach into my make-believe holster, quick-draw my invisible remote, and point it at him. He does the same.

"You know, I was thinking," Dad begins.

"Uh-oh."

"I was thinking that maybe it's time I hired a Northwestern student to help in the store. You're busier now, training for State. And finals are coming up soon—"

"In a month."

"Before you know it, you'll be dealing with college applications—"

"In six months."

"And even though I haven't met him properly, you seem to have a boyfriend now."

"I do not have a boyfriend."

"And you have better things to do than sit in this musty old store every other night, don't you think? It would be a great job for a college student."

"No, it wouldn't, because it's already a great job for me. Thanks, Dad, but I'm fine. I like working here." Besides, I've got to make money for my travel fund somehow, and it might as well be here.

He pulls me into a hug. "Are you sure?"

"Positive," I say, but my voice is muffled by his wool sweater.

He finally lets me go, pulls on his coat, and grabs the bag of cash. He's no sooner out the door than the bells jingle again.

I look up and see Bennett walking right toward me.

"Hi."

"Hi," he says to me.

We stand there awkwardly shifting our weight between our

feet and trying to think of something to say.

"I'm glad you came by." I wring my hands. "I wanted to thank you again for the postcard. That was really sweet."

"Sure." I watch *his* face get red and am grateful that it's not about me, for a change. "I got one for myself, too. To remember the day." He looks as nervous as I am. Which somehow makes me feel a lot better. "Anyway, I just came by to say hi and to get that book. On Mexico. For Argotta's class."

"Oh, right, sure."

He follows me over to the Travel section and I run my finger along the bindings, stopping to extract my favorites. After I've removed a good selection of six or seven, I sit down cross-legged on the Berber carpet and lean back against the shelves.

"Sit." I gesture for Bennett to join me, and he mirrors me on the floor. I reach into the pile of books and I hold up the first one. "This one sucks. Hardly any pictures." I put it down, starting a new pile on the floor, and pick up another. Suddenly I feel a strange sense of déjà vu. "Whoa."

"What?"

I look at him for a minute. "Did we sit like this the other night? Before the robbery and your do-over thingy?"

"Yeah. Pretty much exactly." He smiles. Then he looks surprised. "What? Do you remember it?"

"I don't know. Maybe not."

He picks a book out of the pile and holds it up. "This one's fine for budget travel, but that's not really what we're after." He grins as he puts it on top of the one with hardly any pictures. It sounds like something I'd say.

He grabs another. "This one has high-end hotels and restaurants, so it's a little too pricey for us. But the pictures are nice."

Yeah. That's true. And this is kind of freaking me out.

He picks up another book, and when he opens his mouth—presumably to repeat more of my words—I interrupt him and say, "Why don't you just tell me which one I recommended?"

He leans over me, reaches back into the shelves, and removes a book. "Excuse me." He brushes up against my arm and returns to his spot on the floor, but closer. So close our knees are touching. "This one's your favorite."

I nod.

"Best details. Vivid photos. Recommendations for budget hotels, but not, like, hostels or anything. And it has recommendations for three-day tours, five-day tours, and longer stays, so we can just put them togeth—"

"I want to hear the rest of the second thing."

He looks at me for a moment. "Where did I—"

"You can do over minor details in the past to affect the outcome, but you can't erase an entire event. You can travel to any place in the world *and* into other times, but only within certain dates."

He looks at me like he's surprised that I remember his words so exactly, but how could I not? They spent the night tossing and turning in bed with me.

"Right." He smiles a little. "I can only travel within my own lifetime. I can't go back before the day I was born, or even one second beyond the current date. The first time I tried it, it worked, but, well, things went wrong. I've tried a thousand times since, but nothing happens."

I picture a timeline in my head that starts at the year he was born and continues on until today. "So, you can't travel before 1978 or after today?"

He reaches down to one of the Mexico travel guides and starts playing with the pages like it's one of those little flip books, studiously avoiding my gaze. "No. I can go further into the future than that."

"But I thought you couldn't—then how—" I'm not getting this. And he's not helping much. "Okay, let me ask it this way: How far beyond 1995 have you gone?"

He inhales sharply. He doesn't look at me. "Two thousand and twelve."

"But isn't that 'beyond your lifetime'?"

But he's looking at me like it's not, and I feel a knot in the pit of my stomach.

He raises his eyebrows, like he's just waiting for me to catch on. "Wait . . . when were you born?"

I think a full minute passes before I get my answer. At least it feels that way.

"March 6. Nineteen ninety-five."

I just stare at him. "That was last month."

"Yeah. I know."

"March 6, 1995?"

"Yes."

That's when it hits me. The photos in his grandmother's living room. The framed pictures of her daughter holding a baby. Named Bennett.

"No way." He's still not looking up at me. "The pictures on Maggie's mantel." I don't even realize I've said it out loud, but I must have, because he finally looks up and nods.

"Maggie's your grandmother."

He nods again.

"And the 'real you' is . . ." I can't bring myself to say the words: *an infant.* "In San Francisco." That's the reason there aren't any older pictures of Bennett on Maggie's wall.

"Well, I'm the 'real' me." He holds his arm out and hits it to prove that it's solid. Then he looks at me. "But, yeah. In 2012 I'm seventeen. In 1995, technically, I'm . . . not."

I picture a completely different timeline. One that *starts* in 1995 and ends in 2012.

"What about the . . . other you? The one in the pictures."

"I'm still in San Francisco, probably lying in a crib, staring up at a mobile or something." I cringe and he looks at me sideways, but I shake it off and try not to look like the Baby Bennett thing isn't weirding me out. I must look confused instead, because he clarifies. "I can be in two different places in the same time, just not in the same place at the same time."

"What happens if you are? In the same place at the same time?"

"Well, I never let it happen accidentally. But if I do it on purpose, the *younger* me disappears and I take his place, just like I did at the robbery the other night. Then it's a do-over."

I look down at the books and play with the pages. "You lied to me about your grandmother being sick?"

"Not exactly. She *does* have Alzheimer's, she just . . . doesn't have it in 1995."

"And why does she think you're a Northwestern student?" This time I look up at him.

He sighs. "That's what I told her when I applied for the room."

He's still pressing my hand to his arm, but I pull it away so I can fidget with a string that's pulling loose from the carpet while I try not to hyperventilate.

He can go forward from 1995, because everything from this point on is his future.

He lives with a woman who has no idea he's her grandson.

He's not supposed to be here in 1995.

"This is your past," I say.

"Yes."

"How long have you stayed anywhere in the past?" I close my eyes again. I can't look at him.

"Thirty-six days," I hear him whisper.

"And when was that?"

There's a pause. "Tomorrow will be thirty-seven days."

I close my eyes. I don't think I'm handling this well.

And I still haven't heard everything. I don't know who he was mumbling about in the park that night, or how he got here, or where he came from, or what he's doing in Evanston, or why he was only supposed to be here for a month but he's still here.

I finally open my eyes and take him in.

I'm sixteen years older than him. But I'm not.

He's one year older than me. But he's not.

He looks me straight in the eye. "Look. I know this is weird. And even now that you know the rest of the second thing, you still only know two out of the three." He glances up at the ceiling and it's quiet for a moment before he looks at me again. "The point is that I'm not supposed to be here, Anna. Not in Evanston. Not in 1995. I'm not supposed to know you, or Emma, or Maggie. I'm not supposed to go to this school, or do this homework, or hang out in your coffeehouse." He takes my hands in his like he's about to transport me somewhere, but we don't leave the room—we just move a lot closer to each other. "I don't stay anywhere. I visit. I observe. I leave. I don't *ever* stay."

I'm not sure what I'm supposed to do with this information. Tell him to leave? Tell him to stay? But I don't have time to consider any other alternatives, because he scoots in closer and brings his hands to my face, and I fall back into the bookcase as he kisses me with this intensity—like he *wants* to be here, and if he kisses me just long enough, deeply enough, none of what he just said will actually be true. And as much as I know it's *all* true and that it's incredibly stupid to feel this way about someone who doesn't belong here—who, when he leaves, will hardly be a plane ride away—my hands leave the Berber carpet, find his back, and pull him toward me until I'm flat against the shelves. Because he's here now. And because I'm pretty certain I don't want this to stop. Ever.

Then he pulls away. "I'm so sorry."

"It's okay," I say as I try to catch my breath.

"No. It's *not* okay. This isn't how I planned it—I shouldn't have made it more complicated than it already is." He stands up and combs his fingers through his hair. "I've gotta go. I'm so sorry."

"Bennett." I try to smile at him—try not to look like everything that just happened doesn't have me slightly freaked out—but he won't even look at me. "It's okay. Bennett, please don't go."

But he's already out the door, leaving me alone with the rest of the second thing and the words he said just before he kissed me: "I don't *ever* stay."

16

"Hey, Anna! Wait up!" Courtney slams her locker and starts walking with me. "Did you finish your plan yet?"

"No, not yet." We smash in close to each other as we squeeze past a group of kids huddled around a locker and then we spread out again. "I'm working on it. How's yours coming along?"

"Good. I was just thinking last night I should probably add some ruins or something, you know—something educational." She looks at me like she's waiting for me to agree, so I nod. "But the beaches just look *amazing.* I swear I could spend the whole time just pancaked on different patches of sand."

"Just do beaches, then."

"Are you doing beaches?"

"Some." I have no idea what I'm doing. Last night, I tried to get beyond the pathetic two-column list I started in the bookstore last Tuesday, but I spent most of the night distracted by a time traveler who visits but never stays. An incredible, beautiful boy with eyes I can never seem to get out of my head, a body I never want to be more than two feet away from, and hands that can take me anywhere I want to go at the speed of thought. The same boy who isn't supposed to be here in 1995, but sat on the floor of my bookstore last night like there was nowhere else in the world he'd rather be and kissed me like there was no one else in the world he'd rather kiss. The boy with secrets, who still has one more to tell.

"Where else are you going?" she asks innocently, like we're not in the same competition to win the same five-hundred-dollar travel voucher.

I bring myself back to the hallway and try to think of what to say. "I've got a bunch of—" I begin, but I lose my train of thought again, because there's Bennett, leaning against the locker bank in front of Argotta's room, looking sweet and shaggy and gorgeous and clearly waiting for me. I try to keep pace with Courtney despite the new gear my heart has just leaped into.

"What? Ruins? I knew it. You're doing ruins. I should do—" I don't hear anything else after that, and when we finally reach Bennett, I come to a stop. My heart, on the other hand, speeds up even more.

"Hi," he says as he shoots me this incredible smile, and Courtney practically disappears from my side while I try not to look quite so happy to see him.

"Hi." Great, and now my hands are shaking.

Courtney's still here after all, and I see her look around

like she's trying to figure out where all the electricity is coming from. She looks back and forth between the two of us as a weird little smile forms on her lips. "Oh . . . interesting," she says and heads into the classroom with a mocking "Excuse me."

"Can we talk?" Bennett asks.

I peek around the door and into the classroom. "Spanish is about to start."

"I know. Come on." He leads me out the doors toward the side of the building and to a pathway obscured by overgrown plants and shrubs, and I hear the bell ring in the distance. We climb the slope to a clump of trees near the top of the ridge and stop at the base of the largest one. Bennett sits down and pats the ground next to him. Once I'm sitting, I know exactly where we are; the floor-to-ceiling glass wall of the dining hall is hard to miss, and even from here I can clearly see our table.

"So, I just wanted to say I'm sorry again . . . about last night." He reaches down for a pebble and plays with it nervously, rubbing it back and forth between his fingers. Then he looks up at me with a sad expression I've never seen on his face. "It's just—I've wanted to kiss you so many times." I lean in closer, hoping my proximity will help make this another one of those times, but he leans back with a sigh and rests against the tree trunk. "I told myself I had to hold back, because I knew starting something wouldn't be fair to you. I didn't want to complicate it. You know? I wanted to tell you everything and let you decide how you felt about it. About me."

"I know how I feel," I say as I close the gap he created between us a moment ago and muster a brave face. "But in that case, I guess you'd better tell me the rest—so I can decide." I give him an encouraging smile so he knows I'm ready to hear it. And I am, even though I also know it involves a girl. It was more than a month ago, but that doesn't mean I've forgotten how he looked the night I found him in the park, rocking back and forth on the bench and mumbling that he had to find her. How he told me in the coffeehouse that someone disappeared and it was his fault.

"I lost my sister." My eyes grow wide. "Brooke and I go to concerts. It's sort of our thing."

Brooke. I hadn't thought about the little girl with the dark hair and the bangs, holding her baby brother in a picture frame perched on Maggie's mantel. His sister. Who is two. Or nineteen.

"It's become a kind of hobby. I research bands I like and find the earliest shows I can travel to. Well, Brooke's the one who always travels with me."

He's struggling to talk. Apparently, telling me how he went back in time to save my life and that he didn't really belong here in 1995 were just ways of warming himself up for the hardest one. Brooke's a big deal.

"Remember how I told you I could only travel within my own lifetime?"

I let out a nervous laugh. "Yeah, I haven't forgotten that part."

"Well, if I try to travel earlier, it doesn't work. I close my eyes and picture the date, and . . . well . . . nothing happens. But Brooke wanted me to take her to this one show, so she convinced me to try it. It was a total experiment. Neither one of us really thought it would work." He smiles at the memory. "We held hands, closed our eyes, and I pictured the location and a date in 1994. And—"

"It worked?"

"Yeah, but only for a few minutes. I was there, and then I wasn't. I got knocked back to San Francisco."

"Knocked *back*?"

He shrugs, like it's a minor inconvenience he has to tolerate. "I usually have total control over where and when I go, but if I push the limits, it's like time *rights* everything. I get sent back where I'm supposed to be."

"But if you traveled there with Brooke, why did you get knocked back and she didn't?"

"I couldn't stay because I didn't *exist* in March 1994."

I stare at him, waiting for the rest.

"Brooke did. She was born in '93."

"Whoa. Seriously?" I ask, and he nods. "Where were you taking her?"

"March 10, 1994. Chicago Stadium." He looks me in the eyes and asks, "Does the date sound familiar?"

I think about it. March tenth. Last year. March tenth. I have no idea what he's talking about.

"The ticket stub," he says. "On your bulletin board. Pearl Jam. It wasn't a particularly epic show or anything. She just wanted to see them play stuff from *Ten* and *Vs.*"

"No way." I say the same two words I heard him say when he saw the ticket stub upstairs. "I was there. With Emma. We were *there*."

"Probably a lot longer than I was. I didn't even have enough time to buy a T-shirt."

I think I'm supposed to laugh along with him, but I'm still staring at him in disbelief. "How will you get her back?"

"I'm not entirely sure yet. At first, I just assumed that if I went back as far as I could—to March 6, 1995—Brooke would have lived out the year and been waiting for me at Maggie's. But she wasn't there and clearly hadn't been. So now I have to wait and see; either she'll 'catch up' to March 1995 and hopefully know I'm here, or time will right itself and she'll get knocked back home to 2012 . . . or, I guess, somewhere else between now and then."

"God, she must be terrified." I picture her roaming the streets, lost in time and looking for shelter.

"I know Brooke, and I'm sure she freaked out a little at first, but she's got plenty of money with her, more than enough to get by. I think she'll be fine. But my mom's a mess, and wow, is she pissed at me. Though maybe my screwup proved she's right and I can't handle this little *gift* of mine."

I have no idea what to say.

"Anyway, I returned alone at a total loss and had to break the news that it could take a while. My mom insisted I come back and stay here until I found Brooke. I explained I could be gone for weeks or more, so she made excuses to people at home and had me bring my dad to Evanston to enroll me in her old school." I can hear the bitterness in his voice. "So, here I am. I go back home every once in a while to check in."

The migraines. The rocking. The murmuring: *I've got to find her. I can't leave yet.* It's all making sense. "You were coming back from San Francisco."

"Yeah. It happened a bunch of times in those first two weeks. I would just disappear from Evanston and reappear in my bedroom back in 2012, so I'd close my eyes and force myself to come back here. In fact, that night you came to Maggie's, I'd just returned. And that's why I kicked you out, because I thought I was about to be knocked back. But I wasn't. It hurt like hell, but I kept myself here, and I haven't been knocked back since." I remember my visit, the coffee cups and water bottles strewn across his room, how he stared me down in Maggie's living room. No wonder he acted so weird when he found me in his house, chatting with his grandmother and staring at a photo of him and his two-year-old sister. No wonder he made me leave.

"So you're only here until Brooke comes back." He nods, and I feel sick. But I've known it all along—deep down in a part of me I keep choosing to ignore—that when I learn his secret, I'll also learn why he can't stay.

"We should get back to class." He grabs my hands, and without even thinking, I close my eyes. But we don't move. The wind is still cold on my face when he says, "Anna." I open my eyes again and see him looking at me. "We're not supposed to know each other. I want us to, but there's a lot at stake for you in this—more than I think you even understand yet."

I think I nod. I'm not sure, but I feel him reach forward and softly brush my eyelids closed. He grabs my hand again, and I feel a twist deep in my gut.

When I open my eyes, we're standing on the path lined with overgrown shrubs and my stomach is contorting. He reaches into his backpack, and pulls out a little bag of saltines, and I immediately start nibbling. Then he pulls out a bottle of water, unscrews the cap, and downs it without stopping. He puts the empty water bottle back in his pack and leads me through the doors and into the hallway. He stops at the exact spot we'd been standing in earlier. I peek inside the room and see Courtney taking her seat.

"Well, you know all my secrets now."

I nod and look around the hallway. We're back.

"So, promise me you'll think about it, okay? And ask me more questions."

Questions. I have plenty of those. What I need is time alone with him, with nowhere we need to be and no reason to stop talking until I understand what the hell he means when he says I need to think about what's "at stake" for me.

He turns to walk into the classroom and I grab his arm. "Hey, when can we talk again?" I'm not about to sit around all weekend wondering when I might bump into him.

"Soon." He gives me a smile. Then he walks into the classroom and I follow him, lost in my thoughts but still taking in the details of the room. Argotta's perched at his usual spot in the front of the room, leaning against his desk. Alex and his too-white teeth are already in the seat across from mine. And

Courtney's in the first seat in the first row, shooting meaningful glances at Bennett and me. Just as the bell rings, she gives me a little wink.

⟋⟍⟋⟍

"Wanna hear the buzz?" Emma asks as she slides her tray onto the table and sits down.

Danielle tosses her hair and turns to look at her. "There's buzz?" Her eyes are so wide they look like they might just pop out and roll across the table. "Who's the buzz about?"

"Anna . . ." Emma purrs. "And Bennett . . ."

"If you follow that with anything about sitting in a tree, I'm leaving." I lean back in my chair and bite into my apple. I don't really want to be the subject of "buzz," but I'm grateful for something else to think about besides do-overs and getting knocked back and a nineteen-year-old girl who's trapped in time.

I turn around in my seat and find Bennett making his way through the lunch line, filling his cup with Coke. Emma follows my gaze and then shoots me a sly grin. "People are talking. Don't you want to know what they're saying before he gets here?"

"Nope." I look uninterested, because I am. "Not really."

"It's *good*," she presses in a high-pitched voice that sounds like she might break into song.

"Don't *care*," I sing back and take another bite.

"I hear he lives with his grandmother," Danielle pipes up, and I stop chewing. Emma and I turn to look at her. Then

Emma looks back at me. "He does?" She wrinkles her nose. I can't tell if she's put off by this new information or just irked that someone else heard it before she did.

My head spins toward Danielle. "How do you know that?" I ask, but I stop and force a grin instead, hoping to cover up how defensive I just sounded.

"Julia Shepherd told me."

"Oh. Julia?" My tone is light and casual now, but only because I'm working hard to make it sound that way. I take another bite of my apple to emphasize how little this topic matters to me. "How does Julia know?"

Danielle touches her palms together in prayer position and bends her head to meet her fingertips. "The Donut keeps no secrets." She laughs and takes a bite of her sandwich.

"Clever."

"So, does he?" Emma asks.

I wipe all traces of irritation from my face and say with a voice calm and steady, like it's no big deal, "Yeah. Her name's Maggie. He takes care of her."

"Oh, that's sweet," says Danielle, and I shoot her an appreciative grin.

"Where are his parents?" Emma whispers as she watches him across the room. "Weren't they supposed to be back by now?"

I wish she'd drop this, because I suddenly realize that I don't know his cover story. He told me his parents were in Europe, but that was before I knew where they *really* were.

I have no idea what he's told the school about his family, but I'm certain he didn't leave emergency contact information for people who live in 2012.

I twist around in my chair again and see him coming right toward us. "Ask him," I say, gesturing in his direction. I hope he has a good answer.

"Hey," Bennett says, sliding his tray onto the table.

"Hey," Emma and Danielle say in unison, with far too much enthusiasm.

At least the two of them have the decency to let him take a couple of bites before they start the inquisition. Then Emma raises her eyebrows at Danielle. Game on.

"So, Bennett." Danielle rests her arms on the table. "I hear you live with your grandmother."

Bennett takes a sip of his Coke, looking unfazed by the fact that she's in his personal space, and nods. "My parents are in Europe, and I'm living with her while they're gone."

"Right," Emma says. "In fact, I thought you were just going to be here for a month. Did they decide to stay longer or something?"

"Yeah. Now I'm not sure how long I'm going to be here."

I think about Brooke and wonder where she is, what she's doing right now. Selfishly hoping she's having the time of her life and won't be returning to 2012 any time soon.

"My dad's working on a big project in Geneva," Bennett says.

I smile and roll my eyes at him, and he gives me a wink.

They all talk about how beautiful Geneva is.

"So," I ask at the first break in the discussion, "how's the auction coming along?"

That's more like it. Bennett and I sit back and watch Emma and Danielle talk over each other with excited intonations and an impressive host of superlatives like *coolest* and *most stellar.* He keeps shooting me little glances while they're talking, like he's trying to guess what I'm thinking, but that's impossible; *I* don't even know what I'm thinking. I'm sure it will hit me at some point, but for now, all I know is that he's sitting here like he belongs.

When the bell rings, Emma and Danielle stand up and start walking to the trash cans while they continue their conversation. Bennett and I follow them, and his arm brushes against mine as he whispers, "So, what are you doing tomorrow?" I don't think he notices that Emma and Danielle have instantly stopped talking.

"Tomorrow night?"

"No. Tomorrow. All day." He smiles at me and adds, "Unless that's too much of me?"

I don't have a meet. And the idea of too much Bennett is impossible to comprehend. I beam. "No. I mean, I don't have plans."

"Great. Can I pick you up at eight?"

"In the morning?"

"Yes."

Danielle lets a giggle escape and Emma elbows her.

"Where are we going?"

"It's a surprise."

I light up again. Or maybe I'm still lit up. I can't really tell.

"Oh, and wear your running clothes."

"Why?"

"Part of the surprise. Excuse me." He nudges past Emma, dumps his trash in the garbage can, and strides out into The Donut. No one speaks until he's left the room.

Then Emma turns to me and squeals, "Okay, that was cute!"

"Yeah, but what's with the running clothes?" Danielle asks.

Emma empties her tray and brings her hand to her hip. "Isn't it obvious? He's going to drive you to the track and make you run while he watches from the bleachers." She cracks up at her own joke.

"Shut up!" I punch her hard in the shoulder but laugh right along with her.

"Yeah, he's cute," Danielle decides.

"He is," Emma agrees. "I'm still watching him," she says, like she's a member of British Intelligence, "but I admit, that boy *is* growing on me."

"And it's sweet that he takes care of his grandma," Danielle adds.

Emma looks at me as if she's just had an epiphany. "Ha! Now we *both* have dates tomorrow! Sunday morning. Coffeehouse. We'll compare."

17

At precisely eight a.m., a blue SUV pulls into the driveway and I slam the window shut and bound down the stairs. For the hundredth time, I wonder where Bennett's taking me. I was sort of hoping our next trip would magically transport us to Paris, but all night I've been studying my map for locations that might require athletic attire for visitors. The Swiss Alps? Machu Picchu? Borneo? It doesn't really matter where we go, but the running-clothes part does have me stumped.

Dad beats me to the door and shakes Bennett's hand while he shoots me a chiding glare, and I know he's already eager for me to get home so he can lay into me about not having introduced them properly. He gives Bennett the lecture about driving carefully and having me home before curfew, and as we're walking toward the door he stares at me and mouths the word *dinner.* I nod and close the door behind us.

"This is your car?"

Bennett holds open the door of the shiny new Jeep Grand Cherokee and waits for me to climb in. It figures. Like everyone else I know, he drives something far too nice for a high school kid.

"It's Maggie's." The inside is immaculate and has that new-car smell. He closes my door, walks around to his side, climbs in, and turns the key in the ignition. The car starts with a purr.

"Are you ready?" he asks, still sitting in the driveway. He leans back against the leather, head cocked to one side, watching me as I study him for clues.

"Of course. Where are we going?"

"Road trip." He clicks his seat belt into place and grins at me.

"We're driving? How far?"

"A little over three hours each way." He looks over his shoulder and backs out of the driveway.

"To go . . . where, exactly?"

He raises his eyebrows and gives me a sinister look. "Still a surprise."

"Do I need to bring anything?"

He scans me from top to bottom. I'm dressed in my long running pants, running shoes, and a fleece zip-up. All as instructed. "Nope. You're perfect."

"Okay. So why drive so far when we can, just, you know . . ." I make a weird gesture, as if I know the universal sign for time travel.

"Ah, look who's getting spoiled!" He navigates through the

neighborhood toward the interstate, heading north. "First, driving gives us plenty of time to talk. Second, I haven't been outside Evanston since I got here. And third, well, I wanted to do something normal for you."

"Normal."

"You know. That has nothing to do with my weird little talent."

I settle into the seat and try not to look disappointed.

We talk and listen to music, and three hours and twenty minutes later we pull into Devil's Lake State Park. I know this because the sign tells me so and not because Bennett has given me any information along the way. He pulls into a parking spot, and we get out and walk around to the back of the car. He clicks open the hatch. Inside are two overstuffed red backpacks, and I feel myself take a step back, confused by the neoprene, Velcro, and shiny pieces of metal that hang from the external loops.

"What is that?" I gesture toward one of the packs.

"That, Anna, is a backpack."

"Yes, I can see that, thank you. What's it for?"

"It's for you."

"What's *in* it?"

"Well, you have the lunch. And the shoes. And the harnesses. I have the rest of the equipment."

"The equipment."

"Ropes, carabiners—"

"You've brought me all the way out here to kill me and bury me?"

"Nope, you'll love this. Trust me."

"Love what, exactly?"

"Rock climbing."

I don't have the heart to tell him that, while I consider myself to be particularly brave and up for most challenges, I tend to avoid sports that require one's feet to leave the solidity of the earth. Like parachuting. And bungee jumping. And rock climbing.

He gives me a pat on the back like I'm an old chum. "You're athletic. You'll love this." He grips my shoulders, turns me around, and lifts the pack onto my back. He heaves the second pack over his shoulders, pulls on the straps to tighten it, and reaches up to shut the rear window. He's a little too chipper as he grabs my hand and leads me to the trail, and I try again not to look disappointed that I won't be drinking a café au lait on the banks of the Seine.

We walk in silence along a peaceful trail, and a half a mile later arrive at some spot deemed by Bennett to be "perfect." To me it looks a lot like a very, very tall rock. And if I'm not mistaken, we're about to scale it.

"Stay here," he says as he opens both of our packs and begins to sort the gear. I watch him change his shoes, strap a thick harness around his waist, and throw a rolled-up bundle of rope over his shoulders. "I'll be right back." And with that, he's off, pulling himself up the sheer face of the rock with what looks like minimal effort. It doesn't take long for him to reach the top, pull himself over the shelf, and disappear from sight. He's gone for a few minutes and I start to wonder if he's left me here.

"Are you okay up there?" I yell.

His face pops up from above the rock. "Great. I'll be right down. Stand back."

I follow his instructions, taking a few more steps than he probably intended, and two thick, white ropes appear from the top of the rock and land a few feet in front of me. Then he's on them, sliding down and bouncing off the rock as he descends. He's all happy and shiny when he hits the bottom.

"Are you ready?"

"No."

"Here, start by putting on your shoes." He reaches into my pack and pulls out a pair of funny-looking red shoes with thin rubber soles and pointy toes.

"Classy." I turn the shoes over. They look brand-new. "Did you buy these for me?"

He smiles. "A little gift."

"How do you know what size I wear?" I slide my foot inside. It fits perfectly.

He shrugs, reaches into my pack again, and pulls out a second, smaller harness, also presumably for me. He takes out a small bag and clips it to the belt. "This is your chalk."

"Chalk." I stand up. The elf shoes feel funny.

"To help your grip," he explains as he holds the harness open for me to step into. He tightens it around my waist and then picks up one end of the rope, wraps his arms around me, and starts fiddling with something on the back of the belt. He smells good.

I look up at the sheer wall. "No amount of chalk is going to help me climb that thing."

"Follow me. Chicken." He picks up the other end of the rope, feeds it through some metal contraption, and clips it onto his harness. "This is a belay device. It keeps you connected to me." I'm still not sure about the climbing, but the last part makes me smile. "All I want you to do right now is learn to trust the device. To trust me and know that you aren't going to fall." He leads me to a part of the rock that has lots of grooves and deep cracks. He calls it a great "beginner's rock" and shows me where to place my feet and hands for the first few moves he expects me to make.

"I'm not sure about this," I admit.

"Why not?" He looks genuinely let down by my apprehensiveness. "You're safe. What's going to happen?"

"Well, for starters, you could disappear into thin air while I am halfway up that rock."

"Never happen."

"Okay, but unlike most people, you could actually vanish."

"It won't happen." That damned grin of his shouldn't put me at ease, but it does.

"You're just mean." I laugh and move toward the rock, dipping my fingers into the chalk bag.

"So, the first thing you want to do is check to be sure I have you securely on the rope. You say, 'I'm ready to climb.'"

"'I'm ready to climb?'"

"And I say, 'On belay.' Then you say, 'Climbing.'"

"Climbing," I say, annoyed.

"Climb on." He's far too cheery.

I lift my right leg up into the grove the way he showed me, reaching up and pulling myself into the spot. I can feel my butt jutting out at an awkward angle, so I find a new hold and pull myself into it.

"I knew it. You're a natural!"

I look for another crack and grip it. It feels like a puzzle, finding just the right hold for my hands and an equally strong foothold at just the right distance.

"Okay, stop for a second."

But I'm just getting the hang of this. "Why?"

"Let go completely, like you're falling."

But I'm not. "Just . . . let go?"

"Yeah. Push yourself away from the rock and let go."

I take a deep breath. Push myself away from the rock. Let go.

I suck in my breath sharply as I swing backward. Hang. Dangle.

"I just want you to feel that. I have you. Right now you're only about ten feet off the ground. But when you're higher, that's exactly how it would feel if you missed your hold, or needed a break, okay?"

"Okay." I do feel safe, even though this sensation is so strange.

"So just swing yourself back to the rock when you're ready and say, 'Climbing.'"

I do as I'm told.

"Climb on," I hear from below.

I continue to look for the right places for my hands and feet, maneuvering into them and surprising myself when I don't fall. I don't look down. I don't even want to. I'm focused on solving this puzzle of a rock, figuring out how to crack the code that will get me to the top, and without my expecting it to be there, there's sunlight. And sky.

I pull myself up and throw my arms in the air, Rocky Balboa style, as I dance back and forth at the summit.

As it turns out, getting down is scarier.

Bennett yells instructions from below, telling me how to maneuver myself back onto the face of the rock, and where to plant my feet.

"I don't hold the rope?" I shout, without looking down.

"No, just plant your feet on the rock and lean way back. I know it feels weird, but I've got you. Just let your arms relax."

I can't seem to let anything relax.

"What if I fall?"

"You won't. Anna, let go of the rope, or you'll flip around." I force my arms to hang by my sides. "Trust me," he says, and I close my eyes and let him lower me.

It's all I can do to keep my feet in front of me, my legs parallel with the earth below, but I manage to get the rhythm, and soon I'm back on solid ground.

"You were amazing!" Bennett says as he throws his arms around me. "How was it?"

"Good." I'm euphoric, though my arms are still a little shaky. "That was actually really cool."

"I knew you'd love it." He loosens his grip on me and I start to move away from him, but then I feel his hands leave my shoulders and move down, pausing at the harness so he can untie the rope. He's so close I can feel the rise and fall of his breath, and it's all I can do to stand still while his fingers work to untangle the knot behind me. A minute later, the rope falls to the ground and his hands leave the belt and settle on the small of my back. He pulls me to him and kisses me, and I feel my adrenaline pumping even harder. He smiles and says, "My turn."

Somehow I manage to respond. "What?"

"Ready to learn to belay?"

"Really? You trust me to hold you?"

"Absolutely." He steps back and I miss his hands the minute they leave me. He opens the metal carabiner, unclips it from his harness, and clips it onto mine.

He takes his place on the rock. "Climbing," he says.

And I reply: "Climb on."

18

By the time I've reached the top of the ridge for the ninth time, my forearms are shaking. I take a deep breath, pull myself up onto the shelf, and kick my leg up onto the surface. I push myself into a standing position and look around at treetops that go on for miles, interrupted only by the bright blue lake in the middle. I smile down at him, awestruck and victorious.

"Stay there," he shouts from the ground as he throws his backpack over his shoulders and free-climbs the rock face in half the time it took me to climb it using the rope. He dusts himself off at the top.

"Hungry?" He sits down, unzips the pack, and removes a bunch of plastic bags and four bottles of Gatorade. "I wasn't sure what you'd like. Turkey and Swiss or roast beef and Cheddar?"

"Gatorade." I reach forward, parched, and thrilled to see the bright yellow bottles, and I open the lid and gulp. Out of the corner of my eye, I watch Bennett do the same, and when he's finished, he reclines against a tall rock and closes his eyes.

The sun is high now, and even though it's still cool outside, the surface of the rock is warm. It really is the perfect day for this, and I sit down next to him and reach for the turkey and Swiss. I'm suddenly famished, and I guess he must be too, because even though we stop and smile at each other a few times, neither us of us speaks as we polish off our sandwiches.

"So," I finally say. "Rock climbing."

"Good date?"

"Unexpected."

"Disappointed?"

I look around again at the painting-like scene. "No way." A trip to Wisconsin may not do much to expand my midwestern clump of pins, but at least, I think, as I look around the forest with the sunlight gleaming through the branches and the rock formations piercing the sky, unlike Ko Tao, I can always come back here when he's gone. When I'm missing him, like I already know I will be.

I've been thinking about it all night, now that I know everything. He's from a time seventeen years from now. He can travel anywhere in the world just by thinking about it. He lost his sister, and when he finds her, he'll have to leave 1995 and return to 2012. And apparently, all of this means something important to me, but I can't figure out what. But he's here now, and he wants to be with me. And even though the first part makes me feel a little bit queasy, the last part leaves me smiling to myself. I look at him.

Bennett pats the surface of the rock in front of him, and I scoot over and settle in, rest my elbows on his knees, and let my head fall forward. A groan escapes my mouth as he squeezes my shoulders. My muscles are ridiculously sore.

"So, how did you get into rock climbing?" I have a million questions for him, but this one is the easiest to ask.

He presses his thumbs into the base of my neck, and I breathe into the pressure until I feel the muscles release. "There's a little coastal town in Southern Thailand called Krabi." I can't see his face, but I can hear the smile in his voice. "Railay Beach is known for its rock formations, but I didn't know that until I ran into some backpackers who told me about it. They took me on my first climb, and I've been hooked ever since."

His hands move with a slow, coordinated rhythm up my back until they reach my shoulders again. I open my eyes just in time to see him reach forward, grab a piece of my hair, and twist it around his finger. Then he unrolls it, gives it a gentle pull, and lets go, and I feel the curls spring back into place. "How does your hair do this?"

"What? Look like a mess of miniature Slinkys?" He's so close I can feel his breath on the back of my neck, and I grimace at the thought that my hair must smell more like sweat than vanilla-scented shampoo.

"I've been sitting behind you in Spanish for the last month, wishing I could to do this." He pulls down on another bunch of curls and laughs when they bounce right back where they belong. "How about you? How you did start running?"

I turn my head so I can see his face, and he lets the curls fall from his grasp. "Oh, no, you don't."

"What?"

"I thought I'd get to ask all the questions today. You told me to keep them coming." I lean back into his chest and rest my head on his shoulder. My head rises and falls with the gentle rhythm of his breath, and when he softly brushes my hair off my forehead, I let out a sigh and sink further into him. "Besides, you're far more interesting than I am."

"That's not true." I feel him start to play with my hair again.

"Fine," I say, "we'll take turns. One for one. But ten bucks says you're going to run out of questions first." I lift my hand in his direction and he shakes it.

"Deal," he says.

"And I'm going first." I smile up at him. "What do you miss most about home?"

He doesn't skip a beat. "My cell phone."

"Come on, I'm serious." I wait for him to laugh, but he doesn't. "Seriously? You miss a phone?"

"What did you think I would say?"

"I don't know. I guess I was expecting you to say your family."

"Families seem pretty much the same. You haven't seen a twenty-first-century cell phone."

"What's so special about your phone?"

"Lots of things. But I can't tell you about them."

"Well, that's no fun," I say as I let out a little laugh. "What good are you if you can't tell me about the future?"

"I'm good for lots of things," he says as his fingers leave my hair, settle behind my ear for a moment, and then slide their way down to my collarbone. I close my eyes and try to match my breathing to his as he traces. "Besides, I've got to leave you some surprises. You do like surprises, don't you?"

"I'd better. You're certainly full of them." I inhale deeply and try to concentrate on my questions. "So what are you saying, I'll never see the future? Never see where you really live?"

He softly makes the sound of a game-show buzzer. "That's another question. It's my turn."

"Come on. . . ."

"Hey, you're the one who made the deal. One for one," he says. I let out an exasperated sigh. "Where were you when you heard about Kurt Cobain's suicide?"

"Hmmm. Wow." It's been a while, but I remember the day well. "That was almost exactly a year ago. I went to Emma's after school, and we were up in her room listening to the radio, and the DJ announced that he shot himself. So we pulled out every Nirvana CD she had and listened to them back to back."

His fingers linger on my shoulder for a moment, then slide down my arm.

"That week was weird," I continue. "People were crying, like . . . really crying, like they knew him or something. I didn't get that so much. Anyway, the whole thing was really sad." He's running his thumb back and forth against the back of my hand and when I look down I realize that I'm doing the same thing to his. "Where were you?"

I feel him shrug. "That was in 1994," he says, and for a moment, I don't get it. But then I do.

"Wow." I stop rubbing his hand. "Okay, that's kind of creepy."

"Sorry."

"And I can't believe I wasted a question."

He brushes my hair to one side and kisses the back of my neck. "I'll tell you what; I'll give you that one," he says with a whispery breath near the back of my ear. I squirm a little.

"Stop it. You're making me forget my questions."

"Good. I want that ten-spot," he kisses my neck again and I lose my train of thought entirely. "You wanted to know if I'd take you into your own future."

"*Mmmhmmm.*"

"I can't. Well, technically, I guess I could, but I've never done anything like that before and I have no idea what would happen if I did."

"Why? Are you afraid I don't exist in 2012 or something?"

"No, that's definitely not what I'm worried about. But I can only travel back and forth within the time I've already lived, and you just haven't lived beyond this moment yet. I'll take you anywhere in the world you want to go, but never before or after this exact date."

"Really?"

He rests his chin in the crook of my neck and nods. I guess I can live with that. I've never needed to leave this date or time, only this place.

"Besides you can't know what happens in your future. That would take all the fun out of it." He kisses my shoulder. "So, tell me about Emma."

"Emma?"

"Yeah. Tell me about her. How did you two become friends?"

I feel the corners of my mouth turn up at the memory. "I met her my first day at Westlake." I look at Bennett and he raises an eyebrow, asking for more.

I let out a little laugh. "Mom wanted me to make a good impression, so she made me wear the jumper." I grimace and shudder as I picture the uniform. "We used to have this ugly plaid dress that was one of the approved options but no one *ever* wore. And she made me put on *tights* and wear this lace ribbon as a headband. It was, like a hundred and six degrees outside, and all day long, all I wanted to do was change into shorts and a T-shirt. I was hot and itchy and my hair was out to here." I hold my hands up to the side of my head, and he laughs. "But then this girl bounced right up to me after sixth period—all cheekbones and braces—and asked if I wanted to hang out with her after school. And even though I really wanted to go home and change, I said yes. And that was just kind of it. Emma has been my best friend ever since."

When I look back at Bennett I can't help picturing the place I'll be tomorrow, sitting in the coffeehouse and telling Emma every single thing about this day. I'm definitely winning for best date.

"Tell me about your family," I say, officially changing the subject back to him.

He lets out a heavy sigh. "There's not much to tell. My mom's a little . . . difficult to talk to. If I ask her about something that happened in the news, the conversation eventually leads to doctors. If I ask her about the weather, the conversation eventually leads to doctors. I don't ever ask her about scientific advancements, because that immediately leads to doctors. She thinks I'm broken. She just wants a normal kid."

I pull his arms tight around my waist and start tracing his palm with my fingertip. His hands are dry after climbing, and the lines are filled with dirty chalk dust.

"Now Dad thinks I'm some kind of magical creature. After he discovered what I could do, he wouldn't leave me alone. He spent the first year researching all the catastrophes that took place between 1995 and the present day, and created this massive document that listed each event—and every smaller event leading up to it—so I could go back and prevent it."

"Did you?"

"No. I mean, I don't think I should change things that happen just because I *can*. You've heard of the butterfly effect, right? One small change can have a massive impact on something else. I don't even think I could manage that massive a do-over." He's quiet for a while, and I lean into his chest and listen to the silence. "Eventually, he found a way to use my gift for another kind of good. *His* good."

I keep tracing the lines in his palm, because that seems to keep him talking.

"We didn't have much money when Brooke and I were little. I mean, we had a decent apartment and everything, but my mom was a bit spoiled, I guess, growing up here in Maggie's monstrosity of a house. And Dad hated his job—he worked in a bank downtown; I don't even know what he did—but he was always in a bad mood, and the two of them always fought.

"Then Dad had his big idea. He went back to his research, this time focusing on companies and the positive trajectory of their stock."

"What?" I stop tracing and turn to look at him. "You didn't."

"I did. I'd travel back to each date he listed, a week or so before a major company event, and when I arrived I'd send my dad a letter with a stock tip. He'd buy. The stock would skyrocket. I'd go back and send him another message to tell him when to sell. And Dad had a new job."

"Isn't that illegal?"

"Not technically. Insider trading laws say you can't buy or sell based on nonpublic information. The information we used was always public."

I give him an incredulous look.

"Okay, it's definitely sketchy. But hey, it's kept them off my back . . . until recently, at least. Brooke and I got to travel and see all the live music we wanted. Mom got the fancy life she expected, and Dad got to feel like he gave it to her. Everyone's happy, no one's getting hurt."

"I take it your dad made some good money."

"Well, the economy has had its ups and lots of downs, but if you know exactly where to invest—"

"You could make a lot?" I guess.

"Sure. Millions, even."

"Millions?"

"Well, we didn't mean to."

"Oh, sure," I say with a laugh. "As long as you didn't mean to." He's an accidental time traveler *and* an accidental millionaire. "So, how do you have access to this money?"

"That's another question."

"I know."

He shakes his head but smiles as he gives in to me. "Cash. For this particular trip, lots of it, minted pre-1995, and hidden in my room at Maggie's."

"And Brooke?

"Backpack. Loaded with cash." He pulls his hand out of mine and grabs my chin so I have to face him. Then he kisses my nose. "That's it, I'm cutting you off now. My turn."

As much as I've loved reclining against him, I'm tired of twisting my neck to see his face. I sit cross-legged and spin around in place, scoot in closer, and rest my knees on his legs.

"Hi."

"Hi." He smiles, but as I watch him, his expression goes from playful to serious. "You know, I meant what I said the other day. The fact that I'm here . . ." His voice trails off, and he gets quiet for a minute. "It impacts you more than it does me."

I don't like this turn toward the heavy, so I copy his

game-show-buzzer sound. "Please phrase your statement in the form of a question."

"Do you understand what all of this means for you?"

"No." And I know I'm supposed to care, but I don't, not right now. I don't want to think about what he can do and where he can go and when he might leave, because at this moment we're both in the exact same place at the exact same time. Right now I just want to kiss him.

He brings his hands to my waist. "It's like my dad's list of world events. I could go back and change a bunch of little things that would likely change the outcome, and my life wouldn't be *any* different as a result. But other people's lives would be. And maybe they'd be better. But maybe they'd be worse. My being here with you *right now* is a change. Not for me—for you. You exist in 2012, just like I do, in a future that doesn't include me. Just knowing me here in 1995, where I don't belong—"

"Will be fun," I interrupt.

"Will change your whole life."

"Maybe for the better."

"Maybe. Maybe not."

"Well, I already know you, Bennett. What choice do I have?"

"Remember what I said at your house that first day—that I would tell you everything, but I'd let you choose."

I wrap my arms around his neck and kiss him. "Yes. Let's hear my choices."

He inhales sharply. "First choice: I can go back to being the strange new kid at school, keeping my distance from everyone until Brooke returns and I can go home again. You and I can say hi in the halls, and maybe we'll exchange little glances now and then, like people who share a secret do. But that's it. Your life from this point on won't be any different."

"No way." I kiss him again. "What's the other choice?"

He smiles. "Second choice: I spend the time I have here with you, and we'll hang out like normal people and travel the world like abnormal ones. When Brooke returns, I'll go back home, but then I'll come back here. And I guess I'll keep coming back until you decide you're sick of me." He pulls back to get a better look at my expression.

It seemed pretty easy up until this point, but now that he's forcing me to really think about it, I can see how enormous this decision is. Two futures: the safe but mundane life I know so well, or one filled with adventure but constant uncertainty. He'll take me around the world, but he'll leave. There will be times when we're together, and times when we're separated—not just by miles, but also by almost two decades. Every rational part of my being tells me to take the safe route, as unappealing as it sounds. But then I look into his eyes and I'm somehow confident in my decision. Still, there's one more thing I need to understand.

"I don't get it. Why would you uproot your life just to be with me?"

"Because you—" He stops. Takes a breath. Starts over. "I liked your sense of adventure. I thought it would be fun to take you somewhere you'd never go otherwise. But now it's more than that. Now I just want to know you." His words have my heart racing again, and I close my eyes and take a deep breath. When I open them, he's still looking at me.

"Didn't you once say something about this being a really bad idea?"

He laughs under his breath. "Yeah. I think I did."

"You were right, you know."

"Told you."

"Still, I'm choosing option two."

"Are you sure?"

"Yes."

His face breaks into a huge grin and he pulls me tighter and kisses me, warm and sweet and long and slow and never-ending, and I know this is what I want.

And I know I need to invite him over for dinner, because there's no question. This is serious.

⁓

We continue trading questions the entire way home, and as we pull in to the driveway, I feel like I've achieved the impossible: I actually know Bennett Cooper. As he puts the Jeep in park, I look up at my house and feel my chest constrict. I've been with him for nearly eleven hours, and I'm still not ready for him to leave.

He turns the car off and leans over to kiss me, but I reach up and put my finger to his lips. "Wait. I have another question." He stops midway and waits for me to continue. "Why were you watching me at the Northwestern track the day you started at Westlake?"

"That again?" He settles back into his seat.

"Well, yeah. You haven't answered me yet."

"I have. I didn't know what you were talking about the day Emma assaulted me in the lunchroom, and I still have no idea what you're talking about."

"It really wasn't you?"

"Look, you know everything there is to know about me. And I'm telling you, I wasn't there that day. I still haven't been to Northwestern. Certainly not at six thirty a.m. in sub-thirty-degree weather. That's your twisted thing, not mine."

He laughs lightly, and I want to believe him. Everything about his words and the look on his face says that I should. After all, he's right—there's no reason for him to lie to me now that I know everything.

"Since I've answered that one before—multiple times, in fact—you get one more question."

I'm ready to go back to our comfortable question-and-answer session, so I smile and think of another: "Where is your favorite place in the world?"

He smiles from ear to ear and his eyes shine as he starts to speak. "Easy. Vernazza. It's a small fishing village on the northwestern coast of Italy, in the Cinque Terre, and you have to arrive by train—well, at least most people do. It's the most amazing little village. Narrow, cobblestoned streets. Colorful boats lining the harbor. Row after row of tiny, brightly painted houses built straight into the hillside. It's spectacular."

His eyes fall on my lips and he leans forward and this time I close my eyes and wait for him. "You'll love it there," he says, and as we kiss, the little village comes to life with the two of us in it.

⌒

"I'm home!" I yell in the general direction of the living room, and I start heading up the stairs in an exhausted little daze. My forearms are sore, and my hips hurt, and I have blisters from my new little elf shoes. I can't wait to get into the shower and then into bed and drift off to sleep with nothing but thoughts of Bennett to keep me company.

"Annie, can you come here?" Dad calls, and I turn around and drag myself toward the sound of his voice. Just as I turn the corner and enter the kitchen, I see Mom and Dad push their chairs away from the table and start walking toward me.

Here it comes. "What's up?" I ask, steeling myself for a lecture about spending the day with a boy they don't even know. But as they get closer, I can see that Mom's been crying.

"What?" I repeat, looking back and forth between the two of them. "What's going on?"

"It's Justin . . ." Mom pulls me into a hug, but I resist, stepping back from her.

"What do you mean? What about Justin?"

Mom starts crying again, so Dad jumps in. "Sweetie, he's been in a car accident. I guess it happened earlier today, but we just found out about it an hour ago."

"A car accident? Are you sure?"

Mom tries to pull herself together, rushing to wipe the tears from her cheeks. "We don't have much information yet, honey. I guess he was on his way into the city and someone ran a red light. The Reillys are at the hospital now, and I'm sure he'd want to see you—we've just been waiting for you to get home so we could all go over there together."

"Why was Justin going to the city? He doesn't even have a car."

Then it hits me.

"Oh, my God. He was with Emma."

19

Dad's driving, Mom's in the passenger seat, and I'm in back. No one's said a single word for the last fifteen miles.

We're taking the same route that Emma always takes into the city, so I'm searching out the window for leftover flares. Or tiny balls of tempered glass. Or pieces of red plastic tail-light. Something to indicate where they were when their date took a turn for the worse. I can't find a thing.

When we reach the hospital, Dad drops us off at the main entrance and goes to look for parking. It doesn't take Mom and me long to locate Justin's parents. When we enter the waiting room, they stand up, eyes all red and puffy, and thank us for coming. Mrs. Reilly explains what happened, and even though I'm standing right next to her, her words fade in and out of my head and I process only the pertinent details. The accident happened just after two. They didn't get here until four thirty. The girl's parents arrived just after it happened, which is a good thing, since she's in much worse shape. They're up on the seventh floor in the ICU. She's out of surgery now, but her condition is still considered critical. Justin will be fine, but they're keeping him overnight for observation.

I must have found a chair, because I'm now sitting in one. I watch Mom—who looks like she's moving in slow motion—pull Mrs. Reilly toward her and whisper something into her ear.

Mrs. Reilly's voice rises an octave when she asks, "Who? Who's Emma?!" Strangers turn to look in her direction, relieved, I imagine, for any activity that distracts them from whatever reason they're sitting in the ER on a Saturday night.

"The girl who was with Justin today. That's Emma, Anna's best friend from school." Justin. Emma. And Justin. Emma and Justin. I can't breathe. This can't be happening.

Mom talks with Mrs. Reilly in low, hushed tones designed for me not to hear. It doesn't matter. Everyone sounds far away, anyway.

After a few minutes, Mom gets up and comes over to sit next to me. "Sweetie." She rubs my back in small circles. It feels so familiar, even though it's been years since she traced the invisible pattern that used to make me drop right off to sleep. "Justin is going to be okay, but the other car collided with the driver's side, so Emma got the brunt of the impact. The Reillys had been trying to find out who Justin was out with, but no one would tell them anything, and I guess Emma's parents have been with her in the ICU all afternoon.

"If this was Northwestern Memorial, I'd be staff, but

here—" I can hear the frustration in her voice. She hates that she has no clout. "Stay here. I'll go upstairs and see what I can find out."

I haven't said a word since we left the house, but now I find my voice. "No." I stand up. "I'm coming with you."

⌒

Emma looks small and frail against the while sheets. Her eyes are closed, and the skin underneath them—all the way down to her trademark cheekbones—bulges, black and shiny. Red marks speckle the left side of her face, indicating—as her parents explained when they prepared me to see her—where the doctors had to dig the glass out of her skin. There's a clear plastic tube running up her nose, and even given all the rest of the damage, I think that would piss her off the most.

As bad as she looks on the outside, that was all fairly easy to fix. The real mutilation is invisible. Her spleen ruptured on impact and had to be removed, but it took the surgical team two hours to find the source of the internal bleeding. There's a small skull fracture that they say should heal by itself, but they will need to run an MRI before they can determine whether there was any permanent brain damage. When her internal injuries are healed, she'll have to have her left shoulder reconstructed. She has three broken ribs, but at least they didn't puncture her lungs. The doctors delivered that last part as "the good news."

The other car hit them going fifty miles per hour, just as she and Justin reached the middle of the intersection. "A

T-bone collision," Mrs. Atkins called it. Emma probably never even saw it coming, she had said. No, I'm quite sure she didn't.

I sit next to Emma on the bed and cradle her soft and perfectly manicured hand in mine, still caked with chalk dust, with dirt still wedged under my fingernails. The accident happened around two o'clock. While I was reclining against Bennett, laughing and cuddling and kissing him, my best friend was being ripped apart by metal and glass, transported by a speeding ambulance, and then torn apart all over again so that she could be reassembled. It took me six hours to find out. Another hour to get to the hospital. And yet another to get here to her hand. Eight hours.

The whirs and thumps and beeps of all the machines are inescapable in the tiny room. I want to unplug them, one at a time, and give her the peaceful silence she deserves, but then I remember she might not be here without them, so instead of being annoyed, I try to find their musical qualities. *Thump-beep. Thump-beep-whir. Thump-beep.*

We sit like this, Emma silent because she can't speak, and me silent because I can't think of anything to say. I think I'm supposed to talk to her. To let her know I'm here. But every time I open my mouth to say something, I can't quite get the words out.

I hear the door slide open and my jaw drops. Justin is standing there in a hospital gown, bruised and bandaged, unable to move his head because of the blue plastic brace wrapped tightly around his neck. His hair is matted and speckled with something that looks like blood. His wrist is in a cast.

"Justin." I rest Emma's hand on the sheets and run to him. I stop short, afraid to hurt him, so I'm grateful when he reaches out to hug me first. The scratches on his face and body may be superficial, but they make him look like a porcelain doll that's been dropped on the floor and put back together. I'm pretty sure the glue's not yet dry.

"Are you okay?" I grip a spot on his arm that doesn't look damaged, but he sucks in a breath and I recoil as if he were hot to the touch. "I'm so sorry."

"It's okay," Justin says. He gives me a wobbly half hug. "How is she?"

I just shake my head.

I watch his face fall as the information sinks in, then follow his gaze across the room to Emma. I'm pretty sure we're both thinking the same thing. He's okay. She's not. Justin walks over to where I was sitting on the bed and takes my spot. He picks up her hand and strokes the back of it with his thumb.

"You know, you're supposed to be home writing about me in your diary right now," he says. I can see him smiling at her, and I watch her face to see if she'll return it, but she doesn't. She's too far away. But that doesn't keep him from talking. "I had a bunch of great jokes lined up. I read the newspaper this morning so we could talk about current events. I'm telling you, you would've been hooked. Now look at me." He glances at his chest. "I ripped my best sweater."

He keeps smiling at her. Talking to her like I should have but couldn't.

"She was looking for a CD." He's still looking at her, but I know the comment is meant for me, so I sit down on the opposite side of the bed and take her other hand in mine. I watch Justin's face contort. "We were talking about this British indie band that we like and she asked me to find her CD case on the floor." I picture the hot pink suede case I gave her for her birthday last year and my stomach lurches. I was always putting all her CDs in that case. I should have left them loose, piled up in the glove compartment and on the floor where she had them. I shouldn't have given her that case in the first place. "She started to flip through it and . . ." He trails off.

I just squeeze her hand. There's nothing more to say, because our shared silence confirms what I already know. She wasn't paying attention—the accident was her fault. And she crashed holding on to my gift, which shouldn't make me feel so responsible, but it does.

There's a knock on the door, and it slides open before we can react. The nurse pokes her head in. "I'm sorry, kids. That's all the time I can give you." Her voice is just loud enough to be heard over the machines. "I wasn't even supposed to let you in," she says, like we're about to argue with her. "Family only." We know. She's told us this three times since Mom pulled whatever strings she pulled to score us these ten far-too-short minutes.

I squeeze Emma's hand again, reach forward, and run my finger across her unstitched cheekbone. "I'll be back tomorrow," I say into her ear. I walk to the door and wait for Justin.

He brushes her hair back and kisses her forehead. "I'll see you tomorrow too." He stands up, looking around the bleak and sterile room. "And I'll bring you some music. Maybe that will help."

At first, I think he means that the music will help drown out the incessant beeps. But as I watch him watch her, I think he may mean that the music will help bring her back from wherever she is right now.

⟳

Emma doesn't look any better on Sunday, but the room is cheerier. Enormous bouquets of bright flowers hide all the sterile surfaces, cards have been taped to an empty wall, and a collection of Mylar balloons with *Get Well* written on them in fancy script decorate the corner over by the small window. "Ten minutes," the ICU nurse tells us flatly, "just to keep her company until her parents come back from lunch. You're not supposed to be in here." She looks behind her to be sure no one's watching and then draws the curtain and closes the door.

Justin hasn't been home yet, but his mom has brought in this enormous boom box and a series of CDs as he instructed. Now he comes around to the side of Emma's bed, plugs it into the wall by the monitors, and pops open a CD case. It's one of his homemade mixes, though I can't help noticing that there are no watercolor swirls on this one. He presses play, and the sounds of the machines are instantly masked, their *whir-thump-beep* pattern fading into the background as accompaniment to the music. I take a seat on the bed next to Emma and watch her, wishing I could talk to her, the way Justin did yesterday, but every time I open my mouth I feel awkward.

He's watching me. "Do you want me to leave for a bit?" That would be even worse. I'll have no reason *not* to talk to her, but I still won't be able to.

"No," I say.

He walks around to the other side of the bed and lifts her other hand in his, and we just sit like that. Our ten minutes pass, then twenty, but the nurse never returns to kick us out, so the two of us just stay put. I'm silent, watching her chest move up and down. Justin is silent, too, mesmerized by the glowing red blips on the monitor. The music does help make this horrible room feel less sterile, but that's about all it's doing. Emma is still far away.

The Atkinses return, and I look over at Justin. He was discharged a half hour ago, and his parents are still downstairs, filling out paperwork. He looks exhausted, like he can barely keep his eyes open.

"You wanna get some air?" I ask, and after some thought, he finally nods. I leave all my things inside so I have an excuse to get back into Emma's room.

Once we're in the hallway, Justin leans against the wall. "This sucks." He starts to rub his forehead, forgetting about his stitches. "Ow. Damn it."

I lead him to the elevator. "You should go home, Justin. Go rest. Come back tomorrow when you're feeling better." I wish I could say Emma wouldn't be here tomorrow, but we both know she will.

The elevator takes us to the bottom floor and we follow the

signs to the courtyard. We walk around for a few minutes, but it's windy and freezing and it doesn't take us long to get the requisite air and decide to go back inside and find Justin's parents. We locate the registration office easily, and Justin's parents are still sitting there, waiting for the clerk to finalize his discharge papers. Mrs. Reilly assures us that they'll be a while, so the two of us go in search of the cafeteria.

When we're sitting, drinking the worst coffee I've ever tasted, and taking turns picking at a stale doughnut, I say, "So . . . you and Emma."

Justin looks at me with a guilty smile.

"What?"

"Nothing." He picks off a piece of the doughnut and stares out the window. "I'm so sorry. I should have told you about us. I don't like keeping secrets from you, Anna. But I guess the whole thing just seemed a little . . . weird. I've known you my whole life, and—" His voice trails off and he brings the Styrofoam cup to his lips again, takes a sip, and looks right at me. "I should have told you."

"Yeah. You should have." I smile so he knows I'm not angry. "Really. It's okay. Emma told me. And besides, you're my friend. Emma's my friend. This is good."

"So, you're cool with us going out?"

I decide not to tell him that I still can't put their two names together in my head without a question mark showing up. "Definitely. I'm definitely cool with it."

We both look down at the table. He starts tracing the

design of the Formica with his fingertip, and I push my doughnut crumbs into a little pile.

"Tell me about your date. It was obviously going well, until—" I immediately wish I could take back that last part, but Justin doesn't seem affected.

He smiles down at the table. "It was a really good day. We went out to dinner once before, you know, and had coffee one other time, and that was nice, but it was fun to just be together at her house. See her room and her stuff. And just hang."

He stares out the window behind me. "We had the most amazing talk about . . ." He trails off, but his mouth turns up in a small smile.

"About?"

He shakes his head and looks at me again. "Never mind. . . . Anyway. She's very cool."

I rest my chin in my hand and smile at him. "You really like her, don't you?" I ask, and he nods. He leans back and crosses his arms.

"Yeah. I admit, I didn't expect to, and I wasn't even totally sure until yesterday. But yeah, I really do. She sort of surprised me, I guess." I don't know if Emma feels the same way about him, but for his part, he sure looks hooked. Apparently, some guys really *do* make CDs for girls who are only friends.

"She surprised me too," I say, and I find myself repeating the words I said to Bennett on the rock yesterday, describing Emma's cheekbones and braces and how kind she was to the frizzy-haired new kid. And I smile as I picture her now. Or rather, the way she was until yesterday. Same cheekbones, but no more braces. No more awkward stilts for legs. Just gorgeous, funny, charming Emma, who wins over everyone she meets—even a jock-nerd like me and a skeptic like Justin. I suddenly realize we're looking at each other with matching sad expressions, like we're both wondering what we're doing here, talking about her like this.

Justin breaks the awkward silence. "So-o-o-o . . ." he says, drawing out the word. "Better topic: How was *your* date?"

The question makes me flash back to yesterday, and I feel a grin start to form as I think about Bennett and me, curled up on a rock exchanging questions and stories and kisses and chalk dust. But then I'm overcome with guilt. I can't smile while Emma lies unconscious six floors above me. "It was good."

I keep my emotions in check as I tell Justin about rock climbing and how it felt to reach the top and look out at the view. I tell him how Bennett and I talked and talked, about music and running, about traveling and our families. And suddenly it hits me. I'm supposed to be in the coffeehouse right now trading date stories with Emma, not in a sterile hospital cafeteria talking with Justin. I get quiet and start staring past him, fixing my eyes on the vending machine at the far side of the room. "Sounds fun," I hear him say, but his voice sounds quiet and far away. We both look off in opposite directions, and neither one of us speaks again for a long time.

"What time is your mom coming to get you?" he finally asks.

"Six." I look down at my watch. It's only three.

"I should go find my parents, but I can stay here and catch a ride home with you if you want. I don't want to leave you alone." He looks sincere but exhausted. It's clearly taking all his energy just to stay awake.

"I'm okay. It'll be good for me to have some time alone with her."

He stares at me. "Okay. As long as you're sure." He reaches across the table and grabs my hands to give them a comforting squeeze.

I give him a weak smile. "I'm positive." I sound so certain, lying to him like this. But I'm doing it for him. If he didn't look so tired and pained, I'd say what I really want to say. That right now, as we sit here like this, Justin seems exactly like the person he used to be—my comfortable friend who gives me music and makes me laugh and is the one person I can talk to about anything—and all I want is to have him hug me tight and tell me everything's going to be okay, because if he did, I might just believe him.

20

After Justin leaves, Danielle stops by, and the two of us get caught trying to sneak back into Emma's room. The nurse is just about to kick us out when Emma's mom shows up and convinces her to let us stay. But Danielle can't take it for long; ten minutes later, she still can't bring herself to walk all the way back into the room and Mrs. Atkins finally wraps her arm around her shoulder and suggests she come back tomorrow instead. Danielle says she will be back in the morning, since she has no intention of going to school anyway.

Emma's mom and I spend the next three hours making small talk and staring out the window, and when the clock finally strikes six, I can't help feeling relieved. I give Emma an exhausted kiss on the forehead and hug her mom good-bye.

I'm heading to the waiting room to meet Mom when I hear the faraway *ding* of the elevator. I round the corner and literally collide with someone, and we both step back, muttering apologies until we each realize who the other is.

"There you are," he says at the exact same time I say, "What are you doing here?"

"Looking for you." Bennett's face is all scrunched up with concern. "Why didn't you tell me about Emma?"

I don't have an answer. It probably should have occurred to me to call him and tell him, but it just didn't. I can only shrug as he pulls me to him and asks me if I'm okay. I nod against his chest.

I think at this point I'm supposed to cry. If there were ever a good time, this would be it—with me all nestled into him like this, his head resting on mine and his hand on my back—but I can't. Instead I tell him about the tubes and the machines and the stitches, the doctors and the rehabilitation she'll have to endure when she comes to. That she looks awful, like someone I don't know. And that I feel horrible for saying so.

The elevator dings again, and this time Mom steps out. She looks surprised to see me curled in the arms of a boy she's seen exactly one time and whom I've never mentioned on a Tuesday family-dinner night. "Well, hi."

"Hi, Mom," I say nervously. "You remember Bennett . . . from that night . . . at the bookstore."

She nods and extends her hand. "Yes. Hi, Bennett." She keeps shaking his hand and staring at him. I'm waiting for her to give him her signature smile—her nurse smile—the one that makes people warm up to her so quickly, but she doesn't.

Even though there's nothing cold about the look on her face, there's no warmth there, either, and when she finally drops his hand, Bennett looks a little relieved. She turns away from him and looks at me. "How's Emma?"

I shrug. "The same. Her mom's with her now."

"I'm going to go check on her and see if I can do anything to help. Do you want to come?"

I can't even imagine walking into that room again. "I've been here all day, Mom. Do you mind if maybe . . . Bennett takes me home?"

She whirls around to face him again, her expression full of worry as she looks him up and down. "How's your driving?"

"Good. I'm very careful." She still seems concerned, so he adds, "I'll be *especially* careful."

"It's really windy."

"I'll drive slowly, Mrs. Greene."

"Okay, then." She pulls me to her and gives me a big hug and a kiss on the forehead. "I'll see you at home, Anna." But instead of heading toward Emma's room, she lingers for another moment. "You know, Bennett, Anna's father told me that she was supposed to have you over for dinner so we could get to know you a bit. Has she invited you yet?"

He looks at me, then back at her. "Not yet, Mrs. Greene. But I'm sure—"

"How's Tuesday?"

"Tuesday?" Bennett looks at me. I cover my face with my hand. "Tuesday's great," I hear him say.

"Excellent. We'll see you then." Mom kisses me on the forehead again before turning and disappearing down the hall.

In the elevator, Bennett looks at me. "Dinner." He nods. "Tuesday."

"Sorry about that."

"No. It's good. I like family dinners." The elevator stops and we hold hands and walk toward the lot. "Actually, I can't remember the last time I had a family dinner. We're not too big on them."

"We just have Tuesday. We close the store early so Dad and I can get home, and Mom never takes a shift. She insists on one night a week, and that's Tuesday."

Bennett opens the door on my side of the car, and I slide in. We're alone again, back in the Jeep, just like we were at this exact same time last night. But now we're driving in the opposite direction and there's no laughing or punching each other across the console. No question-and-answer game.

"You okay?" Bennett keeps asking in a whisper and I keep nodding, untruthfully.

The streetlights and traffic signals pass by in a slow-motion blur, like Bennett's driving far below the speed limit. Mom must have terrified him. Or perhaps it's me—maybe everything is moving in slow motion.

"They were alone." I finally say to the passenger-side window. "Justin was alone for four hours before his parents got there. Emma was alone for two." I run my finger across the glass and stare out into the dark. "I don't know why that part's bothering me so much, but I just keep picturing them in separate parts of the hospital, surrounded by total strangers. Maybe that's what happens, you know—maybe your parents have to wait outside—but how could they just leave them all alone like that?"

"They knew everyone was on the way."

"Did they?" I ask, and Bennett reaches over the console and grabs my hand.

We're silent for a few moments, until I finally say what I'm really thinking. "I wasn't there."

He looks over at me.

"It took me *eight hours* to get there."

"It's okay, Anna. You got there as fast as you could."

He squeezes my hand in his, and even though there's really nothing he can say to make me feel better, his grip is somehow reassuring. I look down at our fingers intertwined, resting on the console—his nails still a little dirty from yesterday's climb—and remember how I traced the grooves in his palm while I happily reclined against his chest. His hands feel so normal that sometimes it's easy to forget how extraordinary they are.

"Oh, my God." I recoil from him. "Pull over."

"Why? What's wrong?"

"Pull. Over." I'm shaking and feeling stupid and having a hard time believing I didn't think of this earlier.

Bennett turns in to a residential street and puts the car in park. He stares out the windshield, and that's the moment I realize that I might not have thought of it before, but he certainly did. He knows exactly what I'm about to ask, because even if I've briefly forgotten about the ability Bennett Cooper possesses, he never does.

"Do it over." I twist in the seat to face him. "Bennett. Please. Do it over. Do the day over."

"I can't." He won't look at me.

"You can. You can fix this. Take us back before the accident. We'll stop her from driving. We'll fix it! Bennett?"

He gets out of the car and slams the door, leaving me trembling in the passenger seat. The headlights illuminate the fury on his face as he slams his fists hard on the hood, and I jump. He paces back and forth, then turns his back to me and leans against the front of the car. I watch his shoulders rise and fall. I think I'm supposed to regret asking, but I don't.

After a while he comes back to the car, opens the door, and gets in. He's calmer now, but he's still shaking with rage. He grips the steering wheel so hard his knuckles turn white.

"Please don't ever ask me to do that again."

"Look, I understand all your rules." I stress the word *your* and hope he hears my point. "I get your butterfly-effect thing and your superstition about affecting the future—"

"It's not *my* butterfly-effect thing. It's *the* butterfly effect, and it's a major concept in chaos theory, which has *nothing* to do with superstition. A small change in one part of a complex system can have large effects somewhere else—I didn't come up with this stuff, Anna."

"Okay, I get it. But you can make little changes, right? Affect small details? How is this any different from what you do for your parents? What you did last Friday before Spanish? What you did that night in the bookstore, when you changed what could have been a *horrible* future for me—it might have been the *end* of me—but it wasn't, because you intervened. And look . . ." I put my arms out to my sides and gesture around the car. "Nothing terrible happened. We're still here. No butterfly mayhem."

"It's not that simple. Eventually *something* has to backfire. I just *can't* do it over."

I stare at him, willing him to look at me, and he finally does. "Can't or won't?"

"Won't."

"Why not?"

"Look, I shouldn't have done either of those do-overs, Anna, but they were different. I went back five minutes, an hour, I didn't go back a whole *day*. I didn't stop the guy from holding you at knifepoint or attempting to rob the store, I just got you out and got the cops there sooner. And that day in school, we still went to class, and it was like that hour just never happened. They were minor little changes. But stopping the car accident entirely? That's erasing a major event."

"Sorry, I don't get the difference."

"Yeah? Well, neither does my dad." He bites his lip hard and turns to look out the window. "Look, it's a slippery slope—I affect one bad thing that happened to one innocent person, and suddenly it's up to me to keep every plane that's ever crashed from taking off and be the one-man-early-warning-system for every natural disaster. Until something even more catastrophic happens *because* of what I did to prevent the last tragedy. This is *my* ability, and *I* don't think that's what I'm supposed to do with it. I'm supposed to observe. *Not* change the future. Period. I'm already breaking all the rules just by being here."

"They're not *the* rules, they're *your* rules. And how do you know your rules are right? Maybe you're *supposed* to test them."

"I'm not." He stares me down. "And if you recall, Anna, the last time I tested the rules for a girl, it didn't turn out so well. For *her*."

He has a point, but still, I'm not giving up. I can't. Not when my best friend has spent the past day being sliced open and reconstructed, with parts of her missing, other parts now held together by string. She may be a crappy driver, but she deserves a future. "Well, this isn't about me. And it shouldn't be about you."

He looks at me with sad eyes, and I know he wants to help her. To help me. To be the hero, even though he doesn't think he's supposed to be. "It's not about me, Anna. It's about . . . everyone involved. I can't. I'm sorry, but it's just too dangerous."

"Will you at least think about it?" I give him a small smile and hope he'll smile back, but he doesn't. He just puts the car in drive and makes a U-turn.

"No. Don't ask again."

21

"Travel plans, *por favor.*" I twist around to take the stack of plans as they're passed forward to me. One has a laminated cover. Another one is spiral-bound. Mine—which I'd planned to staple—is still handwritten on individual pieces of notebook paper, wedged in a travel book, and stuffed in my backpack. I won't be turning mine in today, but apparently I'm not the only one who's blown the assignment.

Bennett's chair is empty. When he pulled up to my house last night, I got out, slammed the door without saying goodbye, and walked into the house without looking back. Once I was out of sight, I looked through the kitchen window for a minute or so, long enough to watch him lay his head on the steering wheel before smacking it and peeling out of the driveway.

Argotta gives a lecture today but doesn't make us converse, and when the bell rings at the end of class, I linger and wait for the room to clear. Then I stand up, stop at his desk, and wait for him to look up at me. "How am I going to like your plan, Señorita Greene?" he asks as he pats the stack of travel itineraries.

"You'll love my plan, señor. But it's not done."

I expect him to look at me like I've let him down, but instead he gives me an understanding smile, stands up, and walks around to the front of his desk. I tell him about Emma's accident on Saturday (he's heard), and I remind him about the robbery last Monday (which makes him look sad), and I emphasize that I'm not one to make excuses, but it's been one hell of a strange week (he agrees).

"I'd like to announce the winner soon. Do you think you can have it done by Thursday?" he asks. I nod. "If you need more time, just let me know. We can announce the winner next week instead."

"*Gracias*," I say. I amble out of the room and into The Donut, drop my books off at my locker, and walk into the dining hall. I take one look at our empty table and decide I'm not hungry.

⌒

Mom drops me off at the hospital. I lug my backpack into Emma's room, plant myself in the chair, and start working on my travel plan. Thirty minutes later, the nurse comes in to check Emma's chart. She looks at me with a sympathetic smile and leaves the room.

I look over at the bed. Emma's just lying there, looking

far away and isolated, so I grab my copy of *Lonely Planet: Yucatán* and settle in next to her on the bed. I open the book and start reading to myself about "sugary beaches" and "scandalous nightlife" and "pork slow-cooked in banana leaves." And then I get to the shopping. Now, this is something she'd love.

I start talking, just whispering at first. "This place sounds incredible, Em. Listen to this: 'Shoppers will appreciate the handicrafts found on the peninsula. . . . exquisite silver ornaments that reflect the filigree technique introduced by the Spanish, wonderful models of galleons carved from mahogany, and panama hats so tightly woven that they can hold water.' Doesn't that sound amazing?"

I look down at Emma's still features and wait for a reaction. I speak a little louder. "You know, you look really good in hats. If I win Argotta's travel challenge, I'm going to go to Mexico and bring you back a hat." I consult my travel guide again. "Oh, and get this, they make some of the world's best hammocks, too." I look down at her. "Maybe I'll get you a hammock. What do you think? Do you want a hat or a hammock?" I look for a reaction. Any reaction. There's no movement. "I'll just get you both."

I go back to reading, scanning the pages for another section she might like. I'm just about to start telling her about the "famous cuisine" when I notice that there's a drop of something on the page. Then another. Then another. I bring my hands to my face and find that my cheeks are wet, and the tears are falling in a steady stream, faster than I can stop them—on the pages, on the sheets, on Emma's hand. I look at her face, at all the tubes, and my chest feels tight.

"I'm sorry, Emma," I whisper as I lay myself over her right arm, the only part of her that I know isn't stitched or internally wounded, and I finally let myself cry because she's not supposed to be here. She made one small mistake. One tiny little move that changed everything. Would we be sitting here like this right now if just *one* thing about her day had been different? What if Emma and Justin had decided to go somewhere else, like the movies or the mall? What if they had left ten minutes earlier? Or ten minutes later? Or if Emma had committed to a single CD before she left the driveway? What if she had come to a full stop at every stop sign, slowing her progress to that intersection? What if the driver of the other car had forgotten something, run back into the house, and left three minutes later? What if I hadn't insisted that her CDs live in that stupid case? What if, if, if, if, *if*? If any little detail had been different—just one single detail—Emma and I would have spent yesterday in the coffeehouse, sipping lattes and comparing our dates.

He just needs to change *one* little thing. He's the only one who can make things right, and he's too afraid to do it.

I kiss Emma on the cheek. "I have to leave now, Em," I whisper in her ear, "but I'll be back. I'm going to go fix this and make it right, and after I do, you won't remember any of this."

22

Mom shoots me an impressed look as she pulls up in front of Bennett's house. "Wow. Nice digs."

"It's his grandmother's," I say, but I'm pretty sure the one his dad bought with their stock market "luck" is equally impressive. "I'll be home later, okay? Thanks for picking me up. And tell Dad I said thanks for taking my shift today." I shut the car door and walk across the snowy grass, because the walkway hasn't been salted and it's looking a little slippery. I knock.

Bennett opens the door and I blurt out, "I just spent the afternoon with Emma." He looks nervously back into the house and finally closes the door behind him and joins me on the porch.

"How is she?" At least he has the decency to sound concerned.

"The same. Critical condition. No better than yesterday."

"Give it some time, Anna. She'll be better."

"And you know this how? Because you've seen her in the future and know she's happy without her spleen?"

"Technically, you don't need a spleen."

"That wasn't my point."

"I know it wasn't."

"How can you live with yourself, knowing you could fix this and not even bothering to try?"

He grabs my arm hard and leads me away from the door.

"Ow. You're hurting me."

He lets up on the pressure.

"How can I *live* with myself?" he whispers, checking around for eavesdroppers. "Are you kidding? This is killing me, Anna. I want to try—trust me, I do—but what if I can't change it? What if I make it worse? What if the accident happens anyway, no matter what I do? What if I change the wrong thing and it ends up ruining her whole life? Or mine? Or yours?"

"I don't know! Nobody knows! But how can you have this gift and not use it to find out? Maybe you try to do it over and the accident happens anyway and Emma lands in the hospital and nothing changes. But at least you'll know you tried—"

"That's my point! I'm not *supposed* to try. I'm not saying it's fair, or right, but what if this was—"

"Don't you dare say something lame, like 'supposed to happen,' because this was *not* supposed to happen. She is *not* supposed to be there."

"How do you know?"

"What?"

"How do you know that the accident wasn't supposed to happen?" he asks. I feel my face turn red with fury. "Look, I know no one wanted this to happen, but it did. Maybe she's *supposed* to be in the hospital and wake up. Maybe she's *supposed* to heal and go through physical therapy and fight for something important for the first time in her pink-bubblegum life. Maybe she's *supposed* to get better and learn to drive more slowly." I glare at him. I head for the stairs, but he grabs my arm again. "Anna, I'm not saying it's right. Or that I agree with it. I'm just saying that it happened. And whether it was supposed to or not, it's not my place to change it just because I *can*."

I've heard the words before, but there's something new in his voice. "Wait. Is that what you saw?" I stare at him. "Did you go see her in the future, Bennett? Does she get better? Is that what happens?"

He shakes his head, and I feel his grip on my arm loosen, and I can't tell if I'm right or not, because he's just staring at me, like he doesn't know what to say next. And neither do I, because whether he saw her future or not, I still can't let Emma lie on that sterile bed with those loud machines, just because this might be part of some grand plan to make her a safer driver or a better human being.

I try a different tack. "Look, you don't have to stop the accident itself. You just have to bring us back in time by"—I'm quiet as I do the math in my head—"forty-six hours." I look at my watch. "Forty-seven if we have to stand here in the cold talking about this for another hour."

"That's still playing God."

I cross my arms. It's silent while we wait each other out like we're in a Mexican standoff. Or a third grade staring contest. "I have homework." I turn for the stairs and this time he lets me go. I'm almost at the bottom when I hear his voice.

"Anna."

I stop in midstep and whirl around. "What?"

"That's not enough."

"What do you mean? What's not enough?"

"Forty-six hours. That's not enough." I feel a lightness in my chest, like I'm taking the first full breath after being held underwater. He's been thinking about it. No, he's not only been thinking about it, he's been doing the math.

He lets out a groan and I know what it means: he's about to do something he doesn't want to do. Minutes pass while I stand there and wait for him to make the next move; then he finally speaks: "Come inside. I want to show you something."

23

Bennett's room looks cleaner than it did the last time I was here. His desk is neat, with nothing but a cup full of pens and a textbook, splayed open. Bennett grabs a tattered red notebook and undoes the rubber band that holds it closed. He flops down on the bed and gestures for me to join him as he opens it to a page near the end. Every available surface is covered with ink. I bend my head closer and take in the dates, times, and mathematical symbols, the complex equations that stretch across both pages.

"I have to be really precise." How long has he been working on this? All night? All day? "I have to find the perfect moment for us to arrive."

He points down at the calculations. "Like I said, forty-six hours isn't enough—that would bring us to two o'clock on Saturday, and we were in Wisconsin, almost three hours away." He points to a timeline that stretches across the page.

"We have to be together, and it can't be while we were in the car, because we can't be moving. So we would have to go back to the morning, right about the time I picked you up."

"Okay. Let's go." I sit up and open my hands on my lap, but he doesn't take them.

"Slow down, Speedy, there's more." He turns the page. "Here's the thing: As soon as we get within range of our other selves, they'll disappear. So we need to go back to the exact moment we were in the car, in your driveway, but before I put the car in reverse." I think back to the morning. How long did we sit there? It must have been just seconds. Just long enough for us to put our seat belts on and for me to ask where we were going. Then we left. He points down at the page. "I think we need to land at about seven minutes after eight."

"Okay." I don't rush him this time.

"But I can't screw this up." He sits up next to me. "I want to test it first. We're going to go back five minutes and land in the hallway just outside my bedroom. By the time I open the door, the two of us will be gone, and we'll replace them." He walks over to his desk and returns with a little sandwich bag of saltines. He leaves them on the bed. "Those are for you, in case you need them when we get back."

"Thanks." I stand up and hold my hands out to him. This time he takes them.

"Just because we're testing this doesn't mean we're going to do it for real," he says. "I'm still not sure I can go through with this."

"Okay."

"You ready?"

I nod.

"Close your eyes," he says.

I do. And when I open them, I'm in the hall, staring at his mother's high school graduation photo. I look to my left and find him there, nervously watching for Maggie. "You okay?" he asks.

"Yeah." My stomach's churning, but before I think too much about it, Bennett grabs my hand with one of his and twists the knob of his bedroom door with the other. He peeks in, then opens the door wide and pulls me inside. It's empty.

I grab my stomach and head straight for the bed, but the saltine-filled Baggie isn't there. "Where are the crackers?"

"Shoot. I forgot." Bennett crosses the room, reaches into his backpack, and returns, holding the bag. "Well, at least we know it worked."

I don't get it. "You do? How?"

"The crackers aren't on the bed because I hadn't put them there yet."

"Okay, wow." I grab the crackers and start nibbling slowly, again hoping I don't throw up in his bedroom.

Bennett recrosses the room and grabs the two red backpacks off the floor—the same ones that just yesterday were decorated with ropes and carabiners, and held shoes and sandwiches and plastic bottles of Gatorade. Today, they look much lighter.

"Stay here, okay? I'll be right back." He leaves the room and returns a few minutes later with heavier-looking packs.

Another full bag of saltines.

Two Starbucks Frappuccinos.

Two bottled waters.

He goes to his desk, takes something from the top drawer, and walks over to the armoire. Removing everything inside, he makes a tall pile of photo albums, scrapbooks, old Westlake yearbooks, and several boxes of loose photographs. When it's empty, he reaches inside and pulls out a wad of bills.

"How much cash is that?" I ask.

He's all business. "A thousand dollars each, in case we get separated. Here." The bundle lands in my backpack with a thud.

While he puts everything back in the armoire, I think about Brooke and her backpack of cash. "Have you and Brooke ever done a do-over?"

He shakes his head. "No. Not that Brooke hasn't tried." He talks while he puts the books and photos back where they belong. "There was the time she failed her History final and almost didn't graduate. The time my dad caught her smoking. A really bad prom date named Steve." He closes the door and walks back to his desk. "Man, now that I think about it, you two have far too much in common. I'm terrified for the day you finally meet."

I feel my face brighten at the thought. "I'll get to meet her?"

He shrugs. "Sure. Once she's home I'll bring her back here to meet you. We always come back to see Maggie anyway."

"Really? You come back here to see Maggie?"

"Yeah. All the time." He nudges me with his shoulder. "I don't mean to be rude, but any chance I can tell you about it later? After I'm done changing the course of history and all?" He gives me a teasing smile.

"Yeah. Of course."

"Thanks." Then he's back to business. "We're going to land at 8:07, just next to the shrubs on the side of your house. Wait for my signal; then run to the car."

"Got it."

He offers me my backpack and I throw it over my shoulders while he does the same with his.

"Oh, and don't let go of my hands—even though it will be hard to move quickly that way. No matter what happens, we need to be sure we stay together." His command reminds me of our rock climbing date, when he introduced the belay device and told me it kept me connected to him.

He grabs my hands. I look right into his eyes. I've never seen him look scared before.

"Bennett?"

"Yeah?"

"Will I . . . remember everything from Saturday?" I don't want to forget the anticipation of our drive, the exhilaration of climbing, or the view from the top. I want to remember the moment when we pulled into the driveway back home and I felt like I finally knew him.

"You'll remember both days—"

I interrupt him. "But how? I don't remember anything at the bookstore before you left and came back."

"That's because you weren't with me. This time you'll remember both versions, just like I do. Now, close your eyes."

But I can't. I'm getting nervous now, and I'm sure he can feel my hands shaking in his. "Are you sure we should do this?" I ask.

"You're kidding, right?" He humphs and looks at me with a puzzled expression. "No, I'm not *sure*. I'm testing fate. I'm messing around with *time*."

I bite my lip, picture Emma, and feel my conviction return. "Thank you," I say. It's not enough, but it's all I've got.

His grip is tighter than usual. "Close your eyes."

I open them to the somewhat familiar sight of our side yard. It's not like I'm over here much, but the chipping yellow paint verifies that we've landed at Bennett's intended location. On the other side of the window above us, Dad has probably just sat down to finish his coffee and read the *Sun-Times*.

"Ready?" Bennett asks.

I nod.

"Go!"

We race from the shrubs into the driveway, pulling each other along like we're in some strange Fourth of July event wedged in between the three-legged race and the egg toss.

The car is empty. We've done it. I start to let out a relieved laugh until I realize the car is moving backward down the driveway, picking up speed. Bennett pulls me toward his side of the car; we work together to lift the door handle, and it rises, but nothing else happens.

He swears under his breath. "It's locked!"

I look up at the kitchen window, my heart racing at the thought of Dad's seeing this, but thankfully, no one's there.

Bennett and I run alongside the car until it reaches the end of the driveway, then watch as it rolls across the street, slows when it reaches a snowbank, and comes to rest against a tree. The wheels spin on the ice.

This time when I look up at the window, I see Dad standing there, watching us. He disappears from sight and reappears when the front door flies open.

"What the hell—?" He runs across the lawn and stops when he reaches us. Bennett and I drop our hands. "What the hell?" he repeats.

"Hi, Dad."

"Annie?" He's looking back and forth from me to Bennett and I have to remind myself that this moment is completely different from the one in his mind. As far as Dad's concerned, the three of us were just standing in our foyer, and he has just shaken Bennett's hand and told me to invite him over for dinner. And now we're standing in the middle of the street.

"Dad, Bennett's coming over for dinner on Tuesday, okay?" I say, and then I just start laughing, loud and hard, and I can't seem to stop. Dad's looking at me like I've lost it completely.

Bennett's trying not to look at me at all. "Any chance you have a slim jim, Mr. Greene?"

This gets me laughing even harder, and I can tell Bennett's trying to keep a straight face.

Dad cups his hands against the glass and looks into the driver's window. "How on earth did you lock your keys in a car that's in *reverse*?"

I have no idea how Bennett's going to answer this, but at least the mystery is keeping Dad from noticing that we're wearing backpacks and completely different clothes. I start laughing again.

"I was starting the car and . . . I thought I felt a flat tire, so I—we went to check it out, and I guess the car was in reverse, and when the doors shut I guess they . . . locked automatically." He leans over to Dad. "I think I'm a little nervous today, sir."

Dad stares at Bennett, and then shoots me a questioning look.

Now I'm laughing so hard I have to walk around to the back of the car so I don't make Bennett lose it too. He's doing so much better than I am. I lean against the back of the SUV, trying to breathe, but when I peek in through the back window, I let out a gasp.

When Bennett opened the hatch in the parking lot at Devil's Lake, I saw two red backpacks overstuffed with climbing gear. Now those same packs are on our backs, and when I peer through the window, I see piles of ropes and colorful metal climbing equipment. Two harnesses. The new shoes Bennett bought me, lying on top of the heap next to the plastic bags of food and four bottles of Gatorade. We went back, but all the gear has stayed right where it was fifty-two hours ago.

Some things may remain the same, but this whole day is clearly about to change.

24

I'm glad we're not in a hurry, because it takes forty-five minutes
for the tow truck to get here, two minutes to get the car door
open, and twenty minutes for Bennett to sign the paperwork
and get the guy to stop making fun of him. But once we're in
the car driving toward Emma's, I think we both feel a little
giddy.

He just did something he'd never done before, and I got
to be there for it. I know Bennett's still waiting for the dark
hands of time to snatch us up and throw us back where we
belong, but I can't help being caught up in the moment. If my
stomach hurt, I didn't even notice.

"Hey, how's your head?" I ask.

Bennett rubs it with his fingertips. "Fine, actually. I didn't
even think about that."

"Maybe it *is* the adrenaline, like you thought."

We pull up to Emma's house and find the Saab sitting in

the driveway. No broken glass. No broken taillights. No dents. No blood.

"She's here! She's okay!" I bound out of the car and run to the door. When Emma opens it, I throw my arms around her. She's wearing a bathrobe and slippers, her hair's up high in a ponytail, and she doesn't have a stitch of makeup on—which is perfect, because this way I can see her skin, smooth and unblemished, free of road rash and deep purple bruises. She shrieks when she notices Bennett standing behind me on the porch.

"Bloody hell!" She pulls away from me and tightens her robe. "What are you doing here?"

I don't know how to answer her. I was so caught up in the do-over, I hadn't planned what to do when we got here. "Well . . ." I begin. I point back to Bennett, who is looking down and playing with a button on his coat. "We have a date today. And I know you and Justin have a date today, so we thought we could, you know, combine our dates."

"Combine our dates?"

"Yeah. We thought it would be fun!"

"Fun?"

I look at Bennett. "Would you give us a minute alone?" He nods and returns to his car, which buys me a few seconds to improvise. I turn back to her. "I'm a little nervous, Em. I don't know, I just feel like everything would be better if you were there. You and Justin."

"You don't need me to—"

"I do! Please. Let's just go together. It'll be fun," I repeat.

"Fine. Justin's coming here first; we'll be at the coffeehouse by eleven. Meet us there." She starts to close the door.

I look back at the Saab in the driveway, and know that no matter what happens today, it has to stay parked right where it is.

I stick my foot in the door so it can't shut. "Let's let Bennett drive. His car's nice and roomy." Nice and roomy? When did my mom get here? I take my foot back out of the door and start down the front steps. "We'll pick you up in an hour and a half," I call behind me. "Justin can meet us there."

I practically skip down the driveway, thinking about how healthy she looks. When I catch Bennett watching me through the windshield, I think he looks a bit proud of himself.

⁓

Emma walks into the coffeehouse to meet Justin while Bennett and I wait in the car, and when she points at us through the window, we both give a little wave. Justin looks confused by our presence, but, like Emma, perfectly healthy and unblemished otherwise. No neck brace. No cuts. And as he walks to the car, he looks strong, not at all like someone who was in a T-bone collision.

"Keep cool," Bennett reminds me. And that's enough to keep me from jumping out and running to hug Justin.

"So," Bennett says when everyone's buckled in, "we don't want to change your plans. What were you going to do today?"

Justin replies, "We were going to check out this record store in the city."

Emma adds, "I thought we'd go to the Art Institute."

"Perfect," Bennett says. "Music and art it is." I turn toward the backseat to shoot the two of them an enthusiastic grin, and I catch them exchanging awkward glances.

By the time I've turned to face the front again, Bennett's pulling up near the elevated train station. "Okay if we take the El?'"

"The El?" Emma asks.

"Yeah. It's better for the environment."

"The environment?" Emma asks skeptically as she scrunches up her nose at the train tracks and the grimy-looking staircase that leads to them. "No, really, let's drive. It's so much easier. I know all the great parking places."

"This will be more fun," Bennett says, and he gets out of the car and shuts the door behind him before she has a chance to say anything else. The rest of us get out, and I grab his hand and laugh under my breath. I've never seen Emma get "Emma'd" before.

We start the day at Reckless Records, deemed by Justin the most amazing music store of all time. First, we all take off in separate directions. Then we reconnect as the couples we are. And even, once, as the couples we aren't: Justin and me, looking through the ska titles, and Bennett and Emma chatting about the bands in the Classic Rock section.

"Hey," Justin says in a whisper. He looks around to be sure

we are out of earshot of the others. "I'm so sorry I didn't tell you"—he gestures across the room—"about Emma and me. I don't like keeping secrets from you, but . . . it just seemed a little . . . weird. But I've known you my whole life, and . . . I should have told you." I smile, remembering when he spoke almost the exact same words in the hospital cafeteria.

"That's okay, Justin. Emma told me. It's good. I'm happy for you guys."

He bumps me with his shoulder. "Cool. Thanks. In that case, can you give us a little time alone at some point? Your boy Bennett's making me nervous, and I'm forgetting all my best material. I have some good jokes lined up. Oh, and what do you think of this sweater?"

I stand on my tiptoes and muss his hair. "It's perfect." Justin smiles, and I watch his freckles disappear as the flush takes over.

We spend the rest of the afternoon browsing through shops. We eat lunch in a crowded restaurant. We make sure that by two p.m.—the time of the accident—we're in the safest location Bennett can think of: the third floor of the Art Institute. The hour comes and goes. We take the El back to the Evanston station and pile into Bennett's car again, and because no one's ready to go home yet, we drive to the closest theater and decide to see whatever movie is playing next. It turns out to be *While You Were Sleeping*, which wouldn't have been my first choice, given that it centers on the story of a man who falls onto the El tracks and spends weeks in a coma.

It's ten o'clock when Bennett pulls in to my driveway: Two

hours later than it was the last time we returned from our date. For a moment, I hesitate, picturing Mom and Dad inside, sitting at the kitchen table, waiting for me so they can break the news about Justin.

"Will you come in with me? Just to be sure—you know—it's all different."

He nods, and we walk into the house. It's quiet. I can tell right away that Mom and Dad aren't at the table, and I let out a sigh of relief. Bennett follows me as I lead him through the dark kitchen and toward the sound coming from the living room. When we turn the corner, we find my parents, dressed in sweats and cuddled up on the couch, watching a movie. There's a fire going in the fireplace.

"Hi," they say in unison. Mom shoots Dad a knowing smile that seems meant for my benefit.

"I see you told her about the car," I say to Dad. I smile and look over at Bennett. He hides his eyes behind his hand.

"Are you sure you can make it here for dinner on Tuesday, Bennett?" Mom looks up at him wearing her huge smile—her nurse smile—and Bennett melts like everyone else does when she puts it on. "Because, you know, we'd be happy to drive over and get you if that's easier." She looks at Dad again. "We know how complicated it can all be with the keys, gearshifts, locks . . ." She laughs, and I can't help joining in. Dad buries his face in her shoulder and cracks up.

"Not one of my finer moments." Bennett's still hiding behind his hand. He slides it down to reveal his eyes and laughs along with the rest of us.

"It's okay. We like that around here, Bennett," Dad says. "Now we have something we'll never let you live down."

Bennett looks at the three of us and smiles. "Awesome."

And for the first time since we began the second version of our day date, Bennett looks like he's starting to relax and accept what I knew was true at 8:08 this morning. Our do-over has been a success. Emma and Justin are safe. Nothing bad has happened. And Bennett can do a lot more than he thought he could.

25

"I've had the most incredible week!" Señor Argotta announces after the bell rings and we've all taken our seats. Bennett and I look at each other and grin. I'm not sure what made Argotta's week so "incredible," but I'm pretty sure we can top it.

"I've had the unique opportunity to travel through Mexico on twenty different routes. It was exhilarating! All of them were just fantastic!" He paces around the room, and we stare at him with rapt attention. "But three trips," he continues, "three trips stood out. I'd like to share these with you and see if I can get your help deciding who should go home today with this." He reaches into his jacket pocket and pulls out a folded strip of paper. "A five-hundred-dollar travel voucher." He snaps it taut a few times and sticks it on the whiteboard with a magnet.

I turn around to steal another quick glance at Bennett. At first, I thought working with him on our travel plans would be cheating, but all it took was a smile and a latte to convince me otherwise. On Sunday afternoon, the day after we completed our successful do-over, Bennett showed up for my shift at the bookstore and we sat in our spot on the floor, pulling books from the shelves and reading descriptions aloud. And four hours later, we had mapped two circuitous routes, each different enough to keep Señor Argotta from thinking we'd collaborated, and overlapping only once, in the little beach town of La Paz.

Now, Señor Argotta flips the light off and the projector on, and the screen lights up with a colorful map of Mexico. The route is highlighted in yellow marker, and each destination is marked with circled letters that correspond to points in the written itineraries. This isn't my map. Or Bennett's.

"This first plan comes courtesy of Courtney Breslin." The highlighted route circles the perimeter of the country, avoiding the interior entirely. "You can tell from this plan that this unusually long winter has caught up with Señorita Breslin. She's after some serious beach time."

Everyone in the room laughs.

"At first glance, this looks like she's missing out on a lot of the country. But I chose this one because—even though she selects a few high-tourist destinations—she also found some wonderful secret beach gems." He tapes her map to the whiteboard at the front of the room. "Let's call this one *Hora de Playa*."

When he clicks the button on his remote again, my map appears. I feel my shoulders tense up. "Señorita Greene has a little of both—some beaches, some ruins—but it's well-paced.

Too often, people plan a trip and try to cover too much ground. They're trying so hard to be sure they don't miss anything that they overschedule themselves. In my opinion, that's how you miss out on all the good parts of a country. I like all three of the trips I chose because they don't try to get everything in. They all save time for surprises. Spontaneous decisions. Señorita Greene's trip is aggressive, but she's left room for mystery! For impulsiveness!" He walks to the front of the room. "I call this one *La Aventura!*"

Atrevida. He left out the daring part, so I add under my breath: *"La Aventura Atrevida."*

"Our final travel plan is from Señor Camarian." Alex and I steal a glance at each other at the same moment, and we both look surprised. "Señor Camarian is interested in archaeology and Mayan culture. He avoids the tourist spots altogether. He flies into Cancún, but gets out as quickly as possible. He is the only person who found one of my favorite spots, the Kohunlich ruins, which show more of the influence of Mexico's neighbors in Belize." He turns to Alex. "Go there at dusk, when the howler monkeys come out. It's eerie. And *fantastico.*" He walks to the front of the room again and tapes Alex's map to the whiteboard. *"El Camino Menos Viajado."* The Road Less Traveled.

He walks over and switches on the light. "I have to tell you, I enjoyed my side of this assignment. You found some places that I've always loved, and others that I'd never even heard of. I was extremely impressed, and now, my friends, I am terribly homesick." He sighs, smiles again, and says, "So, do you want to know who won?"

I already know. Alex has clearly won. I don't have monkeys, howler or otherwise.

Argotta paces back and forth across the front of the room, letting the tension build. "These were all great trips, but there was one that was the best-paced, most well-rounded plan. If I were going to see the country for the first time, it would be the trip I would choose." He walks to the whiteboard and gestures dramatically in front of the three maps. "And the winner is," he says, pulling my map off the wall and holding it up high, "*La Aventura*."

The class claps as the bell rings.

I walk to Argotta's desk to collect my winnings. Bennett walks past me and tells me he'll meet me in the hall.

"*Muchas gracias*, Señor Argotta," I say as he gives me the voucher. I can't tell which of us looks prouder.

"You deserve it." He looks at me with an earnest expression. Then he holds his finger up and gestures with his head toward the room, as if he has more to say but can't speak openly until the rest of the students are gone. I start to fidget as I picture Bennett standing outside the door, waiting for me.

"Señorita, as you probably know, I run the summer exchange program," he says when we're finally alone. I nod. "Well, this year, we had more families participate than usual, but we didn't get as many applications as we typically do. I know it's rather late notice, but there's still a spot." When I don't reply, he fills the silence: "If you're interested."

I haven't even considered my summer plans. Come to think

of it, since Bennett arrived, I haven't considered much beyond the current day.

Argotta opens his desk drawer, pulls out a shiny yellow folder, and hands it to me. "It's a really fantastic opportunity. You'd get to spend ten weeks in Mexico with a wonderful host family. Here, take this and talk it over with your parents."

I take the folder. A few months ago, I would have considered this the opportunity of a lifetime, but now, with the ability to see any location in the world, a single one doesn't sound quite so appealing. "Thank you. I'm really honored that you'd consider me." I unzip my overstuffed backpack and push the folder down into it. "I'll think about it."

"Good. The family knows they might not be getting a student, but we need to give them some time to prepare either way, so just get the paperwork back to me as soon as you can—end of May at the very latest. I'm not expecting any more applications at this point, so if you think you'd like to take the spot, it's yours."

"Okay. Thanks again." I race toward the door, and when I round the corner, Bennett throws his arm over my shoulder.

"You did it!" He smiles and pulls me to him as we start down the hall. I lose my balance in a good way. "So, where are you going with that ticket?"

"Mexico, of course. It would be a shame to waste a perfect, well-paced trip that allows time for surprises." I mimic Argotta's accent and look up at him with a flirty smirk. "I happen to like surprises."

"Yeah," Bennett says, "I've heard that about you."

may

26

I put my bookmark in between the pages of *Rick Steves' Best of Italy 1995* and turn off the light, thinking about museums and cobblestoned streets and gelato. It's been almost a month since Bennett took me to Thailand, told me the first of his secrets, and handed me a postcard. He promised to take me to Italy next, but ever since the do-over with Emma, he's been reluctant to use his little talent, even for tourism. I haven't asked—I've been happy just having him here, and pretending that everything about him is normal—but I'm studying my phrase book just in case.

I close my eyes and think about him, and just as I'm starting to drift off to sleep, I realize that something doesn't feel right. Like a weight is pulling me toward the edge of the bed.

"Hey," a voice says into my ear. "It's me." My eyelids shoot open and the beginnings of a scream escape my mouth. "*Shhhh*," the voice says, and a hand covers my mouth to muffle the sound. My heart is racing and my eyes are wide with terror, and I blink until I can finally make out his form in the dark.

"It's me. It's okay." He repeats the words while I try to talk my heart into slowing down. "It's okay, Anna, it's just me."

"*Whan aer ew uing er?*" I whisper-yell it into his palm, so it comes out garbled.

"What?" He laughs under his breath and removes his hand from my mouth.

"What are you doing here?" I repeat, clearly this time, as I sit up straight and punch him in the arm. "You scared the crap out of me."

He's still trying not to laugh. "I'm sorry. I would have knocked, but—" he says as he taps his watch. "Your mom loves me, but I don't think she'd appreciate a visit at eleven thirty on a school night."

I feel my heart slow down a little, and I pull the covers tighter around my waist. "Is everything okay?"

"Yeah, everything's fine. I'm sorry. I didn't mean to scare you. I was just lying in bed, and suddenly, I couldn't wait until tomorrow to see you. So I got up, put on my sweats, pictured your room, and *poof*, here I am."

"*Poof?*"

"*Poof.* You weren't asleep, were you?"

"Nearly." I rest my head on my pillows again and sigh.

I'm not sure how I feel about him—*poof*—appearing in my bedroom uninvited.

He lifts the covers up to my chin. My room is dark, barely lit by the full moon outside, but he must see the look on my face. "Hey . . . are you mad?"

I shake my head. "No, not really."

"But a little?"

I crinkle my nose. "Yeah, maybe."

"I'm sorry. I didn't mean to just show up. I'll go."

Now I feel bad. He looks so sweet, flustered like this, and just as he's about to stand up, I reach over and grab his arm. "Don't go," I say.

"Really, it's okay. I'll just see you tomorrow," he whispers as he plants a soft kiss on my forehead, and that's all it takes for my heart to start racing again, but this time it has nothing to do with fear. Five minutes earlier, I was missing him, and now he's here in my room, sitting on my bed and backlit by moonlight.

"Really. I'm not mad." Without even thinking about it, I grab his arm and pull him down on my bed, and he lands sprawled out next to me, looking a little surprised. I roll over onto his chest and smile down at him. He looks adorable on my pillow. "Don't go."

He looks at me for a moment, and then his hand finds the back of my neck, and he kisses me, harder than usual. And even though there's still a bit of the bulky comforter between us, I can feel the heat radiate from his body, feel the intensity of every one of his kisses, regardless of where it lands. On my lips. On my neck. On my chest. And for a good five minutes, I'm completely lost in him, kissing him, running my fingers under his shirt so I can feel how the muscles in his back tense up every time he pulls me tighter. But then I find myself again, realize where I am, and move away from him, so I can sneak a look at my bedroom door.

"It's okay." He's whispering in my ear, but I can feel his breath on my neck. "Don't worry about it."

I pull away just a little. "My parents . . ."

"Don't worry about it," he repeats. And for a few minutes, I follow Bennett's lead and let myself get lost in his kisses. But I can't seem to ignore the door for long. I steal another glance at it and he catches me.

He stops, breathing hard, and smiles up at me. My hair is everywhere, and he sweeps it to the side so he can see my face. He rests his hand on my cheek. "It's me, remember?" he says. "If they come in, I'll just . . . disappear and come back five minutes earlier." His smile grows more mischievous. "They'll never know. *You'll* never even know. Then you can pull me down on the bed like you just did, and we can do this," he grins, "all over again."

I look away from the door and lean in close to kiss him again. But suddenly, I have this thought. I have no idea where it comes from, why it would be here right now, or why I've never thought to ask it before, but here it is, coming at me full force. I pull away and look down at him. "You've never actually done that to me, have you?" I'm smiling, but my face is all crinkled up. "Done something over. And I never even knew?"

His smile disappears too quickly.

"Bennett?"

He doesn't say anything. His head falls back and sinks deep into my pillow. "Once." The word floats out with his heavy exhalation.

I feel the lump forming, growing in my stomach as I glare at him and wait for more. He doesn't say anything else. He just lies there, waiting for me to make the next move.

"When?" I sit up, tighten the covers against my body, and wait.

He faces me. "Remember that first night—the night you came to Maggie's and I was so rude to you?"

I nod.

"I went to the bookstore to apologize, and we went for coffee."

I nod again.

"And I walked you home."

I just keep nodding, because, yes, I remember all that. I want to know about the part I *don't* remember.

"I kissed you."

"You kissed me?" I would have remembered that.

Now it's his turn to nod. And I can only stare at him. Because that's impossible. All I wanted that night was for him to kiss me, and instead he spoke some nonsense about whatever happened last time not happening again. I didn't know what he meant at the time, but now I do. He'd kissed me. That's what happened.

"It was too much. I was afraid of what it meant for you and—" He grimaces. "I kissed you. And then I went home and realized what I'd done. So I went back and did it over again, the way I'd meant to do it. I walked you home. I said good-bye." While I stood on the sidewalk, shivering and confused, watching him walk away and thinking I'd done something wrong. While I spent the twenty-four days that followed wondering why I felt something for this person who didn't seem to care about me at all.

I can't look at him anymore, so I recline against the headboard, close my eyes, and rub my temples. When I open my eyes again, he's looking at me, sincere and apologetic. I shut my eyes tighter this time.

"When did you do it?" I ask. "I want to know the exact moment you went back." He couldn't risk running into himself and, that night, there were no moments when we were apart. And it all comes back to me. I'd made a dumb joke about him losing people, and he had gone to the bathroom. I remember how I thought he came out a completely different person. Turns out, he had. "The bathroom," I say.

He nods.

I huff in exasperation. "You weren't ever going to tell me, were you?"

"There was no reason to, but I'm telling you now," he says,

and I stare at him, fuming. "Look, I didn't want to hurt your feelings. It was before—"

"So you lied to me? To protect my *feelings?*"

He shushes me. "I didn't lie to you. I just didn't tell you. That's not the same."

"It is to me."

"Keep your voice down, Anna. You don't want your parents to come in."

"My parents? Why do you care about my parents? You'll just disappear and I'll be the one left here to come up with some way to explain why I'm yelling. Alone. In my bedroom." I lower my voice anyway and continue in a whisper. "Or, better yet, why don't you just do it over? That way you won't have to have *this* conversation again."

"I would not do that." The five words come out one at a time, like he means every one.

"Why not? It's perfect. Just go outside, come back ten minutes ago and do it all over again. I'll tackle you and make out with you like I did this time. Not that I'd *know* there was a 'this time.'"

I feel the tears start to well up and I fight, with everything I have, to keep them locked behind a wall where they can't do any permanent damage. If I cry now, he'll think I'm sad. But I'm not—I'm furious. These are hot, thick tears filled with the kind of anger that make some people punch holes in walls.

"Anna," he says in a calm voice, "I did it once. I didn't do it again. Not after I decided to tell you everything. Not after I decided to be with you."

I nod. "Oh. I see. After *you* decided." I think back to those weeks—nearly a month—when I walked into Spanish every day, wondering why he'd stopped looking at me after that night. Wondering why I felt such a strong connection with someone who seemed to hate me. "Well that night you *undid*, even before you *undid* it, that was the night *I* decided I wanted to be with *you*. But I guess that doesn't count for anything, does it?"

The room is silent. I stare at him. He looks down at the bedspread.

"I made a mistake," he finally says. "I did it once. I haven't done it again. I would *never* do it again." I feel my face soften, so I press my lips together to keep from caving in. And to keep these damned tears where they belong.

"I think I need you to leave."

"What?"

"Leave. Now. Please." I intentionally use the same words, the same tone of voice, that he used to kick me out of his house two months ago.

"Come on. . . . Anna."

"You're a hypocrite." I shut my eyes, and for a moment, there is no movement except my trembling. No words except the words that have already been said, still crowding the space in the room. I open my eyes, shoot him a stern look, and say, "Go. *Poof.*"

I feel the mattress rise back up as he lifts his weight off the bed. I open my eyes, expecting him to be gone, but instead I find him standing there. He looks sad as he closes his eyes, but I don't move or say a word. I just watch the map on my wall come more sharply into focus as his transparent shape disappears from in front of it.

27

The May mornings are still cold, but I can run in my lighter clothes now, without the gloves and the wool socks and the beanie. I hardly recognize the man with the gray ponytail, in shorts and a light T-shirt, and when he gives me a friendly wave, I return it with a dim smile. It's sunny and green and beautiful, but it's not enough to make up for my dark, angry mood. So my feet connect with the pavement harder than they should, and before I even reach the track I can feel the pain burn my shins from the steady drumbeat of abuse. Later today I'll pay the price for letting my feet do the screaming I can't seem to do.

When I arrive at Spanish, I find Bennett sitting at his desk, exactly where he's supposed to be, and his eyes bore into mine as I walk down the aisle in his direction. I take my seat wearing a frosty expression.

A few minutes later, I feel a tap on my shoulder. Argotta's

back is turned to the class as he writes a series of conjugations on the board, so I reach back, grab the folded slip of paper, and open it.

We need to talk.

I squeeze the note into a little ball and throw it on the floor in Bennett's direction.

Argotta turns to face the class, and we spend the next ten minutes talking as a group through each of the conjugations. When he turns around to write out another set of verb infinitives on the board, I feel another tap on my shoulder.

Bennett shoves the crumpled paper at me again.

I'm so sorry. It will NEVER happen again.

I stick the note in my pocket as I rise from my seat, walk to the front of the room, and lift the bathroom pass off the hook. I sprint through the safety of The Donut to the bathroom and splash cold water on my face. Now that I've seen him, I don't know how to be this angry with him. I'm too drawn to him, too completely caught up in everything I've come to know about him, to feel this way. I want to understand why he did what he did, and I want to tell him why it hurt me so much, and I want to believe that he's sorry, so that I don't need to be this angry with him anymore.

I stare into the mirror for a long time, watching my own reflection until it blurs and morphs and no longer looks like anyone I know, and I breathe and stare and gather my strength. As I walk back to class, I practice what I want to say.

But when class ends, there's no time to stop and tell him what's on my mind. As soon as we're out in the hallway,

Bennett leads me upstream, defying the laws of The Donut, moving against the current of hungry bodies making their way to the dining hall. He pushes open the double doors that lead to the quad and stops in his tracks. The bright day has pulled nearly everyone outside, and there's not a quiet spot to be seen.

Without talking, we both turn back toward the hall, looking for a quiet corner. "Follow me," he says, as if I have a choice, and he pulls me along, weaving through the remaining groups of people until we're at a bank of lockers clear on the other side of the school. He stops at locker number 422, which I realize, for the first time, belongs to him. He dials the combination and lifts the metal lock with a click. Unlike my locker, decorated with pictures and schedules and stuffed with books and packs of gum, his is empty and completely devoid of personality. Like his room at Maggie's—functional but temporary.

He piles our backpacks inside and slams the door. "Can we get out of here?" He grabs my hands and looks around the empty hallway to verify that we're alone. Before I can comprehend what's happening, I feel the not-yet-familiar sensation of having my intestines twisted and wrung. I keep my eyes closed, breathe in, and know a moment later from the smell around me, from the sound of the birds calling to each other, that we aren't in The Donut.

I open my eyes.

It's early morning, but the weather is already warm in the small harbor, and I spin around and take it in. Everything around me is yellow, blue, or red, a sea of primary colors, surrounded on three sides by hills and by the open sea on the fourth. I see a church topped with a bright green cross. A hillside covered with brightly painted houses, divided into sections by twisted staircases built into the steep mountainside. With the exception of a few fishermen on the dock, we're alone in this small, beautiful town, with its residents still sleeping before making their way down for coffee and breakfast.

I smile at the ground so he can't see me—he doesn't deserve the satisfaction. As incredible as this moment is, he's not playing fair. "Okay," I say, with venom seeping into my voice, "I give up. I have no idea where we are."

"Somewhere quiet."

He leads me past the harbor filled with colorful fishing boats toward the boulders jutting out like a pier into the sea. When we reach the shore, he steps up onto the smooth rocks, and I follow him as he hurdles them. He finally sits down in between two giant stones on a shorter one in the middle that creates a narrow bench just wide enough for the two of us to squeeze onto. He looks at me sideways, his face right next to mine, and gives me a hopeful smile. "Still mad?"

I can't decide if I want to hug him or shove him off the rock.

"Yes, Bennett, I am *still* mad. What, you're just going to bring me to an island every time you screw up? You didn't even ask my permission."

"I was just looking for a quiet place to talk. And it's not an island. It's a fishing village." He looks more miserable than I think he should. "It's Vernazza."

I close my eyes and listen to the sound of the surf hitting the rocks instead of the sound of my heart hitting my rib cage. Vernazza. Italy.

"I'm so sorry." I've lost count by now of how many times he's said it. He holds my chin and forces me to look at him, but I pull away. "I should have told you."

"It's not that you didn't tell me earlier." I look down at the rocks and collect my thoughts again. I can forgive him for not telling me. I can almost understand why he wouldn't have. What I can't get past is that he did it in the first place; he stole my free will.

"What is it, then?"

"You have the power to change people's lives, Bennett. And I don't mean that in a cheesy, romantic way. You can *literally* alter my life. That night, you changed it without giving me a choice, and you just can't do that."

"You didn't give Emma a choice. Or Justin a choice," he says. "We changed their lives, and if I recall, we didn't get their permission first."

"That's totally different."

"No, it's not," he explains. "We have no idea what happened from the time they each woke up that day to the time they got hit by a speeding car. Maybe one of them did or said something especially important, and we just wiped it out. We changed it. But we did that because we thought we were doing the right thing; we wanted to protect them from pain. My reasoning was no different."

"And I had to *beg* you to even consider that do-over. What

happened to you not changing things, huh? What? The rules only apply when they're convenient for you?"

"I was protecting you."

"You can't protect me. Not all the time."

"See, that's the thing. I can. I will. Even if I have to lie to you to do it."

I can't look at him. Instead, I look out at the small waves and watch them wash up against the rocks and roll back out again. "I don't want you to protect me, Bennett, not like *that*. Just because you're *special* doesn't mean you get to choose what I experience. You don't get to decide what I know and don't know. What I get to feel or don't feel. That isn't the way it works."

"Look, Anna, when I changed what happened that night, things were different. I was trying to stay as far away from everyone as possible. I didn't want this."

I glare at him.

"I do now," he says, clarifying things. For a long time after that, we're silent. "I haven't done it since," he finally says. "I'd never do it again."

He's looking directly at me, and I can tell he means every word—and I can tell how much he wants this to be over—but I still don't think he understands how hurt I am that he crossed a line I never thought I needed to define, especially for him.

"Remember when you asked me to make the choice to be with you or not?" I ask. "You told me all your secrets, and you let me decide if I wanted this."

He looks out toward the water and nods.

"That meant so much to me—the fact that you had *me* choose. And that's what makes it so hard to understand how you could have made a choice *for* me."

"I made a mistake."

"And—" I begin, but I feel the words catch deep in my throat. "We lost three weeks. We could have been together three weeks longer."

He lets out a sigh and his face falls as everything clicks; he took something away from me, but he also took something away from *us*. When he apologizes again, I finally hear the remorse I've been waiting for, and when he wraps his arms around me and pulls me tightly to him, I feel the anger begin to melt away. "It won't happen again."

"I know," I say with a sad nod, and I pull away so he can see my eyes as I say the next words. "Look, Bennett, I'm somehow okay with the fact that you can alter the events of my life— bizarre as that is." I give him a little smile, the first genuine one he's seen since I found out what he did. "But this is my life. I'm the only one who decides what comes next." I hold out my hand. "Deal?"

"Deal," he says, and he shakes it.

"So, are you going to show me around this place, or what?"

Vernazza is just like he'd described it. We walk away from the harbor toward what looks to be the main part of town, through narrow streets paved with large cobblestones and lined with small shops that haven't yet opened for the day. Bennett walks up to a door with an Italian flag hanging above a striped awning and pulls it open for me, and I walk in. The bells on the door jingle, and for a moment I think I'm walking into my dad's bookstore. That is, until I smell the bread, sugary and warm, filling every crevice of the bakery.

The woman behind the counter shuffles over, slides a mountain of twisted rolls onto a platter behind the glass, and looks up at us. *"Buon giorno."*

"Buon giorno," Bennett says. *"Cappuccini, per favore."* He holds up two fingers, and she takes her place behind the oversize espresso machine.

A rack of postcards near the window catches my eye and I walk over to it and give it a spin, watching the colorful photos of Vernazza and the surrounding towns pass by me. I feel Bennett watching me. I turn around just in time to see him point at a glass jar on the counter. The woman removes two chocolate-dipped biscotti and places them on bright blue plates. Bennett points to me, standing just under the sign that reads *6/£1,000* in a flowing script I assume to be hers. "Will you add six postcards to that too, *per favore?*"

"Six thousand lire, dear," she says.

"Can I borrow these?" I hear Bennett ask, but I·can't see what he's talking about. He balances the biscotti on top of the coffee cups and pushes the door open with his hip, leaving me inside. "Pick six you like. I'll meet you out at a table." The bells jingle as the door closes behind him.

When I arrive at the table, Bennett is leaning back in his chair under one of the bright yellow umbrellas, sipping his coffee. I sit down in the chair next to him, and he motions to the stack of postcards. "What did you get?"

I spread them out across the glass-topped table.

"Pick one."

"Any one?"

"Any one," he says. "Pick one and give it to me."

I select the picture of the harbor and the small fishing boats, the first things I saw when we arrived here, and I hand it to Bennett. He pulls two pens out from under the rim of one of the little blue plates and passes one to me.

"Now, you pick another for yourself. I'll write you a postcard, and you can write one to me." He leans secretively over his card and begins to write. I look down at the little boats on my postcard, and it hits me for the first time in a while: *He doesn't stay.* Someday soon we may not be together the way we are now, and these postcards will be what we'll turn to when we're missing each other most. The pressure to live up to a high romantic standard starts to close in, and I compose my thoughts before taking pen to paper. Then I write:

Dear Bennett,

For as long as I can remember, I've dreamed of seeing what lies outside the only world I've ever known—outside my safe, normal life. And now, here I am, in a

small fishing village as far away from home—as far
away from "normal"—as I can possibly be. And as
amazing as that is, I know one thing for certain—none
if it would matter if you weren't sitting here next to me.
You can take me anywhere. Or nowhere. But wherever
you are in this world, that's where I want to be.

I stop and hesitate, looking over at Bennett before I write the next two words. Maybe the word *love* is too much, but I feel it pushing against my chest, wanting to make its way onto the paper. So I let myself write the words:

Love,
Anna

Before I can chicken out, I slide the postcard over to him. I watch as Bennett completes his thought, flips the card over, picture-side up, and slides it across the table to me. We each pick our notes up off the table and read them at the same time.

Anna,
I'm so sorry I didn't tell you, but I promise it will never
happen again. From here on, you'll always have a say
in your own future.
Love,
Bennett

At least he used the word *love* too. I place the card back on the table so his words are facedown in the glass, and I force a smile. "Thanks."

He looks at me, confused, knowing he's missed the mark but not sure how. I can feel him watching me as I pick up my biscotti and take a bite.

"What?" he asks.

"Nothing."

"No, you're disappointed."

I shrug and swallow my bite. "That's just . . . kind of a lame postcard." I look over at him in a forgiving way. "And besides, you don't need to keep apologizing." I thought by now he would have known me better: Once I make up my mind, I don't look back. "Is that what you really wanted to say?"

"No," he says. "I know exactly what I want to say. But I don't need a postcard to do it."

"Okay, I'm listening."

"Okay, here goes." He takes a deep breath, like he's preparing himself for something epic. "I . . . You're . . . You're amazing, Anna. And I love your passion to travel the world, but I have to admit, I don't completely get it. When I look around at this 'normal' life you're so eager to leave, I don't see *boring* or *predictable*—I see friends who love you and a family that would make any sacrifice for your happiness. I see the kind of security I've never had and always wanted. I may have given you access to the world I know best, but you and your family have given me a world that doesn't exist on a map.

"When I'm here, we both have the lives we want—you have

your daring adventure and I have my perfectly acceptable *nothing*. And more important, we have each other."

"Now, there's your postcard. I expect you to write this all down." I slide him a new one and smile, but I'm only half kidding.

He continues as if I never interrupted. "I don't think I can go back to a life without you."

My face goes blank and I just stare at him. "What are you saying?"

"I'm saying . . . I'm completely in love with you. And I guess I'm wondering . . . what if I didn't leave, after all?"

The word that was just pressing against my chest minutes ago is now coming from his mouth, and even though I wanted so much to see it on paper, I guess I wasn't prepared to hear it spoken out loud. He loves me. He wants to stay with me. I can't completely process either idea, but I feel light-headed from all of the hope that's surging through my veins. And I think I'm still staring at him.

"Is that okay with you?"

"Which one?"

He smiles. "Well . . . both, I guess."

"Yeah." I'm just sitting there, nodding, not sure how to say it back but knowing I want to. And instead of telling him how I feel, I take the easier route. "How long will you stay?"

"Through graduation?"

I think again about the words he said in the bookstore the night he first kissed me—*I never stay*—and now I'm pretty sure he can see the disbelief in my eyes. "I thought you couldn't."

He shrugs. "I didn't think I could, but, well . . . I've been here this long."

"What about Brooke?"

"When she finally gets home and I no longer have an excuse to be here, I'll just tell everyone that Maggie needs me and I want to stay here with her. I'll tell them all about you—"

"Come on, do you seriously think they're going to be okay with this? Won't they be furious?"

He shakes his head no but says, "Absolutely." Then he breaks into a huge grin.

I feel my face light up as his words run in a loop in my head: *I'm completely in love with you. What if I didn't leave, after all?* He wants to stay with me. "That's a lot of Tuesday-night dinners," I say. "Think you can take it?"

"That's a lot of traveling," he says. "Think *you* can take it?" and he leans across the rest of the postcards, pushes my cappuccino out of the way, and takes my face in his hands. Buried deep in his kiss is a new kind of promise for our future, but on the surface, all I can feel tickling and teasing every nerve ending is the intensity of what we have right here in the present.

We spend the rest of the day in the Cinque Terre.

And then we spend the night there.

28

I push a pin into the little town of Vernazza and stand back, enjoying the way the newest marker has bridged the gap between Southeast Asia and the state of Illinois.

Thanks to Bennett's talent, I've made it home without my parents even realizing that I was gone overnight, and while I don't know for certain what happened back here, I have a pretty good idea: I didn't return to school. Or show up at the bookstore for work. Or come home for dinner. At some point, my parents may have become exhausted from worrying. Police may have been called. Neighbors could have walked the streets with flashlights. Posters might even have been printed and stapled to telephone poles. But twenty-two hours later, when Bennett returned me to the spot in front of his locker—the place where we had taken a brief hiatus from our fight to hold hands, close our eyes, and leave the hallway the day before—it turned out that less than a minute had passed, and no one was ever worried, because no one ever missed me.

Despite knowing how awful the undone day might have been for the people I love, I can't bring myself to regret it. In those twenty-two hours, Bennett and I climbed the mountain steps to the trail that leads from Vernazza to Monterosso, the steepest of the trails connecting the five villages. It wound us through olive orchards and vineyards, challenged us with rough climbs and narrow pathways, and in the end, rewarded us with the most incredible views of both villages and of the Mediterranean.

We spent the afternoon in Monterosso, but when we tired of the tourists and longed for the more peaceful Vernazza, we chartered a small boat to take us back to where we had begun. As it sped through the blue water, jumping and bouncing over the waves, I reclined lazily against Bennett's chest and smiled up at the clouds. Just before we reached the dock, he enfolded me in his arms, leaned forward, and whispered in my ear, "Spend the night with me." Thinking back, I never even questioned my reply. And I certainly didn't think about panicked phone calls and posters and police and neighborhood searches, even though I should have. Instead I stayed, selfishly wrapped in Bennett's arms, and watched the Tuscan sun rise up over the bay from a tiny *pensione* tucked into the hillside.

29

A shrill series of wailing beeps fills the room, and before I can mentally process the action, my palm comes down hard on the top of the digital clock on my bedside table to buy myself another ten minutes. It isn't until the guilt climbs in under the soft covers and snuggles up next to me that I finally give in, throw both feet on the floor with an audible thud, and mind-over-matter myself through the darkness, arms extended for safety, to the closet.

Ten minutes later, my music is throbbing in my ears as I take the customary turns, pass the man with the gray pony-tail, and reach the spongy surface of the track. I run, lost in my thoughts and singing along with the chorus when a movement in the bleachers catches my eye. I look over and see Bennett sitting there on the metal bench—just like he was that first day, wearing the same black parka and the same little smile—and this time I don't hesitate. I turn and run across the center of the grassy green field, waving at him as I approach. I take the cement steps two at a time. "See? You are stalking me," I pant when I'm finally within earshot. "I knew it."

He stands up, looks around the track, and steps down to meet me.

"Hi. I'd kiss you, but I'm all sweaty." I stand next to him and lift the hem of my T-shirt up to wipe my forehead. "What are you doing here? And what's with the jacket—it's, like, sixty-five degrees out here already."

"Oh, my God. You know me. Anna, you know me?"

"Yeah. Ummm . . . why wouldn't I?"

He tightens his lips and presses his temples with his fingertips, and I start to realize that something's not right.

"I've been trying to get back." His voice is sharp, his eyes wide and panicked. "I haven't been able to get back. What's the date?"

"Tuesday. May . . ."—I think for a moment—"the sixteenth, I think." I add what would be obvious to most people but may not be to him: "It's 1995. Bennett, you're scaring me. What's wrong?"

"Oh, my God," he says again under his breath, "I'm still here." Then, to me, "I'm still here."

He is, in fact, standing in front of me, so I nod. I take a step back and watch his face as he processes the information. "Anna, I'm so sorry. I've been trying to get back to you, ever since—"

It's sinking in. *"What? Ever since what?"*

"Anna, listen to me. This is important. Brooke's home. Tell him . . . er, *me* . . . that Brooke's home. And tell me to show you—" But before he can say another word he's gone.

"What?" I beg. "Show me what?" But I'm talking to empty space as I stand there wondering where and when he'd come from and what he's supposed to show me. I search the bleachers, looking for him like he might still be there, but I know he's not. When Bennett disappears, he's gone.

I sprint down through the bleachers, through campus, and back into the street. *Brooke's home.* Trees are blurring by and I'm stopping only for traffic lights, and I'm trying to block the vision of his fading against his will. My heart's beating so fast it feels like it's going to explode by the time I reach Maggie's porch and knock hard on the door. I double over trying to catch my breath while I wait for Bennett to answer.

"Anna." Maggie's clearly surprised to see me sweaty and flushed, and the tone of her voice as she says, "Good morning," makes it clear she doesn't think I should be here this early.

"Good morning, Maggie." I pant. "I'm sorry. I know it's early. Is Bennett here?"

She opens the door wide and invites me in. "I don't think he's left for campus yet. Go on up."

"Thanks," I say as I race past her, up the stairs, and down the hall to Bennett's door. I knock and listen for movement, and when I don't hear anything, I start to panic. He said he was trying to get back here. *What if he's already gone?* But he opens the door wearing nothing but a pair of sweats, a headful of wet hair, and a smile. I take in a sharp breath. He's still here.

I throw my arms around his neck, relieved to smell his shampoo and feel the warmth of his still damp skin. "Hey, what's up?" he says brightly, but he seems to realize from the vise grip I still have on him that I'm here for a reason. "You okay?"

I back away. "Something's wrong."

He pulls me inside and closes the door behind him. I haven't been here since we sat on his bed and I begged him to do a day over again. That was only a month ago, but it seems like years have passed since then.

"I saw you at the track, just like that time in March."

"That again? I keep telling you, I was never—"

"Bennett. I just saw . . . another . . . *you*." I'd planned to break the news a little more gently, but at least I have his full attention now. "You were at the track again, but this time I could talk to you, and you knew me. And you were shocked that I knew you too."

"Are you sure?" he asks, and I nod, wide-eyed and absolutely certain. "What did I say? Exactly? What were the *exact* words I used?"

"You asked me the date, and when I told you, you were surprised. And you realized that you"—I reach out and rest my hand on his chest—"*you* were still here." He stares at me, eyebrows knit, forehead tight with confusion. "You told me to tell you that Brooke's home."

"What?"

I nod. "That's what you said."

He looks at his watch like the time of day is going to help him puzzle this out. "She's home?" he says, to no one in particular.

I nod. "There's more." I have his full attention again. "You said you'd been trying to get back here 'ever since.' And you told me to tell you to show me something, but you never told me what. You were in midsentence as you disappeared, like you couldn't stop it from happening." *Like you were out of control*, I want to say, but don't.

He looks around the room, out the window, anywhere but at me. "Bennett, what's going on?" I press my fists into my thighs hoping he'll say something, anything, that will make me feel better.

"I don't know."

30

Dad is driving us home from track-and-field sectionals, where I got the top time in the 3200-meter and guaranteed myself a spot in the state finals, when Bennett pipes up from the backseat, "Will you drop me off at home on the way, Mr. Greene?" His voice is robotic, just as it has been since the full impact of my conversation with the other Bennett hit.

I don't know what's going on. I do know that Brooke is back home and he's still here and there's something he's supposed to show me. I know that all week, he's replied to my questions in monosyllables, with forced smiles, before disappearing into his thoughts again. He's already blown me off twice this week to sit alone and think, and now I'm not even sure if we're still going to the movies with Emma and Justin tonight.

"I'll pick you up at seven," he says without looking at me. I watch him get out of the car and disappear through Maggie's front door.

At least now I know one thing.

～⌒〜

The phone starts ringing the second I walk through the door, and I've barely even gotten the word *Hello* out when Emma's voice booms through the receiver. "We're going shopping. In the city. I'm picking you up in a half hour."

I look down at my shoes and at the number still pinned to my chest. "Not today, Em. I just walked in the door from my meet." And, besides, I want to add, I already have plans for today. I'll be spending the afternoon trying to figure out how to get things with Bennett and me back to the way they were.

And on top of that, just the words *the city* and *I'm picking you up* leave me with horrible visions of Emma lying in a sterile room with cuts all over her face, and tubes and needles sticking out of her body like alien appendages. I can practically hear her pout over the phone line, but the mental image only strengthens my resolve. "I am not shopping, Emma."

"Anna. Greene. The auction party is next weekend. What are you wearing?"

"I'm borrowing something from your closet. Like I do every year."

She clicks her tongue like she can't figure out how she got stuck with me for a best friend. "Well, then help me pick out *my* dress. I need something new and shiny and gorgeous."

"I really don't feel—"

"Come *on*," she whines into the phone. "I need your advice."

She doesn't, but I look at the clock and sigh.

"Thank you!" she blurts out. "I'll give you forty-five minutes to get ready!" She barely gets the last word out before clicking off.

"I take it you're going shopping with Emma," Dad says, and I flip around. I didn't realize he was standing there.

"Apparently so."

"Well," he says as he pulls out his wallet and offers me his credit card, "here. Now you don't need to borrow a dress."

~⁀~

We drive into the city—Emma chatting away, me silent and white-knuckled because of my grip on the door handle—and spend the sunny Saturday shopping on Michigan Avenue. Emma picks out a graceful dark orange gown for the auction party that looks beautiful against her olive skin. I pick out a black sheath that's much simpler, and much more *me* than anything Emma owns. As I turn around in the three-way mirror, I picture Bennett leading me past students with their dates, staff members and their spouses, moms and dads, as we round the skydeck on the ninety-ninth floor of the Sears Tower, and my chest constricts with the thought I don't want to have: What if he isn't here next Saturday?

I realize he'll need to go home eventually, but that he'll come back and stay through graduation. *Won't he?* I want to believe the words he said in Vernazza two weeks ago—*What if I didn't leave after all*—but they keep fighting with the words I heard at the track five days ago—*I've been trying to get back to you ever since.*

Two more shopping bags and four hours later, Emma decides we need to return home immediately, before she spends another penny. As we're walking to the car, she has an idea.

"Oh, Anna!" I jump as her squeal echoes through the parking structure. "Come home with me, and I'll get you ready for our dates tonight! I'll put together an outfit and do your hair and makeup! Come on! It'll be fun!"

Fun? I've been her project before, and I wouldn't use that word to describe the experience.

When we're settled in the Saab, bags in the trunk, music on the stereo, Emma turns to me and says, "I know the perfect outfit!"

~~~

Emma and I spend the rest of the afternoon getting ready. She dresses and undresses me, pokes and belts me, tugs and brushes me. And finally she throws her arms up in the air, declares her work complete, and turns me around by the shoulders so I can stare into her full-length bedroom mirror.

"Ta-da!" she yells as I stare. Okay, I have to admit that I look pretty good. She's piled my dark curls up with a clip and pulled some of them down at the sides so they are wispy around my face. The makeup feels thick on my skin, but she's done a great job with the colors, and I don't look like a clown.

I glance down at my feet—I'm practically on tiptoe, thanks to the chunky heels—and back up past the black tights to the clingy little skirt. The tight cotton shirt is a lot more low-cut than what I'm used to, and I cross my arms over my chest like I need to cover something.

"Stop that." She forces my arms to my sides and holds them there. "You look stunning."

I sigh, but relax my arms. "Are you sure?"

"Positive." She walks over to the window and looks outside. "Where are those guys? They're twenty minutes late."

As I stand there, staring at my reflection, my heart starts racing. What if he's not coming? What if he's already gone?

"Stunning!" Emma says again. "Oooohh. And guess who is about to tell you the same thing." I rush to join her at the window, pressing my face against the glass, and watch as Bennett and Justin get out of the car and walk up to the front door. I let out a breath I didn't realize I was holding. "Awww . . . just look at them. Our boys are awfully cute." Emma blows an air kiss down in Justin's general direction, grabs my hand, and pulls me toward the stairs. "Come on."

She races down to the front door like she's about to burst with excitement, and as she opens it to greet the guys, her accent is even thicker than usual. I can't help smiling at her. Or maybe I'm smiling because the guys really are cute. Or maybe it's that even though I'm dressed in high heels, a skirt far shorter than anything my mom would ever approve of, and more eyeliner than Marilyn Manson, there's something about this moment that feels more normal than anything I've felt all week.

Bennett must feel it too, because when he sees me, he launches right into compliments and pulls me into a big hug that signals that he's here—*really* here—and for the first time since we found out that Brooke was home, it feels like I'm all that matters to him and there isn't someplace more important he's supposed to be.

When we get to the theater, we walk in side by side, Bennett with his arm draped over my shoulder and Justin and Emma holding hands. While we're waiting in line for popcorn, Justin tells me, in a brotherly sort of way, that I look really nice tonight. Emma tells me to stop trying to steal her boyfriend, and Bennett jokingly threads his arm through hers, tells her he'll be her date, and leads her into the theater cradling the jumbo-size popcorn.

And that's how it goes for the rest of the night. The four of us are just the four of us, and Bennett and I are just the two of us, and everything feels so normal, not in a pretending-everything-is-normal kind of way but in a real, comfortable kind of way that makes me think that he's found a way to fix things. That this is still the life he really wants—safe and boring and utterly normal.

I snuggle into his shoulder, grab a big handful of pop-corn, and watch the screen, happy to act like I didn't run into *another* him and learn about an *ever since* neither of us has any control over. Like double dates and popcorn with extra butter and Twizzlers are the most important things in the world to us, our daring adventure is still in full swing, and there are no clocks to be seen for miles.

⌒〜

Bennett drops Justin and Emma off at their respective houses, and when he points his car toward mine, my heart sinks at the thought of going home. I don't want my normal night to be over. I don't want to think about when Bennett may leave or when he'll be back, and I certainly don't want him to wake up tomorrow morning so absorbed in his thoughts that he forgets that tonight was fun.

"You okay?"

I reach over and touch his arm. "Not really. I want you to talk to me."

He drives for a couple more blocks, then pulls into the small parking lot of an office building and cuts the engine. The headlights go dark, and the two of us sit there in silence, staring out the windshield at nothing in particular.

He finally twists in his seat to look at me. "I meant what I said in Vernazza." His voice is low and steady, his eyes sad and faraway.

I wait for the word *but*. It doesn't come, so I fill in the blanks for him. "But you don't think you can stay?"

He sighs. "I don't know, Anna. This is completely uncharted territory. Nothing like this has ever happened before." He stares past me out the window into the dark.

"What are you supposed to show me, Bennett?"

He shakes his head. "I've been trying to figure it out, but the only thing I can think he—*I*—might have been talking about is something I can't show you."

"Why not?"

"Because . . . it's in my room. My *real* room, in San Francisco. In 2012. I don't think it's a good idea for me to bring it back here, and I *know* it's a bad idea to bring you into the future."

"But at the track, *you* told me about it. That I needed to *see* it, whatever it is. I think you're *supposed* to show it to me, Bennett."

He presses his lips together. "I'd rather just tell you about it."

"You need to *show* me. That's what you said." I reach down to the console and grab his hands. "And I want to see your room."

"No way." He takes his hands out of mine and grips the steering wheel. Then he looks me in the eye. "I told you, Anna, I'll take you anywhere in the world you want to go, but never before or after this exact date and time. You can't see your own future."

"I'm not—I'm seeing *your* present. I'm observing, just like you do."

"I'm not supposed to bring you forward."

"Says who?"

"Me."

"What if you're wrong?"

"What if I'm not?"

"You didn't think you should undo a car accident either, but that turned out pretty well in the end. Look," I say, "you're supposed to show me something, and besides, if you do go— if for some reason you really can't—" The words get stuck on the way out. I can't say them. "I just need to know where you'll be."

He stares at me for a long time. I have no idea what he's thinking.

"Please," I beg. "Just a few minutes. Just show me what I need to see, and bring me right back."

He closes his eyes, and the car is completely silent as I sit and watch him. Minutes pass, and finally he pulls the keys out of the ignition and stuffs them into the pocket of his jeans. I give him my hands.

I close my eyes as I hear him say, "Five minutes."

31

"We're here."

I open my eyes. It's dark in the room, but we're standing at the center of a curved wall of windows that look out upon the city below, and all I can see is lights twinkling across the horizon and stretching to the dark waterline. "Wow. This is your *room?*" I hate to leave the view, but I turn around and take in the rest of my surroundings.

It doesn't look any more lived in than his room at Maggie's; it's far too clean and devoid of personality, but at least I spot a framed piece of art on one of the walls. His bed is neatly made, and on the oversize glass and metal desk in the corner there's a silver and black screen and a digital clock that reads 11:06.

"What's the date?"

"May 27, 2012." I'm seventeen years away, in Bennett's real bedroom. I walk toward his desk and spot a single framed photo of Bennett with his arm draped over Maggie's shoulders. The two of them are smiling. The fact that he looks younger throws me for a moment, but it's the sight of this completely different Maggie that really jars me. She looks so old and frail, gaunt, and nothing like her 1995 self. Bennett takes the picture away from me and puts it facedown on the desk, and I can tell from the look on his face that she must have died shortly after it was taken.

I look around again. I picture my room—its walls plastered with paper race numbers and photos, its shelves lined with CDs and trophies—and realize there's a lot less of *him* in his room. But then I spot an oversize glass bowl on the nightstand next to his bed, and I know exactly what's inside. Something that's uniquely him.

I sit on the edge of his bed and start removing stubs. U2 in Kansas City, 1997. Red Hot Chili Peppers, Lollapalooza, 1996. The Pixies at UC–Davis, 2004. Lenny Kravitz at the Paramount in New York, 1998. The Smashing Pumpkins in Osaka, 1996. Van Halen in L.A., 1994. The Ramones at the Palace in Hollywood, 1996. Eric Clapton, Cleveland, 2000. I see a bunch of tickets stamped with band names I've never heard of and assume they started playing sometime after 1995. There are hundreds of tickets in here.

I look up and see Bennett at his desk, digging deep in the bottom of the largest drawer, and I watch him remove a wooden box and lift the cover. Then he walks over to me, holding a piece of paper.

"What's that?" I ask.

"A letter."

I drop the tickets back into the bowl. "You're supposed to show me a letter?"

"I think so." He looks at me and inhales like he needs a deep breath of courage. "Last year, I was hanging out in the park with my friends when a woman walked up to me." He hesitates but I keep looking at him, and suddenly his face relaxes into the smile I know so well by now. "She was beautiful. She had these big brown eyes and a headful of dark curls. She asked if she could talk to me in private, and she handed me this." He smooths it flat and pushes it toward me.

"What does it say?"

"You need to read it."

"I don't want to read it." I push it back and look away from the words. I begged him to bring me here, to show this to me, but now that I'm here, I know this isn't what I want. I want to go back to Evanston. I want to go back to pretending that everything is normal.

He pushes the letter toward me again. "I need you to know everything now."

I feel my face contort. "I thought I already knew everything. Bennett?"

"You don't. Please."

I look down and read:

October 4, 2011

Dear Bennett,

I'm worried about saying too much and breaking any of the rules you once taught me. I hope I've chosen my words carefully enough. Someday, my visit and this letter will make a lot more sense. For now, you'll just have to trust me.

The last seventeen years have given me a good, solid life. It hasn't been the daring adventure I'd hoped it would be, but I've been happy. Still, I've never forgotten that you once gave me a choice between two paths and somehow, against my will—and I think against yours, too—I got stuck on the wrong one. The one I didn't choose. Giving you this letter is the riskiest, scariest thing I've done in my whole life, but I just have to know where the path I chose would have led.

Someday soon, we will meet. And then you will leave for good. But I think I can fix it—I just need to make a different decision this time. Tell me to live my life for myself, and not for you. Tell me not to wait for you to come back. I think that will change everything.

Love,

Anna

I've always signed my name with a capital *A* that looks more like a large lowercase *a*—rounded instead of sharp. Apparently, in 2011 I still do.

"This is from . . . me?"

He nods.

"What, like, a future . . . me?" Those words would sound bizarre to anyone but Bennett Cooper, but he just nods like it makes perfect sense.

"How long have you had this?" I ask, as I remind myself to inhale.

He rests his finger on the date. "Since last October." At least his voice sounds guilty when he says it.

"So you read this . . . before you came to Evanston."

"Many times." I watch him nod and think back to that first day in the dining hall, when I told him my name and the color left his face. He knew me. He'd already met me. Five months earlier. Sixteen years later.

He grips my arms with both hands, which is a good thing, since I'm not feeling very steady. "You have to understand, Anna. I went to Evanston to find Brooke. Honestly. I figured I'd find her and be home in a matter of days. I only went to Westlake because I promised I would. Can you imagine how it felt for me that day in the lunchroom? To hear your name and see your hair and your eyes and *know* it was you? That you were *Anna*." He gestures to the letter. "*This* Anna. That you were the person I'd met five months earlier on a random day in a random park in 2011. And there you were, in a high school lunchroom in 1995 in a town I had no desire to even *be* in." His voice cracks.

"I tried to avoid you at first. I probably should have just avoided you. These words were just rattling around in my head those first weeks, and I didn't know what I was supposed to do. I didn't want to create this life for you," he says, looking down at the letter. "I didn't want to hurt you."

And suddenly it hits me. I don't know why I didn't see it before, but now it's there and completely unavoidable. He doesn't come back. He doesn't stay. We lose each other for seventeen years, or longer; maybe forever.

Someday soon, we will meet. And then you will leave for good. And he's known all along.

"How could you not tell me?"

He just looks down at the floor, not speaking. "I don't know; I thought I could stop it," he finally says. "When I kept getting knocked back here, and returning to Evanston, it felt like I was building up strength or something. Like I was teaching myself how to stay somewhere for a long time. The letter never says how long I was there—it just says I *left for good*. I figured if I came back and stayed—if I didn't leave . . ." His voice trails off, and when he looks up at me his eyes are full of remorse. "It wasn't until you saw the *other* me at the track last week that I realized I hadn't fixed it after all."

"You should have told me." I can barely get the words out. He's still too confident in his own ability, still lying to me, thinking *that* will protect me from pain. But he can't protect me. Not when I'm the one who needs to make a different decision—when I'm the one who supposedly knows how to fix it. "What am I supposed to do differently?" I ask, and I wait through the silence for him to speak up and educate me on some finer point of time travel that I've missed somewhere along the way—something that makes all of this logical.

To tell me exactly what happens next and reassure me that everything is fine.

But he brings his gaze to the rug again and says, "I don't know."

The last time he let me down, it took everything I had not to cry in front of him, but this time I don't care. This time, I can't hold back, and I let those hot, angry tears fall without even trying to stop them.

I'm crying because he really has lost control and because he's actually admitting it, because he's been carrying this around with him all along, still keeping secrets he swore he wasn't keeping, all to protect me. But mostly I'm crying for her, the thirty-one-year-old me who spent nearly two decades missing a shaggy-haired boy with smoky blue eyes that changed her life one snowy day in Evanston, Illinois.

How could he not tell me about a letter that spelled out our fate and made it clear he could never stay? And that he'd known all along? "How could you—" I start to say, but I can't finish my sentence. But I need to, because if I don't, I know exactly what he'll think. That he's ruined my life. That he shouldn't have stayed with me in the first place. That he should have left when he first had the chance. That he should do these last months all over again. And I love him far too much let him think that.

I wipe my tears, and before either of us can say another word, my stomach muscles clench and I double over, reaching down to grab fistfuls of his comforter. It feels like my insides are on fire. I can't move or speak, but I can hear Bennett yelling my name and feel him reaching for me. Everything seems far away and muffled. His face is fuzzy and distorted, like I'm looking at him through a camera lens that's out of focus. My stomach twists and curls with a force that makes me double over again, and I hear myself scream. Loud.

Then it's dark and silent.

32

My face is wet and all I smell is leather, and when I uncurl my legs and reach down to steady myself in the seat, all I *feel* is leather. I open my eyes.

I'm in the dark parking lot, back in Evanston and completely alone in Bennett's Jeep. "No . . ." I have no other words, so I repeat the only one I can get out. "No. No. No!" I look around and feel panic traveling through my limbs. I keep looking over at the driver's seat, waiting for Bennett to magically appear like he does, but he never materializes, and neither do the keys, which should be in the ignition but aren't. I remember Bennett leaning back in this seat and stuffing them in his jeans pocket.

The digital clock on the dashboard reads 11:11. I have only been gone for five minutes after all.

Now I know what Bennett was feeling in the park that

night—getting knocked back against your will is nothing like traveling. I can't sit up straight or draw a real breath; all I can do is pant and try not to panic. My stomach churns again, even more violently this time, and I look around the too-clean car, but there's nothing I can throw up into—not even a stray coffee cup—so I cover my mouth and lean back against the seat.

Breathe.

Hold it in.

Breathe.

Hold it in.

I need to throw up.

And then I need a giant glass of water.

Breathe.

Hold it in.

I reach for the latch, but just as I start to pull it toward me, a small flashing light on the dash catches my eye. The alarm is set. As soon as I open the door, it will go off. But I feel a metallic taste in my mouth again as my stomach cramps into a tight ball, and when I throw the door open the alarm yells in the background, covering the sound of my retching over the cement.

When there's nothing left in me, I wipe my mouth on my sleeve and look around while the car alarm continues to remind me that I don't have the keys. I see a light go on in the house across the street and I know I need to get out of here before someone calls the police. I scour the car one last time for keys I keep hoping will magically appear.

I'm nowhere near home, but I take off running, heading for my neighborhood at the fastest pace I can manage in this outfit. If I could run at my usual speed, I would be home in fifteen minutes, but it's closer to a thirty-minute walk, thanks to Emma's tight skirt and chunky heels. And because I keep stopping to look for Bennett's Jeep. There's a small part of me that thinks he'll pull up to the curb at any moment now and we'll stand here in the dark, fighting about the letter, and eventually I'll forgive him, because I'm just so happy to have him back. But his Jeep never comes.

When I finally arrive at home, I trudge up the front steps and let myself in; I try to sneak past the kitchen, but Dad spots me.

"How was the movie?" He peeks out the window, looking for the car. "Where's Bennett? Why didn't he drive you home?"

I don't even want to imagine what I look like right now. Tearstained and puffy, sweaty and frazzled. "We were at the coffeehouse," I lie.

Dad looks down at my little skirt, up at my frizzy hair, and then he stares at me with a hardened expression I've never seen on his face before. He squints at me. "You look like hell. What happened, Anna? And you'd better tell me the truth."

The truth. I was at the movies. Then I was in San Francisco. I was looking at concert stubs, and I was happy for a second, and suddenly I was furious. I threw up in a parking lot, and now I'm home. I say the first thing that pops into my head. "We got into a fight. Bennett doesn't know where I am. I'm sorry." I feel the tears stream down my cheeks again. "It's been a really horrible evening."

"Are you okay?" Dad's face softens as he asks, and I try to say no, but nothing comes out. He pulls me toward him and holds me tight while I sob into his shoulder. Eventually, the tears stop. "Next time, go to the bookstore and call me to come get you, okay?"

"Okay. I'm sorry."

"It's all right. I bet everything will be better in the morning." He pats my back, and I head for the stairs. "Annie." I turn to look at him. "If it's *not* better, come find me. Okay?"

I smile and trudge up the stairs. My room looks just like it did when I left it. I was supposed to wash that pile of clothes this morning before I went shopping. My textbooks and notebooks are stacked haphazardly on the desk. My bed is still unmade.

This can't be it. I walk to the window and look down, hoping to see Bennett's car pull into the driveway. I picture him sitting on his bed, holding the letter, and the helpless look on his face when—for the first time ever—he watched someone disappear before *his* eyes.

The letter.

That day he heard my name in the dining hall, he knew exactly who I was. He knew we were together here. And he knew he would leave and not come back. He knew it all, and I knew nothing.

And suddenly, everything about his first month in Evanston makes sense. He didn't want to meet anyone because he didn't plan to stay, and he didn't want to know me because he knew eventually we'd be separated. But he gave me the choice. I remember exactly what he said that day, when we sat on the top of the rock we had just climbed. *You exist in 2012, just like I do, in a future that doesn't include me. Just knowing me . . . will change your whole life.* He wasn't only letting me choose to be with him while he was here. He was letting me choose whether or not I wanted to be *that* Anna. The girl he left heartbroken at sixteen, who grew up and hadn't forgotten about him.

I remember her words. My words.

I got stuck on the wrong path.

You will leave for good.

I just need to make a different decision this time.

I think that will change everything.

I have no idea what those words mean. What different decision am I supposed to make? What's supposed to change?

The street is quiet and dark, lit by a full moon and a cloudless sky full of stars. I cross the room until I'm standing in front of my map, and I touch my finger to Evanston, Illinois. I run it all the way to the left until it stops on the spot marked SAN FRANCISCO, CALIFORNIA. If only we were separated by this distance. But we're not. We're separated by this distance plus seventeen years.

I take a pin out of the box and stare at it. I spin it between my fingertips. Maybe if I just picture it, maybe if I want it enough, I can take myself somewhere else too. I bring the red plastic tip to my lips and close my eyes, as if *I* have Bennett's gift, and I will myself to disappear from this room and reappear in his. I picture the view from the window and the bowl full of ticket stubs and the desk and the bed, and I close my eyes tighter and let the vision of the space fill my head as I repeat the words "May 21, 2012. May 21, 2012" aloud, over and over again, in a whisper.

When I open my eyes, I'm still here, holding my pitiful little pin and standing in front of my map of the world with tears streaming down my face.

I look at the dot marked SAN FRANCISCO. The pin makes a sad little pop as it pierces the surface.

33

I sit up with a start and grab the clock from the nightstand. Ten twenty-two. In the *morning*? When did I get into bed? How could I have fallen asleep? That's when it all comes back to me: I got knocked back here, and Bennett's still gone.

I throw on my running clothes, race downstairs, and bolt out the door, ignoring my mom's chiding about sleeping the day away, her prodding me to eat before I exert myself, and her questions about why I'm training on a Sunday in the first place. But I'm not training; I'm running.

When I arrive at Maggie's, four blocks away, I notice immediately that Bennett's car isn't in the driveway, and my stomach plummets so far and with such speed that I fear I may throw up again. I leap onto the porch and ring the doorbell.

There's no answer.

I ring again and wait.

I peek through the sheer curtains into the living room for any sign of activity, but there's nothing. No movement. No sound. Where is he? Where is Maggie? I lean my back against the window and bury my face in my hands. What now?

My brain doesn't come up with any good ideas, so I obey my feet instead, which are telling me in no uncertain terms to go back to the parking lot—to the last place I saw Bennett where he was supposed to be. Or rather, *not* supposed to be—but where I wanted him to be. Here. In *my* town.

My gait feels stiff and awkward as my feet pound against the cement, but as the scenery goes by in a blur, it's what my eyes are taking in that's just plain wrong. The sun is casting a warm glow on each house I pass, igniting the patches of rose-bushes and new tulips that act as colorful dividers between red-brick walkways and lawns so green they nearly spar-kle. The air I'm breathing in is warm and humid, and unlike the cold that prickles against the lining of my lungs, this air makes me feel like I've inhaled a pillow and it's suffocating me from the inside out.

Two miles later, I finally arrive at the office building and come to a full stop. Bennett's car is gone, and for a moment, I let myself think maybe the whole thing was just a dream after all. But then I spot the amorphous blob of puke chang-ing color in the hot sun, and that's all I need to confirm that it was real.

I feel the tears start to well up behind my eyes, but I push them down and turn back the way I came instead. There's nowhere else to go, so I run back to Maggie, the only person who might know where he is. Or at least where his car went.

I wind back through the same neighborhood, past the same houses and cars I ran by just minutes before. When I see the street sign for Greenwood up ahead, I pick up my pace, and that's when I see Bennett's Jeep moving toward me. The right-turn signal starts flashing and the car turns and moves out of sight.

I fly around the corner just in time to see his car pull in to the driveway. He's home. I feel my feet kick into a totally new gear I didn't even realize I had. I knew he'd come home. "Bennett!" I yell as I slap my palm against the rear window and race around to the driver's-side door. "Bennett!"

The door opens slowly and I watch Maggie plant her feet on the cement and carefully lower herself onto the driveway. "I'm afraid not." Her voice is soft, controlled. I crowd Maggie's path as I lean past her, looking in at the passenger side, into the backseat. It's empty.

"Where is he? Maggie, where's Bennett?"

She closes the door behind her, shutting off my view of the interior. Her silver hair glimmers in the sunlight, her face is drawn, and her eyes—Bennett's eyes—seem to be searching mine for something she can't quite put her finger on. "You really don't know where he is, do you?" she asks.

I shake my head, even though it's not entirely true. I know where he is. I could tell her, but she'd never believe me.

She wraps her arm around my shoulder and guides me toward the porch. "Come on in. Let's talk." On shaky legs I let her lead me up the steps, and I follow her into the house and wait while she hangs her coat and purse in the closet. I trail after her into the kitchen and stand in uncomfortable silence while she takes two teacups out of the hutch and fills a kettle with water.

She looks back and sees me leaning against the doorframe for support, shuffling and fidgeting. "Relax. Have a seat." Maggie points to the kitchen table and turns her attention back to the tea bags. I sit.

I should be thinking about what I'm going to say to her, but instead I just look around the room, taking in the stark white cupboards, the dark granite countertop, the flower vase on the windowsill. My eyes settle on a stained-glass mountain scene that's affixed to the kitchen window by a suction cup and a hook, and I follow the stream of sunlight as it shoots through the colored glass and transforms itself into orange and blue and green streams of light that streak across the room and land on the white table.

"My daughter made that for me in high school," Maggie says from across the room. She doesn't give me time to respond, which is good, because I don't know what to say anyway. "I love the way the light comes through that window. Those colors just take my breath away." She puts the teacup in front of me, and a streak of blue light bounces off its side.

"I've just come from the police station," Maggie says as she takes her seat. "They found Bennett's car in an empty parking lot last night. The alarm was sounding, and a neighbor finally called to complain." She lifts her cup to her mouth and takes a sip.

"Oh, really?"

She gives me a suspicious look over the rim of her cup. "Weren't you together last night?"

I reach for the tea but my hands are shaking too much, so I just slide the saucer closer to me instead. "Yes, we were together. We went to the movies with some friends. We parked in that lot." I look at her. "And then we got in a fight, I walked home, and I haven't seen him since." To my own ears, I sound rehearsed, but I hope I'm telling her enough pieces of the truth to keep her suspicion at bay.

"And you don't know where he went?"

I shake my head no, even though this time it's a lie. I know where he went, but again, she'd never believe me.

"Well, I have no reason to spend my time trying to track down a Northwestern student who's simply renting a room from me. Why would I go through all that trouble for a complete stranger, right?" There's a certain bitterness and sense of bravado in her words that confirms what I already know: she's come to care about Bennett, too. I hide my hands under the table and clasp them together for stability. "What I find most interesting is that the police called *me* when they found the car." The lines on her face seem to deepen with concern, confusion. "Do you know why I was the one they called?"

I feel my face squish up, and I say, "No."

"First, because I'm on the registration as the *owner* of his car. And second, because, according to Westlake Academy— where he apparently attends high school—I'm his grand-mother." She slowly takes another sip of tea and rests her forearms on the table. "I assume you know I was under the impression that he was a student at Northwestern. I also assume you know, that I am, in fact, *not* his grandmother."

I try again to bring the cup of tea to my lips, but when I start to take a sip I discover it's still hot enough to scald. I return the cup to its saucer.

Maggie takes a big sip of tea, unaffected by the temperature. "Do you have any idea why he lied about me, Anna?" *Stay calm. Breathe. Take a sip of scalding tea.* "Why he listed me as his grandmother?"

All I want to say is "Because you are," and then run through all the events of the last three months, starting with the day Bennett moved to town. But I can't tell her that the boy in the photos on her mantel and the boy who's been living in one of her spare bedrooms are the same person. "I don't know, Maggie." Her expression doesn't change. "I don't know." I repeat the words like that will make them true.

She stares at me with those eyes, and my stomach turns over with guilt. She lets out a heavy sigh. "I really don't know what to do. The police want me to file a missing-persons report if he's not back in twenty-four hours. If you know anything, Anna, you have to tell me. Please."

I look down into my cup and take a sip.

"This boy has been living in my house and lying to me the entire time. I've liked him, but now it turns out I don't even know who he is. I never did." Maggie stares right into my eyes. "But something tells me you do."

She's right, of course. I know. And right now, all I want to do is tell her everything, because I want her to know who he is, and because I'm tired of being the only one who does and, mostly, because I want her to like him again. And she would, if only she knew who he really was and what he'd done for her.

I want to tell her that four years from now, she'll be diagnosed with Alzheimer's. The decline will be gradual, until 2000, when it will speed up and never slow down. By 2001, she'll start forgetting more than small details and minor events. She will forget to pay her bills, forget where her investments are located, forget to tell anyone enough to help before it's too late. By 2002, she'll no longer be able to function on her own. She will have forgotten her family. Her daughter, Bennett's mom, will be too far away in too many ways to make it better. And then, when Bennett is eight years old, Maggie will die.

But five years later, Bennett will start coming back to 1995. To 1996. To 2000. To 2003. Eventually, he'll start bringing Brooke. The two of them will knock on Maggie's door, pretending to be students soliciting donations, just to hear her voice. When she's really sick, they'll show up in the middle of the night to clean her kitchen and pay her bills. When she leaves for appointments during the day, Bennett will mow her lawn, and Brooke will plant new flowers. They'll stuff cash into strange hiding places around the house, because, even though they know it will cause her confusion, they also know she'll find it. And eventually, Bennett will let Maggie in on his secret. Even if she doesn't remember it for more than a moment, she'll die knowing that the last years of her life would have been very different if it hadn't been for Bennett's gift.

"Anna?" Maggie interrupts my thoughts.

"Don't let the police search for him." My voice catches in my throat, and even though I want to say so much more, I don't.

Her eyes grow wide with curiosity. "Why not? Please, you have to tell me. What do you know, Anna?"

I look at her, holding her gaze in mine. Finally, I return my eyes to the tableful of colored light. What do I *know*? Well, at least that's a question I can answer. Sort of. I run my fingertip along a streak of green. "I truly don't know how to find him. But I know he's safe," I begin, my voice a whisper. "I know he's back in San Francisco. I know he didn't want to leave, but he didn't have a choice. I know he didn't want to lie to you. Or to hurt you."

"Who is he?"

Over the past two months, I've never been tempted to divulge Bennett's secret—not to my family, not to my best friend—but sitting here, looking at Maggie's sad eyes, I just want her to know him like I do. But I remind myself that it's not my place. "I can't tell you, Maggie. It took him a long time to confide in me, and when he finally did, I promised I wouldn't share his secret with anyone. It's killing me not to tell you right now, but it's his story, not mine. But he's not a bad person." I want to add *He loves you*, but I stop short of saying too much. "He's just going to have to tell you himself when he gets back."

She leans forward. "And when will that be?"

Another question I can't answer, but this time it's not because I can't break my promise. It's because I truly don't know. "I have no idea. But he told me once that he'd come back, and I have to believe him."

I sit there watching her, waiting to hear what she'll say next. I feel sick.

"What should I tell the police?"

I think quickly. "There was an emergency back at home. An illness . . . in his family. A friend gave him a ride to the airport, and he left his car in the parking lot. But now he's called, and he's fine. He's . . ." I take a deep breath so I can finish my sentence without breaking down. "He's back in San Francisco with his family."

"I'm supposed to lie? To the police?"

"It's not a lie. That's where he is. You can tell them that, or you can say nothing, file a missing-persons report, and let them search for him. But they won't find him."

"If he comes back—"

"When," I clarify. "*When* he comes back, I'll be the first to know. I'll make sure you're the second. And I'll be sure he tells you everything. Okay?"

She nods a few times as she considers my solution. "What am I supposed to do about all his things? What about his car?"

The car. He told me the SUV was Maggie's, and now that I

think about it in context with everything else, it fits. "I think Bennett bought the car for you."

She furrows her brow and stares at me again. "Why on earth would he do that? He doesn't know me well enough to buy me a brand-new car."

I smile at her and let out a sigh. "He doesn't. But he does. And I know that doesn't make any sense. . . ." My voice trails off while those last words echo through my mind, and somehow, I find myself repeating the words I read last night in San Francisco. The words I will write in a letter to Bennett seventeen years from now. They worked on him. Maybe they'll work on his grandmother. "Someday," I say, "it will all make sense. For now, you'll just have to trust me."

34

For the last hour I've been leaning against the foot of my bed, dressed in the oversize sweatshirt Bennett wore after our first date in Ko Tao and staring up the black silk sheath I've bought to wear to tonight's auction party. When I first brought it home and hooked the hanger on my closet door frame, this dress looked almost magical, like something cartoon birds and mice had stitched together from scratch while I slept.

But tonight's the one-week anniversary of the night I got knocked back. Of *ever since.* And now the dress is just another museum piece, in good company with my map, a bag of sand, six postcards, and four new pins. All the things I can no longer look at without thinking of him.

I'm still staring up at the dress when I hear the knock at the door. I've been expecting it, but I'm not sure which one of my parents lost the coin toss.

"Come in," I mutter.

Emma?

I stare up at her from my spot on the floor. She's wearing the dress I helped her pick out, the strapless, floor-length gown in a deep, dark orange that looks as incredible on her now as it did in the dressing room. Her hair is pulled back in a tight twist at the nape of her neck, with a few strands of hair pulled out to frame her face. "Wow. You look gorgeous."

"Thanks." She takes a seat on the floor next to me, leans against the footboard, and reaches for me.

I look at her sideways. "You're gonna get all wrinkled."

"That's okay." She scans me from top to bottom, from my frizzy hair and bloodshot eyes down to my leggings and—to her horror, I'm sure—my unpedicured toes.

"What are you doing here, Em?"

She gives my hand a little squeeze. "Sorry. I know you want to be alone, but your mom put me up to this." I turn my head away from her and roll my eyes. Both Mom and Dad have been bugging me all week about this stupid party, and I've made it more than clear I'm not going. Under any circumstances. But to send Emma in as reinforcement? That's just cruel.

"And I wanted to be sure you were okay."

"I'm fine."

She looks at me in disbelief, then stares at the dress. "It would be a shame if I was the only one who ever saw you in it. You looked so beautiful."

I can't look at it without feeling sick. "Thanks."

We're silent for what feels like minutes, me looking down at the carpet, Emma looking back and forth between me and that dress. "I'm not going to change my mind," I finally say.

"I know. But we should stay here for at least, like, fifteen minutes so your mom thinks I really tried." She turns to me, smiles, and bumps me with her shoulder. "Okay?"

I give her a sad smile. "Thanks." Emma understands. She understood right away. Last Sunday I left Maggie's, ran straight to Emma's, and fell apart on her porch. We sat in her room while she passed me tissues, let me talk for hours, and believed every word of the story I made up. Someone in his family got sick. He had to take a red-eye back to San Francisco after we left the movie theater. He wasn't sure when or if he'd be back and was sorry he wouldn't have the chance to say good-bye. He'd miss us.

The next day, I told a few more people the same story and waited as it made the rounds of The Donut. And that was it. Within hours, everyone knew why Bennett had gone home, and I was the only one who knew it was all a lie.

Now I look at my best friend, all made up and happy and ready to go to the party she's been looking forward to for the last six months, and I know I should go tonight. I should be there to see what Emma and Danielle helped plan and to watch my parents dance and to see Justin in a tux. But I can't go out and pretend to be happy. Not without Bennett. Not yet.

"Are you mad at me? For not going tonight?"

She shakes her head. "No. I'm not mad. I just . . ." I stare at her, waiting for her to continue, but she doesn't. She looks down at the floor and twirls a loose thread in the rug with her finger.

"What?" I ask.

"Nothing."

"What?" I repeat.

She takes a deep breath and lets it out with a sigh. "I just miss you, that's all. I know you miss him—we all miss him too—but . . . I really miss *you*."

I force out a little laugh. "I'm right here."

"No, you're not."

I look at her and know she's right. Ever since the day I saw the other Bennett at the track and he told me he'd been trying to get back here, I've been doing exactly the opposite: I've been slowly disappearing.

She stops playing with the rug and stares at me. "Look, Anna, you're my best friend, and I love so many things about you. I love that you make me laugh, and that you love music and books, and you want to travel the world, and you're so committed to running . . . but you know what I love most about you? You know what I've loved about you since the moment we became friends?"

I look at her and wait.

"You're the strongest person I know. You're independent and you don't care what anyone thinks and you trust your instincts and . . . you've got *fight*. I've always envied that about you. If Justin left town, left me here, *I'd* be a blubbering basket case. But . . ." Her words hang in the air like she didn't mean to say them. *But what?* She expected more from me? She didn't think I'd be so weak?

"Where's your *fight?*" She stares at me for a minute and then reaches down and grabs my hand again. "Listen, I know it's only been a week, it's just—" She brings my hand to her face and kisses the back of it. "I want my friend back."

I look at her and wish I could tell her everything. I want to get back to her and the rest of my ordinary life too—to Mom and Dad and running and travel books—and I just don't know if I can find my fight with all these secrets weighing me down.

Emma doesn't let go of me, and we sit like that, waiting for our requisite fifteen minutes to tick by. "I'd better go. I have to greet the VIPs." Emma stands up and smooths out her gown. Then she checks her hair in my mirror and pats her eyes with her fingertip.

"I'm sorry, Emma."

She reaches for the doorknob, stops to blow me a kiss, and walks out, closing the door behind her.

I can't hear them, but I picture Emma at the bottom of the staircase, talking with Justin and my parents in hushed tones. I go to the window and peek out as Justin and Emma walk out to the car. Just as he's about to open the door, he looks up, sees me there, and gives a sad little wave. He gets in the car and they drive off.

Soon enough, Mom and Dad shout their good-byes and are-you-sure-you're-okays up the stairs and then they're off too. I look down at the sidewalk and stare at the spot where Bennett first kissed me—even though I don't remember him doing it. I look at the tree across the street, where his car rolled backward and settled because he didn't time our do-over exactly as planned. Even if he was a little off here and there, he'd always been in control. If he could get back, he would.

And that's when it hits me. He would have been here by now. Bennett was wrong and the letter was right. He's not coming back. He's stuck, against his will and most definitely against mine. Unless I make a different decision. And I have no idea what that means.

I leave the window open and walk back to the map. I stand there and study it for a minute, and then I reach forward and begin tracing invisible lines between the eight little red pins with my fingertip, running it back and forth, up and down, tracing patterns to connect them. Then I stop. I bring my finger to Evanston and make a tiny circle around the four I started with: Springfield. Minnesota. Michigan. Indiana. And then I rest my finger on San Francisco and make a much larger circle going all the way to Ko Tao, back to Vernazza, over to Wisconsin, and back to San Francisco.

I should have more. I'm supposed to have more.

I reach into the Lucite container and pull out a pin. Look at it. Stare at the map. Stick it into Paris. I pull out another one. Study the map. Stick it into Madrid. I stand back and consider the map again, enjoying the new look, and reach into the dusty container again. I push a red pin into Sydney. Then I grab the container and turn it upside down in my hand, feeling a few stray pins prick my palm.

I press pins into Tokyo.

Tibet.

Auckland.

Dublin.

Costa Rica.

São Paulo.

Prague.

Los Angeles.

And I just keep going and going, picking up pins and stabbing them into the paper until the map is covered with places I'll never see and the clear plastic box is as empty as I am.

june

35

Last week I was sad. This week, I'm just angry. I'm angry at him for not telling me about the letter and angry at my friends for acting like he was never here, but mostly, I'm angry at myself for letting my guard down so completely—for accepting this whole thing as perfectly normal.

My hands are balled up in two tight fists when Señor Argotta announces, *"¡Practiquemos la conversación!"* and walks down the aisle pointing out partners and passing out cards. He points to me. Then to Alex. I roll my eyes as I turn my desk toward him.

"¡Hola!" Alex says with a smile. "Hey, where were you on Saturday? We missed you." I'm not sure why it's taken him until Thursday to ask.

I shrug. "I'm training for state finals."

"On a Saturday night?"

"No, Alex. Every morning. I run *every* morning now. Even

on Sundays." Before I've said the last word I'm embarrassed by my tone, but I don't apologize. Instead I continue talking to him with this attitude, because it's actually making me feel better to see him uncomfortable for once. "So, do you have the conversation card, or what?"

He mutters something under his breath, picks the card up from his desk and reads to himself. "Oh, this one's pretty good." He reads it aloud. *"Partner number one, you are interviewing for a job as a waiter/waitress at one of Madrid's finest restaurants. Partner number two, you are the restaurant owner."*

I look around for something to punch.

"That's not such a bad one, right?" Alex decides without looking at me to notice that I'm gripping the sides of the wooden desk. "Do you want to be the waiter or the owner?"

"Neither." I push my chair away and run for the door, leaving my backpack on the floor and my textbook on my desk. Leaving Alex and that stupid conversation card. Leaving Señor Argotta calling after me in an accented voice that's full of concern, then frustration. But I don't stop. I don't even turn around. I run through The Donut, past the lockers. And I literally run into Danielle.

She crashes into a bank of lockers and her wooden bathroom pass goes sliding across the floor. "What the—!"

I'm wiping tears from my eyes as I help her back up to a standing position. "Danielle, I'm so sorry."

She starts to say something, but then she realizes I've been crying. "Anna? Are you okay?"

"I need to get out of here," I say.

"Anna!" She calls after me, but I'm already gone, through the double doors, racing toward the only thing I think may make me feel better.

~~~

He's here.

Not the way I want him to be, but in the only way I can have him now, in pictures of an infant, framed and displayed on a mantel, and in the eyes of his grandmother, who makes me tea and doesn't even question why I'm sitting in her kitchen at eleven twenty in the morning on a school day.

We sip from our respective teacups. We try to think of things to say, but come up with very little. She has plenty of questions and I have plenty of answers, but she can't voice hers because she knows I won't share mine. So we sit there, stuck in a thick silence that's interrupted every few minutes by the sound of porcelain cups connecting with their matching saucers.

Maggie finally breaks the silence. "I started cleaning out his room last week. I thought I'd put his things in the attic until . . ." Her voice trails off and I smile a little. I like the idea that she thinks he'll come back. "Do you—" she begins, looking at me like she'll let my expression determine whether she should continue her sentence or not. "Do you want to hold on to anything for him? Until he returns?"

I nod. And since there's nothing left to talk about, we carry our cups up the stairs and down the hall, past the photos of Bennett's mother as a child, of Maggie as a young woman, and into the mahogany-furnished room he once called his.

"I'll get you some more tea," Maggie says, and she grabs my nearly full cup and carries it out, closing the door behind her and leaving me alone in his room.

There are a few boxes stacked near the wall under the windows, but otherwise, it looks like it always did. I slide open the closet doors and peer inside. His uniform is there, along with a bunch of clothes I never got to see on him. His wool coat is hanging on a hook within easy reach, and even though it's ninety degrees outside, I put it on, lift the collar to my nose, and inhale his scent.

I shut the closet door and walk toward the desk. There is nothing on the surface—not even a pen or a photograph. I sit down in the wooden chair and open the top drawer. And that's where I find the rest of him. I take each of the items out one at a time and pile them on the desk. His Westlake student ID. One of my red pins. A blank postcard from Ko Tao. The postcard I wrote him in Vernazza. A stubby yellow pencil. A carabiner. A single key.

I push everything aside, take out the key, and walk over to the armoire. I work quickly, stacking the photo albums and old yearbooks in a pile, until I see the small gold keyhole in the back corner. I twist the key in the lock and pull up on the small door. Inside, I find stacks and stacks of rubber-banded dollar bills, hundreds, and twenties.

On top of one of the stacks, I see his notebook and remember how he used it to plot the do-over that probably saved

Emma's life. I pick it up and flip through it. Every page is covered with timelines and mathematical equations, charts documenting age conversions and historical events, and company names with dollar signs next to them. Finally I get the page he once showed me—the time conversions he did that landed us in my driveway and eventually kept Emma from driving to Chicago.

I flip back to the first few pages of the notebook and see something else familiar. My words, but in his handwriting:

> *Someday soon, we will meet. And then you will leave for good. But I think I can fix it—I just need to make a different decision this time. Tell me to live my life for myself, and not for you. Tell me not to wait for you to come back. I think that will change everything.*

He's circled key words and terms like *for good* and *leave* and *fix* and *change everything*, adding his own comments and question marks and exclamation points like he was studying it, attempting to figure it all out. But he didn't. Not after months of trying. And now it's too late—he's gone for good. *Why didn't he tell me?* He was supposed to tell me *everything.*

I check the door for Maggie. Then I put the red notebook back on the top, lock the cabinet, and put the scrapbooks and photo albums back where they belong. Once everything looks just as he left it, I return to Bennett's desk.

I open the drawer and put the key inside, and then I look at the rest of the items. I pick each one up and turn it over in my hands, starting with the postcard from Ko Tao. I remember the day he presented me mine on the lawn at school. I couldn't believe he'd gone back, just for that. "I got one for myself, too . . . to remember the day," he'd said.

"Here," Maggie whispers, and I jump and turn my head. She's traded our teacups for a small shopping bag, and now she's holding it out to me.

"Thanks."

She looks down at the pile of things on Bennett's desk and rests her hand on my shoulder. "Are you okay, sweetie?" I give her a sad nod. "He's such a sweet boy. I hope he comes back."

I hold the bag under the edge of the desktop and brush everything inside. Then I stand up, pull Maggie into a hug, and thank her for letting me hold on to his things. She squeezes me tightly.

"You should go to California for a visit," I say as I pull away from her embrace. "Meet that grandson of yours. I bet it would mean a lot to your daughter."

"I don't know. . . . My daughter and I aren't very close these days."

I stare straight into her eyes, and even though they're exactly the same as her grandson's, I don't see him at all. I just see Maggie. "You should go anyway."

"Maybe I will."

I look at her and smile. There's no need to wait for Bennett to get old enough to start making little changes that will affect her future. Not if I can help her get it right the first time.

I kiss her on the cheek and close the desk drawer, leaving the key inside.

I'm back on campus a half hour after last bell, and as I walk through The Donut I can hear my footsteps echoing in the empty halls. I hope the classroom is unlocked, my backpack is still there, and Argotta's already gone for the day. The probability of all three being true is extremely low.

When I reach the classroom door, the first thing I see is my backpack, propped up against Argotta's desk. When I look up from the floor, I spot him there, correcting papers.

"Señor Argotta?" When he hears the sound of my voice, he stops writing but keeps his eyes on his work.

"Señorita Greene. How nice of you to return."

"I'm . . . really sorry. It's just—" Now he looks at me, first curious, then horrified. My T-shirt is soaked with sweat, my face is all blotchy and red, and the humidity has caused my curls to tighten up and frizz. Argotta blinks fast a few times but doesn't ask.

"No need to explain. Your friend, Señor Camarian, filled me in on the . . . impact . . . that Señor Cooper's departure has had on you." I'm not sure if Alex has the necessary information to explain this "impact," but if The Donut is as all-knowing as Danielle says it is, he probably does. And now my chest feels heavy with guilt. How could I have been so mean to him today?

Argotta leans down and reaches for my backpack like he's

about to hand it to me, but when he feels its weight he sort of scoots it in my general direction instead. I step forward, pick it up, and hoist it over my shoulder. "Thanks." I turn to leave.

I'm almost at the door when I hear him clear his throat behind me. "Are you aware of the date, Señorita Greene?"

I stop. "It's June first, señor."

"*Exactamente.*" I roll my eyes. I'm not in the mood for this.

"Which made yesterday the last day of May." I turn around and look at him. "I was really hoping you'd consider taking that spot in Mexico, señorita. Perhaps now that your summer plans have changed . . ."

I flash back to the day he gave me the shiny yellow folder and realize I never even bothered to open it. I should probably know all the details, but I don't. "Oh. Right. Where is it again?"

"I think you had it as a destination on your travel plan, did you not? It's a beautiful town called La Paz. It's getting very popular. Now is really the time to see it."

"La Paz?"

"*Sí.*" He watches me while I try not to look confused. *La Paz?* "You have your travel voucher and you would have an excellent family to live with. The trip is practically free. I'm sure you already have your summer all planned out, but it really is a great opportunity, and if you're interested, I could still pull some strings."

Argotta watches me while he waits for his answer. And finally, when none comes, he leans back in his seat and folds his arms across his chest. I want to go, but I don't think I can.

What if Bennett comes back? I can't leave. I have to wait here. But my whole body starts to tremble as I remember the words I just read in Bennett's notebook—the words I will write in a letter to him seventeen years from now: *Tell me not to wait for you to come back.*

"Are you okay, señorita?"

I think that will change everything.

I feel far away as I nod, and when I speak, my voice doesn't sound like my own. "This is a good chance, isn't it? To leave?"

"Exactamente!" he yells as he throws his arms up in the air, and I startle. "Go! Go! There's nothing stopping you! Go see the world, señorita!"

He smiles at me, and I feel myself smiling back. Because this is it. *This* is the moment.

I don't know how it happened before. Maybe Argotta never mentioned it again. Maybe all the spots were full from the beginning. Maybe everything was exactly the same, but she decided to stay here all summer, sulking and waiting for Bennett to return. But right now, there's no question in my mind that *Anna* stood here in front of Argotta, politely thanked him, and turned down his offer. And that's not what I'm going to do.

"Do you still have the application?" he asks, and I nod. I'm not exactly certain where it is, but I know I'll find it; and now I can't wait to get home to dig through my desk.

"I'll give you until Monday. Let me know what you want to do."

My parents may need until Monday, but I don't. I rush

around to Señor Argotta and hug him. "Thank you so much, señor!" When I pull back, he looks a little shocked, but it hits him that the hug was my yes, and there's nothing but delight in his expression. "You're making a good choice, señorita."

I hope it's a good choice. I don't know for certain that it is, but I do know that it's a different one.

And suddenly it hits me. I'm smack in the middle of her do-over.

36

Depending on the season, Schiller Woods can be beautiful or eerie; the perfect place for either a wedding or a horror-film shoot. As Dad rounds the corner through the gate, I see that what was once a blanket of gray slush is now a bright green meadow. I step out of the car and take a deep breath; the whole park smells new.

"I've missed this," I say as I close the car door, feeling truly content for the first time in weeks. Dad looks surprised to see me so happy, but I can't help it; I love this event. The cross-country coaches in our division created the noncompetitive but mandatory race, just in case six months of running on a spongy track instead of sticky mud, and leaping metal hurdles rather than downed trees, had caused us to question our true passion. I've run this course enough to know how the path will dip and turn for the next three miles, where the tight spots will be, and where the obstacles are likely to be placed.

My teammates and I gather around a picnic table a few feet away from the starting line, stretching and looking across the open field for our biggest competitors while Dad goes in search of coffee. A few minutes later, he returns with a paper cup and a folded map.

"How are you feeling?" he asks me as he lays the paper flat on the table and huddles over it.

"Good." He looks up, waiting for me to elaborate, but I don't. Still, I do feel good. I've been feeling increasingly like myself since I made the decision to go to La Paz two days ago. Now I just need to find a way to tell my parents.

"Where is she?" Dad asks under his breath.

I lift up my arm and stretch in his direction while I point with my chin. "Over there. Number thirty-two. Blue shirt." I stretch deeper and give him time to find her. Size her up.

"Hmmm." He's watching her, but for what exactly I can't be sure. "Okay, remember to pace yourself. Don't hold back just to blast her at the end. Keep the pressure on all the way. Keep passing, keep in front. Then get that blue shirt in your sights and turn it up even more at the last marker." He's searching the crowd again. He shouldn't be so nervous, since I don't have a scholarship on the line this time.

"Got it."

"Where's your marker?" Dad asks, pointing back to the map.

I rest my finger on the drawing. "This water pump looks like it's about an eighth of a mile before the finish."

He studies the other options and finally nods. "Yeah. That's good. I think that's your best bet. Okay. I'm going to take my place with the other worried parents." He pats me on the back. "Don't break anything."

"I won't." I take a deep breath and drop forward. As I stretch, I stare at the upside-down paper number 54 pinned to my chest and listen as my teammates and competitors collect around me. I shake out my limbs and take my place.

We stand side by side at the starting line. It's only seven a.m., but we're already dripping with sweat from the heat and the humidity as we stretch and visualize the course. When the shot signals our start, we run at a controlled speed across the grass and into the woods. I already miss the mud and the slush. We push ourselves up a steep hill littered with fallen tree branches and debris, and then we drop down into the deeper woods where the footing is even more uneven.

We run as a pack for the first mile, sliding past one another when we reach narrowly spaced trees. At the end of the first mile, we cross a shallow creek and jump over a series of logs. I'm pushing and climbing and hurdling, and I know there are people around me, but as I cross the miles they seem to disappear as I move past them and fight my way to the front of the pack.

This is better. I'm not as light on my feet as I usually am, but at least while I'm running, surrounded by forest and sky, my head starts to feel clear again. I'm in control here, moving with the pack, but I can tell that I'm not pushing and fighting like I should be if I want to win this thing.

I run, feeling both the pounding of my shoes on the trail and my heart beating fast in my chest, and I look ahead at the girls in front of me. And just as we come around a bend and start to descend a narrow trail, I see the water pump far ahead in front of the leader. My marker. At first, I slowly increase my pace so I won't seem like a threat to the five girls in front of me. I slip quickly past one. Then another. I'm in third place when we hit the quarter-mile mark, and that's when I lock my eyes on that blue shirt and chase after it with everything I have left. For a moment, I feel something familiar returning. My feet move faster. *Where's your fight?* I hear Emma ask.

"Right here." I breathe out, without even caring if anyone's overheard me, and I kick it up a notch. Something has changed. Something feels different today. I picture the words in her letter—*I think I can fix it*—and they echo in my ears as I keep my eyes glued on the runners ahead.

The two girls in front of me hurdle the last obstacle, and then it's my turn. I run up on the fallen tree, leap forward, and my feet leave the ground. But I feel the tip of my shoe catch on a knot, and I fall forward in a stumble, taking wide steps to keep from falling. The girls I just passed shoot ahead of me again.

I rebalance myself, take a deep breath, and force myself forward again. I climb the hill at top speed, legs burning, until the two girls fall behind me again. Then I overtake the next. But the girl in the blue shirt is too far in front. I can see the finish line from here—see that she's closer to it than I am— and that makes me switch into a completely different gear. I steady my gaze on the blond ponytail swinging in front of me. I give myself one last push and speed up to catch her.

But she's faster. She's the one to break through the tape first, though I am right on her heels. I come to a stop and fall forward, pulling in breaths, wiping the sweat from my face, and smiling at the ground.

"Good race," I hear her say, and I twist to my side to see the girl I barely beat at state finals doubled over next to me and breathing just as heavily. She holds out her hand to shake mine.

I don't even care that I came in second, and my smile is geniune. "Thanks," I reply between breaths as I take her hand. "You made me fight for it." Her eyebrows pinch together in confusion but I don't feel the need to clarify. I may have lost that first-place trophy, but somewhere on the course I found what I was missing.

At home, I fly up the stairs, flop down on the floor, and start rifling through my backpack until I find the yellow folder I unearthed from the bottom of my desk last Thursday. I open it and read the letter from the host family again, for the hundredth time, and stare at the eight-by-ten picture of them. They're standing in front of their house with their arms locked around one another. Four kids. A girl my age. A boy that looks a little older. Two small girls in dresses, standing in front, who look like twins.

And now when I look up at the map, suddenly all I want to do is make it real again. I pull the pin out of Prague and listen to the *plink* it makes when the metal connects with the plastic container. I pull the pin out of Paris. Cairo. Amsterdam. Berlin. Quebec. A few minutes later, I've removed every false pin that pierced its surface, every destination I've never seen but marked as if I had, and placed them back in the home where they belong.

Only the eight pins remain:

Springfield, Illinois.

Ely, Minnesota.

Grand Rapids, Michigan.

South Bend, Indiana.

Ko Tao, Thailand.

Devil's Lake State Park, Wisconsin.

Vernazza, Italy.

San Francisco, California.

Eight pins aren't nearly enough, but at least they're real. The ninth one will be too.

37

Everyone's in a good mood at dinner, perhaps because I am finally smiling and not casting a depressing pall over the dining room table. But the mood, I sense, is about to change.

"I want to talk with you about this summer," I say.

Mom glances up at me as she chews, and Dad keeps his eyes on his plate while he takes a knife through his chicken. "Sure. What's up?" he asks.

I take a deep breath and go. "I've been talking with my Spanish teacher about an exchange program in Mexico. He organizes the trips and personally selects students to participate and he just told me that there's a great family that can host me this summer. In La Paz." I didn't expect to blurt it all out quite so fast. And now all those words are hovering above the table while my parents look at each other, confused.

"I know, it's sudden," I continue, "but I've thought a lot about this. I've always wanted to travel, and you know, I really need time away . . . from here." No one moves or says anything, so I just keep talking. "It won't cost you anything. I won the plane ticket in Señor Argotta's class, and I'd have a place to stay with this amazing family. It's basically free." I hear myself repeating Argotta's words and feel like he's here with me, cheering me on.

"La Paz?" Mom can't hide her concern.

"Yeah. It's on the Baja peninsula. On the Sea of Cortez. In Mexico," I clarify, just in case she missed that part.

"That's far away."

I smile at her and shrug. "That's sort of the point, Mom."

"No way." She sighs and shifts in her chair. "What do you even know about this family?"

I walk over to the counter where I laid the packet of information earlier and bring it back to the table. I lay the photos and the letter out for them to see, and describe what I've learned about them. He's a businessman. She's a nature photographer. They have a daughter my age. I take the completed form out of the folder and place it next to the photos.

"It just needs your signature."

Mom picks up the form, considers it, and sets in down on the table. "When would you leave?"

"In two weeks."

"Two weeks!"

"It's a bit last-minute."

Dad's too quiet. I can't tell on which side of the fence he is, so I look at him, pleading with him to stand firmly on mine.

"How long would you be gone?" he asks.

This part isn't going to go over well. "Ten weeks."

"Ten weeks? That's the entire summer!" Mom pushes her chair away from the table and walks to the kitchen. Dad looks at me and I look back with pleading eyes.

"Please, Dad," I whisper. I hear the water running in the kitchen.

"That's a long time," Dad says, loud enough for Mom to hear, and I picture her bent over the sink and nodding vehemently. "But even so," he continues, "it sounds like a really good opportunity." Mom returns to the table wearing a panicked look that morphs into an angry one, like she can't believe he's voiced this opinion without consulting her first. But Dad holds his ground. "She's been wanting to travel since she was little," he says to her. "This is a good way to see the world, to experience a different culture."

I mouth the words *Thank you* when she's not looking.

Mom sets her glass down with a little too much force. She sits down and looks across at Dad. "You're seriously considering letting our sixteen-year-old daughter live in a foreign country, for two months, with people we don't even *know*?"

"Argotta says it will really help my diction. It will help me develop an ear for the language. I probably won't be fluent in only two months, but I'll be closer."

"I don't know." Mom's looking from me to Dad, and Dad is looking from me to her, and we're at a stalemate.

"It's a huge honor to be selected," I offer. She doesn't need to know that no one else wanted this spot. It's funny to hear myself argue with such passion, given how dismissive I was when Argotta first made his offer, but that was when Bennett was here and permission slips weren't required for international travel. "Mom. This is something for *me*. I need to do this."

She won't look at either one of us, so we all sit in silence, pushing food around on our plates, and trying to ignore the photos of the happy family on the table in front of us.

⁓

"Drop me off here, would you?" I ask, even though we're still two blocks from the bookstore.

"Why here?" Emma pulls over to the side of the road and when she's stopped, follows my finger up to the bright blue awning of the Going Going Gone Travel Agency.

"Oh." She sounds so sad. "Wait. I'll park and come in with you."

I start to argue with her, but then I decide it might be therapeutic for her to witness me purchase the ticket, to see that this trip is actually happening, because she can't seem to fully process the fact that we'll be spending a summer apart for the first time in three years.

When we open the glass door, we're greeted by the same jingling bells we have at the bookstore. Emma and I sit down in the only chairs in the office just as a youngish woman with thick glasses and a mop of split-ended, outdated hair comes around the corner and takes a seat in the chair across from us. I can hardly see her behind the giant monitor.

"Are you sure?" I ask.

"Yes. Absolutely," she replies, without looking up from the book.

"I'll take the twelve fifteen flight," I tell the agent, and she goes back to pounding on the keyboard.

Emma flips back to the photo of the open-air market. "Look at these hats. It's says they're woven so tightly they can hold water. Why would you want to hold water in your hat?" She looks up at me and shrugs. "I don't know why, but lately I've been thinking I need more hats. What do you think? Do I look good in hats?" she asks, and I suck in my breath. Even though she's sitting next to me, without even a single scar, for a moment all I can see is her lying on a stark white sheet, her frail body covered with cuts and punctured by tubes while I tell her about my Mexico travel plan. I jump when the printer comes to life and starts whirring and plinking just behind the desk.

"Hats?" I ask.

"Yeah. Hats. Those contraptions people put on their head to block out the sun and hide bad hair. Hats." She looks at me wide-eyed. "What do you think? Do I look good in hats? Some people can't pull them off, you know, but I think I might be able to."

I just stare at her, and finally I find my voice. "Yeah, you look good in hats." I feel pale. *You look really good in hats*, I remember saying that day I sat on her bed and held her hand and told her about the Yucatán Peninsula. Then I broke down. Then I told her to hold on and I'd fix it.

"Hi. I need to purchase a round-trip ticket to La Paz, Mexico, please." I reach into my backpack and grab the now-tattered copy of *Let's Go Mexico*, flip to the dog-eared page on La Paz, and pull out the voucher I wedged into the binding.

"I'd like to use this." I slide it across the desk and picture the satisfied look I saw on Argotta's face this morning when I gave him my completed, parent-signed form.

She picks up the voucher, turns it over, and sets it on the desk in front of her.

"Sure! When do you want to leave?" She's a little too perky, and when she turns her attention to the computer screen, Emma rolls her eyes.

"June twentieth, please. It's a Tuesday." The travel agent's fingers begin flying across the keyboard. Every few minutes she stops typing to consult the screen, and then the fingers start flying again.

"Here, let me see this." Emma grabs *Let's Go Mexico* and starts thumbing through the pages, stopping every once in while to show me some photo of a beach at sunset or to tell about the great scuba diving or the delicious food.

"Look at this!" Emma twists in her seat and push book at me. "Look at these markets—all this pott food. This isn't fair; you don't even like shopping."

The travel agent clears her throat and reads me of departure times.

"I'm driving you to the airport," Emma cl that one at noon."

"Here you are." The agent smiles brightly and gives me a thin envelope decorated with colorful fish. "Have a fantastic time on your trip! And come back and see us again, Miss Greene!"

Emma locks arms with me and leads me out of the office. "Now that we did your thing, it's my turn. Let's go see Justin," she says, pulling me down the block to the record store.

38

School ends on a hot, muggy day, and while everyone heads to the lake carrying food, music, and picnic blankets, I spend my afternoon waiting in line with a bunch of sweaty people in the downtown Chicago passport office. Four hours later, passport in hand, I get off the El at the Evanston stop and trudge down the cement staircase toward home. At the intersection, I look down the street and see the sign on the record store.

It's been over a week since Emma and I went to buy my ticket and bounced happily into the record store to tell Justin all about Mexico. After she finished imitating the perky travel agent, he threw his arm around her and made a joke about being stuck all alone with her for the whole summer. He told me to come back next week and he'd load me up with CDs for my trip.

"There you are! I thought you forgot." Justin beams at me

as I push through the doors and walk inside the empty store. The music's loud, as usual.

I shrug. "How could I forget free music?"

He fakes a pout. "And here I thought you were coming in to see me."

"You?" I give him a confused stare. "No. Nothing to do with you. I'm just here for the tunes." I break into a smile.

"You're mean." He takes a step back and grabs both of my hands, just like Bennett used to do right before we closed our eyes and opened them elsewhere. "You excited?"

"Yeah. Very."

"We're gonna miss you."

"I'll miss you guys too." I look around the record store. "But it'll be nice to do something different, you know?"

"I know." Justin's been listening to me talk about traveling the world for the last decade, and the look on his face proves that he's genuinely excited to see me finally going somewhere. "Well, since you're only here to sponge music off me, let's stock you up." He takes my hand again and leads me through the store, down the skinny aisles carved out between roughly sanded wooden bins. He stops at a kiosk of new releases.

"Here, this is brand-new. Just came out this week." He passes me the CD, and I turn it over and read the track list. "She's good. Some pissed-off Canadian chick. Great breakup music."

"We did not break up."

"Of course you didn't, but you know . . ."

I fake a glare and the room goes silent as one song ends and another is about to begin. We start walking again, just as piano notes come in through the overhead sound system and a soft melody begins. Justin stops in the Rock section and reaches into the bin for a CD. "I've been meaning to tell you about this local Chicago band; they're playing at the coffee-house next week," he says, and I try to listen to him, but all of my attention is now focused on the melody being piped in from the ceiling. It sounds familiar, and when the lyrics begin, even though I'm supposed to be listening to Justin tell me about this band he's excited about, I find myself straining to hear the song over his voice.

> *Take me to another place, she said.*
> *Take me to another time . . .*

I feel that hole in the pit of my stomach start to grow again as I listen.

"Here it is," Justin says, and I almost *shush* him.

"The drummer is—"

> *Take me where the whispering breezes . . .*
> *can lift me up and spin me around.*

Now I can't look at him, because I'm afraid if I let go of the wooden bin I might not be able to stand. He's waving the CD around, his facial expressions all animated and enthusiastic, so I know he's still talking. And I think I'm saying, *"Uh-huh,"* or something like that, but I can't hear a word from either one of us. All I can do is listen to the lyrics.

If I could I would, but I don't know how.

"Anna? Are you okay?"

Just when I've stopped looking back at what I did wrong and stopped being angry at Bennett for what he did wrong—just when I've finally found my fight and made a decision that could change everything—the sadness and the anger flood over me again, and before I can talk myself into stopping them, the tears start falling, landing with little splashes on the plastic jewel cases.

"Stay here." Justin leaves and I watch him walk over to the front door and bolt it with one hand as he flips the BACK IN TEN MINUTES sign to the glass with the other. I release my grip on the bin and let my knees bend as I sink down to the floor, and I lean against the shelving, my knees pulled tight to my chest, and listen to the song. The adrenaline surge that makes my hands ball into fists has returned, and I open my eyes to find my short fingernails stabbing little smiles into my palms.

I'm melting into nothing. . . .

First I sense Justin standing over me, then I feel him on the floor, facing me and pulling me into a hug. As soon as I feel the warmth of his body I sort of fall into it. His proximity to me—the position itself—feels far too intimate, and I know I should pull away from him, but I can't. I need this connection. So I cry and breathe and enjoy the feeling of his hand, heavy on my back. We used to just be two best friends who'd known each other since we were little kids. Now he's my best friend's boyfriend, and that means we probably shouldn't be sitting here on the floor, listening to music, and holding each other quite so tightly.

I'm just about to say this to him when he pulls away from me and rests his chin on my knees. When we're eye to eye like this, he looks so different. The sun has tanned his skin, blending his freckles together, and his smile is so . . . Justin, so sweet and kind and ready to be there for me. Something in my expression must change, because he's suddenly leaning forward, closing his eyes, and moving much further into my space than he should. I know what's about to happen, and I know that I don't want it to, but I'm not quite sure how to stop it. I feel trapped between his mouth and the wooden CD bin.

I turn my head so fast that when our lips brush, it's an awkward, almost accidental movement. "Justin . . ." My accusatory tone makes his face fall. To break the tension, I collapse against his shoulder, let out a nervous laugh, and punch him in the arm. "What are you doing, you idiot?"

If it's possible, his laugh sounds even more nervous than mine. "Wow," he says, looking down at the floor. "I guess I misread that. I'm sorry." He can't even look at me.

And now I feel horrible for my other best friend. "Justin, I'd never do that to Emma. I didn't think you would either."

"I wouldn't. I didn't . . . I don't know, I just lost myself for a minute there."

He scoots away from me, and I feel like I need to say something to lessen his guilt. "Don't worry, nothing happened. Besides"—I let out a nervous laugh—"I guess it's kind of nice to know I wasn't crazy. Until you started seeing Emma, I always thought you had a thing for me."

Justin looks up into my eyes. "Of course I did."

"Shut up." I reach out and punch him in the arm again, mostly because I can't figure out what else to do with my hands.

He shakes his head. "How could you not know that?" he asks, and I just stare at him, because I have no idea what to say. "Do you remember that time in the sixth grade, when I came over to your house? Our parents were playing cards, and you and I spent the night hanging out in your room. You kept telling me you had a surprise for me." I smile at him, but so far, I don't remember any of this.

"When the room got dark, you told me to lie down on the rug, and then you clicked off the light and stretched out next to me. We spent the next hour looking at those little plastic glow-in-the-dark stars on your ceiling, making up our own constellations and laughing until we couldn't breathe. You told me how you looked at the stars at night and pretended to be somewhere else in the world until you fell asleep. Then you told me all about your travel plans, how you wanted to be a photographer or a journalist—someone who got to tour the world—and you were planning to live in Paris first. You were going to take a French class that summer and move there right after graduation."

"That sounds like something I would have said." I can't believe he even remembers this. We were eleven. Even now that he's reminded me, the details that are so vivid in his mind are murky and vague in mine. "How on earth do you remember all that?"

He laughs under his breath. "That was the night I stopped thinking about you as my best friend . . . well, as *only* my best friend." I feel my eyes narrow, and I inhale sharply, watching him, waiting for me to tell me he's kidding, but he just smiles and shrugs, like he can't help it.

"Why didn't you ever tell me?"

"I didn't want to ruin anything. I figured if it was going to happen it would eventually." He shrugs again and looks at me.

"So what are you saying? What about Emma?"

He gives me a genuine smile. "Emma's incredible. She's gorgeous and funny and totally amazing. But she's still not you. She's not my best friend."

"That's not fair to her. You've only known her a few months and you've known me my whole life. Give her a chance."

"I know. I am. It's just that, most of the time, I can't even believe we're together. When I first asked her out, I honestly didn't expect her to say yes. Maybe part of me asked her out just to see if it would make you jealous. But she completely surprised me when she agreed, and I don't know . . . she seemed like she was really into me."

"She was. She *is*." And until this moment, I thought he was too. I think back to the day we sat in the hospital cafeteria and he told me about his date with Emma, how they talked and talked—how she surprised him. I picture him huddled over Emma's broken body, stroking her hair and whispering jokes into her ear, with eyes for no one but her. How could I have been wrong?

Then I remember there was no hospital. Aside from Bennett, I'm the only one who knows there were two versions of that day: the first one ended with a horrible accident, but the second one ended with all four of us at the movies, eating popcorn, the two of them wearing smiles instead of hospital gowns. The first one ended with Justin comforting a very broken Emma, but the second one ended with him on a double date with me and Bennett.

Something important happened to them that day— somewhere between Emma's house and the poorly timed arrival at the intersection—that brought them together. Or maybe it was the accident itself that made all the difference. Either way, we wiped it out. We did it over. We changed it.

Maybe Bennett was right—testing fate, toying with it, may not have any obvious impact at first, but eventually something has to backfire.

39

It's six thirty a.m. and already it's eighty degrees outside. I dress in my lightweight shorts, pull my hair through the back of my pink running hat, and pop on a pair of black Oakleys I splurged on for my trip.

When I run past the man with the gray ponytail, I wave and give him the most enthusiastic "Hi!" he's ever heard from me. He's seen me every Monday, Wednesday, and Friday for the last three years. For a moment I want to stop and tell him that I'll miss him and that he shouldn't worry about my absence, because I'll be spending the next two months running on sand.

When I finish my three-mile loop, I stand on the porch, stretch into a runner's lunge against the banister, and look around. I wonder if this place will be different when I return. Maybe the trees will have noticeably grown or maybe there will be new cracks in the sidewalk or maybe Dad will have painted the house.

I open the door and stop cold. There, leaning against the banister, stands a black case with the word TRAVELPRO stamped on it in shiny silver letters and a giant red bow attached to the collapsible handle.

Dad and Mom emerge from the kitchen. She's still in her bathrobe, and he's pulling her along, holding her hand like she might turn and run if he didn't.

"A suitcase," I say. I've never owned luggage. "Thank you." Mom gives me a sad smile, moves to my side, and practically yanks me into a hug.

"Ew. Stop. I'm all sweaty."

"I don't care." She squeezes harder, and I feel her warm tears land on my bare shoulder. "I'm so proud of you," she whispers into my ear.

"Thanks, Mom." I squeeze her back and plant a kiss on her cheek. "Don't be sad. I'll be back before you know it."

"I know," she says. She wipes the tears away and locks her eyes on mine. "You're so much braver than I ever was."

I reach up and take her face in my hands. "That's not true. Look how brave you're being right now." I smile at her and hug her tight.

⌒‿◞

"Annie, your Brit's here!" Dad yells from downstairs.

I look around my room one last time and zip up the last compartment of my suitcase. I don't imagine that I'll need that much for a summer on the beach, so I've packed light. I have running clothes and shoes, my Discman, batteries, a collection of CDs, and a few light dresses. Flip-flops. Some makeup. Hair clips.

I zip my suitcase, roll it to the door, and stand in front of my map. I consider the little red dots sprinkled across its surface, remembering the soft feel of the sand in Ko Tao and the smell of the dusty rocks at Devil's Lake and the deep red of the Vernazza sunrise. And then I stare at the newest one, kiss my fingertip, and bring it to the pin in San Francisco. I close the door behind me and pull my new luggage toward the stairs.

When I get to the porch, Emma's standing there, telling Mom all about her and Justin's plans for the summer.

"Are you sure we can't take you to the airport?" Dad's in the driveway wearing a tight smile.

"Emma really wants to take me."

"So do we."

"Yes, but Emma doesn't have a bookstore to open or a hospital shift to make."

"Okay." He hugs me hard, but quickly, and then pulls the suitcase out of my grasp and rolls it toward the Saab's open trunk. The convertible soft top is down in celebration of this hot summer day.

I hug my parents one last time, say good-bye, and promise to write. Then I open the passenger door and see a small box wrapped in colorful paper waiting on the seat. "What's this?"

"Open it," Emma commands as she backs out of the

driveway, honking like a madwoman while I hold the small wrapped box with one hand and wave good-bye to my parents with the other. When we're out of sight, I rip the paper off and find a black leather case. I flip the top open.

"Em." I remove the delicate piece, turn it over, and twist the leather strap. "I don't need a watch. I have a watch."

"You have a running watch. This is a dressy watch. In case you meet some wonderful, handsome boy and he asks you out to dinner." I'm surprised to feel myself grin when she says it.

"And I need to know when to be home before I turn into a pumpkin?" I touch the glass face with my fingertip and look up at her. "It's beautiful. You didn't have to do this."

"I know. I just wanted you to always remember that I'm here counting the minutes until you return. Har-har-har."

I laugh. "Seriously, Em. Thank you. I love it." We both fall silent while I struggle to fasten the watch around my wrist.

"I can't believe you're missing Pearl Jam at Soldier Field. We've been waiting for this for more than a year."

"It's okay. You'll go with Justin." I feel a pang of sadness when I say his name. I wouldn't change what Bennett and I did for her, but I wish I didn't feel so responsible for the subtle shift in Justin's feelings. I look at her, wondering what's going to happen between them this summer, and hoping Justin gives her a chance like he promised me he would.

She sighs. "Justin thinks Eddie Vedder is 'pedestrian.' That was his word. 'Pedestrian.' The man's a genius." And with that, Emma turns the stereo on. "Case in point."

She twists the knob, and the opening guitar licks of "Corduroy" fill the car. As always, we sing. Loud. Off key. People in neighboring cars stare at us and shake their heads. But then I stop. Emma's still drumming hard on the wheel and singing, but I'm just listening to the lyrics of the chorus.

Everything has chains . . .
Absolutely nothing's changed.

Has anything changed? He blew into our lives and back out again, and on the surface, maybe it looks like he didn't leave any marks, but I know he did: they're all over me. And as painful as it is to be in this town without him, if I could do the last three months again, I'd make the same choice—to know Bennett Cooper. Even though it kills me when the song ends with the words *I'll end up alone like I began.*

Emma pulls into the international departures terminal and screeches to a halt in front of the curbside check-in, punches the gearshift into park, and turns to face me.

"Send postcards, love."

Postcards . . .

"I will. I promise." I hug her tight. "Have a fun summer. I'll see you in August."

I soften my grip on her but her arms remain firmly locked around me, and when she tries to say something, I hear her voice catch in her throat. "Em . . ." I tighten my hold on her again. "Stop. You're going to make me cry."

She lets me go and pulls away. "You're right. Happy moment. No crying." She rushes to wipe the tears from her face and we air-kiss on both cheeks. "Until August," she says.

"Until August." I give her another quick hug and bolt from the car before her tears become contagious. I pull my bag from the trunk and walk into the airport, then stop and look back to give Emma a final wave good-bye.

After the agent hands me my boarding pass, I walk on wobbly legs toward the line of people waiting at security. I've never felt more alone, but on the flip side, I don't think I've ever been braver.

I act like I know how to board a plane. People move quickly. And slowly. My heart races as I make my way through the seats, and it feels like it's about to burst out of my chest when I see 14A. My carry-on bag is filled with magazines and travel books and, of course, the eight things I couldn't leave behind.

After I take my seat and buckle in, I reach into my bag and remove the small stack of postcards and look at each one. Most of them are blank, but the one in his handwriting and the two in mine say the same thing—we meant something to each other. We didn't want it to end.

The plane taxis down the runway, and we lift into the sky. And that's when I feel it. Finally, something I can compare to the feeling of traveling with Bennett. A small twist. A lightness in my stomach. I feel this incredible rush of adrenaline, and I can't help smiling when I think of what's about to meet me. I adjust the pillow between the seat and the wall of the plane, grip my postcards, and lean my head against the small double-paned plastic window. I watch as Illinois slips and shrinks away below.

40

My neoprene belt is strapped tight around my waist, my music is thumping loud in my ears, and the soles of my shoes are leaving little impressions in the damp sand as I run. I look over my shoulder at the sun climbing fast on the horizon, and I let my head keep turning, following the line that divides the turquoise bay from the deep orange sky. I still can't believe I'm here.

I just wish he were too. The change of scenery helped, but it still aches to miss him so much, to look for his face among strangers on the street and to think of him every time I pass one of the hundreds of postcard racks scattered throughout this tourist town. And even though it's Bennett I miss most, I also hate knowing I'll never feel that twist in my stomach again, the one that made me feel queasy but completely alive.

Up ahead I can see the tall rocks and jagged cliffs that mark the end of the beach, and I feel my arms pump harder, pushing me toward them. I fix my gaze on the rock closest to the water and sprint with everything I have, stopping only when my fingertips touch it.

I shake out my arms and legs, walking back and forth along the beach as I cool down. When my breathing has returned to normal, I find a dry spot on the sand and recline on my elbows so I can take in the view. Then I lie back into the heat. I close my eyes, and for a long time I don't think about anything but the feeling of the sun on my face and the sound of the water lapping against the shore.

My head falls lazily to one side, and I exhale as I open my eyes, but instead of seeing the rocks that mark the end of the beach, I find myself staring at a picture of the San Francisco skyline. My heart starts racing again, maybe even faster than it did as I ran. I twist onto my side, reach forward to remove the image from the sand, and stare at it.

I flip it over.

You didn't get your postcard.

I want to look behind me. I have a feeling he's there, but I shut my eyes tight, because I don't think I can handle it if I look around and discover that the beach is still empty. But I remind myself that the postcard is real and tangible in my hands, and I force myself to sit up and look over my shoulder.

Bennett Cooper is sitting in the sand just a couple of feet away from me, and I take him in, from his mess of hair, down to his concert T-shirt, past his jeans, and finally to his flip-flops. I stare at him, my lips pressed together, slowly shaking my head back and forth. This can't be happening.

"Hey, you."

I feel tears slide down my cheeks, and I think I say, "Hi," but it doesn't matter, because within seconds he's right next to me, and all I can feel is his fingers on the back of my neck. His kisses land everywhere, on my wet cheeks and my forehead, on my eyelids and my neck, and finally on my mouth, and we pull each other close, neither one allowing even the smallest gap between us. "I missed you so much," he murmurs into my hair, and I want to say it back, but I just can't.

He brings his thumb to my face and wipes my cheeks dry, and I finally find my words. "You're really here," I say, and he nods and kisses me again.

"Yeah," he says. "I'm really here."

I can't help smiling at him. "I didn't think I'd ever see—" My words catch in my throat, but there's no reason to finish the sentence. He's here, and I just want to remember how it felt when I didn't wonder if he would be. I bury my face in his neck, warm from the sun and salty from the heat, and I stay there for a moment, just breathing him in. "I've missed you." This time I say it out loud, and when my hands find his hair again, I let my fingertips get lost in it, then pull back so I can see his face. He looks gorgeous and sun-kissed and so . . . here.

He stretches out next to me and we prop ourselves up on our elbows facing each other, and suddenly I feel like we're back on Ko Tao, lying on the beach, wishing we were kissing, and wondering what to do with our hands. But this time we both seem to know exactly what to do with them, and when he kisses me again, my hand goes straight for the bit of skin peeking out between his T-shirt and jeans, and I grip his waist, feeling the curve of his hip beneath my fingers. I'm relieved when he tightens his arms around me, because I still can't seem to get close enough to him to believe this is actually happening. We finally separate from each other, but just barely, and I rake my fingers through his dark tumble of bangs and let them linger there as I watch his face, lit by the morning sun but brightened by something else entirely.

"You look surprised to see me," he says.

I laugh under my breath. "How are you here right now?"

"I told you I'd keep coming back until you were sick of me." The corners of his mouth turn up in a half smile. "What?" he asks. "You didn't believe me?"

"No." I shake my head. "I wasn't sure what to believe." I'm still not sure. But right now, I just want to know that he isn't going to disappear at any second. I rest my forehead against his. "Are you back for good?"

"Yeah," he says as his eyes light up, "I'm back."

"How do you know you won't . . ."

Bennett looks at me and his expression turns serious. "I was here yesterday." His eyes move behind us to the grove of trees at the top of the beach and I follow his gaze. "I wanted to be sure I was really back in control again before . . ." His voice trails off and he lets out a heavy sigh. "It was all I could do to stay away, but . . . I was looking at you, and for a second

I thought that maybe it was better if I—I don't know. . . . You just looked so happy."

"I was. But I'm happier now."

He smiles. "Are you sure?"

"Yeah, definitely."

"La Paz, huh?"

"Where else?" I picture the circuitous routes of our travel plans, how the lines crossed in one only place. I rest my hand on his waist again, tracing tiny circles on his bare skin. "Tell me everything," I say. "Where have you been? What have I missed?"

He leans forward and kisses the tip of my nose. "You haven't missed much. I spent the last month and a half watching you."

"Watching me?" I lean back so I can see his face.

"You were right. That morning at the Northwestern track—I *was* there. I just hadn't done it yet." He reaches over my shoulder, grabs a little bundle of my curls, and twists them around his finger. "Ever since the night you got knocked back, I've been stuck in San Francisco. I tried to travel, but no matter what date or time I chose, I'd arrive at the same place: Monday, March 6, 1995, 6:44 a.m. At that damned track. God, it was like being stuck in *Groundhog Day*. I could only stay for a minute or so before I got knocked back, but it was the only place I could go, so that's where I went."

"I *knew* it was you." I knew I wasn't crazy.

He shoots me a small smile and keeps talking. "For some reason, at the beginning of this month, something changed.

Instead of landing at the track on March 6, I arrived on a sunny day in May and you *knew* me. And since then, everything's been slowly returning to normal. Every day I could travel a little bit further, stay a little bit longer, but I still couldn't get back to you—to Evanston or here—until yesterday."

"So what changed?"

"I don't know," he says, "but I bet *you* do. What did you do differently?"

I think back to the beginning of the month and it all comes back to me to me in a rush. *Are you aware of the date, Señorita Greene? June first, señor.* That was the day I decided not to stay in Evanston, moping around town and waiting for Bennett to return. The day I listened to *Anna's* advice and put myself on the other path—the one I wanted to be on. The day I made it possible for Bennett to come back.

"I decided to come here," I say. "You never came back. When Argotta told me about this trip, I just knew I needed to come here."

"Without me." He looks at me with a sad smile and I nod, and for a long time after that, we're quiet. "I should have told you about the letter."

"Yeah, you should have." I bring my fingers to his cheek, and when his eyes find mine I give him a smile that says he's forgiven. He smiles back, but I can tell he's thinking about something. I wonder if he's wishing he could do it over again, but I have a feeling his rules are back in place and we won't be changing our own history again any time soon. "So, do I know everything *now*?"

He lets out a laugh and looks at me again. "Yeah, you're all caught up. I have absolutely no idea what happens from here."

"Good." I watch him, thinking that my whole future suddenly looks different again. I'll get to feel that uncomfortable twist in my stomach and I'll poke the sharp end of little red pins into my wall-size map and I'll kiss him in romantic little villages and we'll drink lattes in hidden coffee shops.

"You know what you need to see next?" he asks, and I smile and shake my head. "Paris."

I remember how we walked along the path back at Devil's Lake, Bennett excited about teaching me how to climb a rock and me wishing we were in a Parisian café. He stops, and an impish grin forms on his face. "Are you hungry for breakfast?"

"Breakfast?" I laugh and look around the empty beach. "Now?" He wants to take me to breakfast. In Paris. Right now. I look down at the running clothes, dried on my skin.

"Why not?" He stands up and holds out his hand.

I consider my clothes again, but within a matter of seconds, I've decided I don't care, because after all, it's *breakfast in Paris.* I let him help me up.

We stand there on the beach, and I put my hands in his. He smiles, and I can see how excited he already is to show me something new. "You ready?"

I start to say yes. But then I stop. I look around at the water, at the rocks and the cliffs and the mountains that serve as a backdrop. And suddenly I don't want to be in Paris. I don't want to be anywhere else but here. I drop one of his hands, breaking our ability to travel in the way to which we've become accustomed, and I wrap myself up in his arms as I lean back into his chest.

"See that yellow umbrella way down there?" I point to the other side of the beach and look up at his face.

He squints as he stares into the distance. "Yeah." He looks down at me with a puzzled smile.

"That place has the *best* Mexican coffee in town."

His smile turns soft with understanding. "Does it, now?"

I nod as if I'm some kind of expert on La Paz. And I am. At least as far as present company is concerned. "It does." Bennett brings his hand to my face and kisses me like there's no better place in the world to be right now anyway.

I knit my fingers together with his. Then I reach down and pick up my San Francisco postcard from the sand and wave it in the air. "Come on," I say as we start off for the umbrella. "My turn to buy you one."

He bumps my hip. I bump his back. And we walk down the beach toward something he's never seen before.

acknowledgments

So many people have influenced this story about love, friendship, and family; I've been blessed to know all three in abundance.

My husband, Michael, is the love of my life and a partner in the truest sense of the word. If I could travel back to 1995, I'd choose you all over again.

My son, Aidan, and my daughter, Lauren, had to share my time and attention with a bunch of imaginary people to make this book possible, and all they asked for in return was a "make-up story" of their own at bedtime. I'm so grateful for their unconditional love and support. I hope I've made them as proud as they *always* make me.

At its heart, this is a story about choosing the kind of life you want to live and pursuing it with tenacity. My dad, Bill Ireland, taught me how to do that, and I owe him big-time. I'm equally thankful for my mom, Susan Cline, who flat-out loves me for exactly who I am—always has. Not every mother would reply to the words "Guess what? I'm writing a book" with "Well, it's about time." Every kid deserves fans like these two.

My family is big and wonderful and ridiculously supportive. Special thanks to: my brothers, Ben and Jeff Ireland; David and Kristen Stone; Randy, Sharon, Brandon, and Sonja Cook; Karen Clarke; and Joanna, Eric, and Kristina Ireland. I'm especially thankful for Jim and Becky Stone's constant love and support, and for their being so enthusiastic about this project; and for my grandma, Edith Ireland, who should have been here for all of this.

At first, I didn't realize how much I needed to tell a story about finding a home with a family that isn't your own. I will forever be grateful to the DeLongs, who, when I needed it most, gave me a world that didn't exist on a map.

I'm still overwhelmed by all the support I've received from my friends, and I love all of them more than they know. My earliest readers, Heidi Temkin, Stacy Peña, Molly Davis, Sonia Painter, Elle Cosimano, and Spencer Davis, were especially generous with their time and kind with their feedback. And I'm especially thankful for my business partners, Molly and Stacy, who whole-heartedly supported me in this new endeavor and never even questioned whether they should. They are the best kind of friends.

There are three extraordinary girls embedded in these pages: Hosanna and Sophie Fuller, my real-life smart, athletic, and worldly heroines; and Claire Peña, a demanding, discerning reader whose love for stories and characters first inspired me to write for young adults. Special thanks to Hosanna for loving time-travel plots and music, and for letting me bend her ear about both when she probably had better things to do.

Huge thanks to: DJ Stacy, for advising on all things college radio; Anita Van Tongerloo for the Spanish lessons; Kate Wolffe for the cross-country tips; Mark Holmstrom for help with climbing technique; Dr. Mike for the medical consults; and Pearl Jam and Phish for allowing me to use their beautiful lyrics.

And there aren't enough words to thank the two remarkable women who brought this book to life: Caryn Wiseman and Lisa Yoskowitz.

My agent, Caryn Wiseman, believed in this story—and in me—from that very first handshake-hug-thing we did, and she never lets me forget it. I'm especially thankful for her early editorial guidance, which opened doors I hadn't considered and led my characters in a beautiful new direction. Huge thanks to Caryn's extended team, Taryn Fagerness and Michelle Weiner, who represent me with such passion and dedication, and to everyone at the Andrea Brown Literary Agency, for all their support.

I'm simply in awe of my editor, Lisa Yoskowitz, whose insights and ideas made this a much better book, and whose patience and high expectations made me a much better writer. She completely *got* this story from day one, asked all the tough questions, and guided me through every twist and turn along the way. Lisa and the entire Disney-Hyperion team embraced Anna and Bennett so quickly and with such enthusiasm, I knew we had found the right home. Special thanks to Tori Kosara, for providing feedback on every draft, and to Whitney Manger, for her beautiful cover design.

10-12